Extra Indians

Extra Indians

Eric Gansworth

milkweed
editions

© 2010, Text by Eric Gansworth
All rights reserved. Except for brief quotations in critical articles or reviews, no part of this book may be reproduced in any manner without prior written permission from the publisher: Milkweed Editions, 1011 Washington Avenue South, Suite 300, Minneapolis, Minnesota 55415.
(800) 520-6455
www.milkweed.org

Published 2010 by Milkweed Editions
Printed in Canada
Cover design by Jason Heuer Design
Interior design by Connie Kuhnz
The text of this book is set in Chaparral Pro.
10 11 12 13 14 5 4 3 2 1
First Edition

Please turn to the back of this book for a list of the sustaining funders of Milkweed Editions.

Library of Congress Cataloging-in-Publication Data

Gansworth, Eric L.
    Extra Indians / Eric Gansworth.
        p.   cm.
    ISBN 978-1-57131-079-8 (pbk. : alk. paper)
    1. Truck drivers—Fiction.   2. Japanese—America—Fiction.   3. Minnesota—Fiction.   4. Stereotypes (Social psychology)—Fiction.   5. Difference (Social psychology)—Fiction.   6. Domestic fiction.   I. Title.
    PS3557.A5196E98 2010
    813'.54—dc   222009028716

This book is printed on acid-free paper.

for the Bumblebee

at a quarter century,

flight paths in tandem,

and for P.B.,

at the old Bell School,

gone from there like a cloud's come up,

but not forgotten.

Extra Indians

Extra Indians

PROLOGUE:

Coming Attractions

Dear Mr. McMorsey:

Enclosed please find directions, and the key to your cabin, "Moonlight Serenade," and your receipt for two nights in November. It is the off-season for us, but we have had occasional winter requests from other stargazers like yourself. You should have a beautiful opportunity as astronomers say we are in the direct path for the Leonid showers this year. Please come prepared, as we do not have a regular caretaker in the off-season. You may leave a message at the office phone, but if you need anything urgently, we recommend you make arrangements with others before arrival. Enjoy your stay.

—the Management,
Kwitchurbeliakin Cabins,
Detroit Lakes, MN

Tommy Jack McMorsey

People are always wishing on falling stars, trying to see them, lying out under the nighttime sky, scanning back and forth, just hoping to spot one, and usually the ones they catch are fleeting, almost out of sight, vague impressions in their peripheral vision. Then they speed-wish, going as fast as they can, the lines they have rehearsed all day, maybe wishes they've written on the steam in the bathroom mirror after their morning showers, or on napkins at lunch, ink bleeding their desires away into accidental coffee spills, but they still do it, and try to get it out before the star burns dead away and cancels their dreams on account of their too-slow brains.

So they don't win the Mega Millions, or they never get that man or that woman to truly love them, no matter how bad they might want it. After a while, maybe they only whisper that person's name as they see the trail flaking off into space, believing that might make their wish quick enough. You know you've done it. Even if you claim you haven't, I know you've done it. Maybe you wish Earl would quit his drinking on his own before he falls down a serious flight of stairs, or gets the cirrhosis on you and dies long before your lives together were supposed to be over. Or maybe it's Roberta, and the way she looks directly at you and smiles that one just for you, over lunch, and you wish to lie naked next to her, even if only once in both of your lives, though she talks about "all those jerks in the personal ads, requesting discreet women when what they really mean is they want to cheat on their wives with you."

Yes, I have been there. The wife and I have been together for a very long time, more than a silver anniversary's worth, but there's a reason silver comes so late in that list. You can build up a lot of tarnish in twenty-five years. My daddy used to proclaim that about my momma, but he was only joking when he would say those things, and she would hit him with the flyswatter and get him another sweet tea from the kitchen, and he would kiss her hand as she passed it to him. Liza Jean Bean, though, was never the forgiving type, and she didn't get any closer to being one when she took my hand and changed her name to Liza Jean McMorsey, either. I am not building up a reason for doing some of the things I've done. I have kept time with some others because they were there. Those women, they have good eyes, and they know when a man is living in a marriage that's become legal only.

I'm not for sure when it happened, or why it happened in the first place. Hell, I'm not even for sure how we wound up married, truth be told. I suppose we did it for the boy. Liza Jean and I were just about living together, anyway, so we decided to go ahead with it, both knowing we could always get a divorce if that was what came to be. It was the seventies and divorce was even on the TV shows, so who would care if two kind of lonely folks from West Texas married and parted at some point? And besides, she had already been through it once and said it wasn't all that bad. It would barely even be a ripple in the coffee cups down at the gas station, where most news gets spread in a town as small as Big Antler.

Yes, I know it sounds like I was planning to continue finding comfort on the road even as I was getting my funeral suit dry-cleaned for my wedding day, but I wasn't really. I was even good for a while, and we had a pretty decent life together, but after a couple years, the old itch came back, right around the time Liza Jean was thinking we were not kids anymore, and gradually had worked us into a once-a-week kind of schedule, late on a Saturday night. By then, other aspects of my life had changed, too. I was definitely not going to New York anymore, among other things.

Maybe you're thinking my falling-star wish is for something steady, or an amazing woman, a Marilyn Monroe look-alike, to come tapping on the door to my rig just once, and keep me company in the sleeper cab, but it isn't. I wish for the same thing any time I see a shooting star, but I might as well be wishing for something that unlikely as to be chasing the things I am chasing.

ACT ONE:

Lights

CHAPTER ONE:
Fall Out

o o o o

THIS IS A TRUE STORY.

*The events depicted in this film
took place in Minnesota in 1987.*

*At the request of the survivors,
the names have been changed.*

*Out of respect for the dead,
the rest has been told exactly
as it occurred.*

—statement from opening credits,
  Fargo

Tommy Jack McMorsey

The first thing you should know is that the papers got it all wrong. Well, some of it's, you know, public record and there is no disputing that she ain't ever coming back this way again. But it's the way things happened. That's what I'm talking about. Yes, I know they asked to interview me, but if words you've spoken have ever wound up in a newspaper at any time, or if you've found yourself on film or videotape that they've cut and rearranged, you already know what I am saying here about the inexact relationship between language and the ways we truly experience the world.

Even some of the basic things, the papers didn't get right. I don't know, maybe they thought it would be weirder or more interesting if she took a cab from Bismarck out to Fargo, or was it a bus to Fargo and a cab to Detroit Lakes? Wasn't it weird enough that she flew into the Twin Cities and by winding up in Bismarck, she totally overshot where she was going by hundreds of miles? I don't know, can't ever remember the way they tell it, because I know the truth. I was the one who found her in the first place, both times, and maybe I should have just kept my mouth shut the second time. None of these new problems would have started for me, and I'd be living out my life the same way I have for the last twenty years or so, but I had to do it, make my yearly wish, hoping one falling star would come through.

I could tell right away when I pulled into the Oasis that she wasn't your average lot lizard. I know that's not too flattering a name to call a lady who will do all kinds of nice things for you just to share some time breathing the same air you do, but I didn't make it up. That name is not one I generally use. It's just one of the many things you learn on the lonely roads of this country. The lizards like to call themselves truckers' wives. They like the way you maybe can't tell if that label means being connected to just one trucker or maybe to an undisclosed number. There are men who wander the lots too, looking for the same thing those women are, but drivers use the standard names for those guys and as often as not, give them a taste of fist instead of the body part they're interested in. I just tell those men *no thank you.* Who am I to be critical about what you want to do with another person, so long as no one gets hurt?

But as I was saying, this woman was not like those other women, though. They have a particular look about them. Hers was not that different, mind you, but different enough so's you'd notice. She was not the type of woman who would share the back of your sleeper cab in trade for conversation, a meal, and a ride to the next place. For most of those others, the "next place" was only a minor matter. They didn't care all that much about where it might be, and they were grateful if you helped them find their next ride after you. If you let them, they'd spin through your CB dial, like some kind of lottery-drawing emcee, risking nineteen if the others come up dry.

There's a lot of good old boys out there. You get to know a man's disposition on the road sometimes watching the way he eats his biscuits and gravy of a morning. The ones who eat with a smile, give you a nod from the next counter stool, flirt with the waitress, those are the boys you might ask about the weather or any Staties taking pictures from the median.

But there's other fellas, too. You can see them at the stops just as often. They blame the cook and waitress if they don't like the food, but they keep eating on it, grinding that food into nothing— chicken-fried vengeance. If they treat a piece of meat like that, I am afraid to think of how they might receive people. When they're sitting at the next stool, I let the sky tell me directly what it might deliver and I watch the road myself for unmarked cars.

If a lady riding with me asks for help finding her next ride, I offer the radio. I let her run through the channels to find her own next rides into the routes. Chickenshit, but I do not want to be a party to sad young women looking for company and meeting the business end of a claw hammer or a tire thumper.

That's blunt, but you can ask the wife. I have a certain way with words, Liza Jean says, and her tone lets you know she means the opposite of a compliment. Some over-the-road haulers ask these ladies if they're riding with someone and then ask to speak to me, like I'm some kind of background check, but that's not the way it is with me. A lady might fit nicely resting up against my belly in the night, and she might not steal anything when I'm looking elsewhere, but that doesn't mean she's not nuts. The only thing that had made me eligible for her talents was eighteen wheels and a full tank. That's not too discriminating. I'm no troll, mind you, not half-bad, even—but no real prize, either. A man's looks don't matter to most of them.

But this lady was different, right off. I wouldn't have done anything with her, anyway. There's two kinds I pass right on by, those who are Asian, and those who look like Shirley Mounter. Some things in your past should just never be awakened. You don't know if you'll ever get them back to sleep again. Even if she hadn't fallen into one of my categories, I still would have not considered her. It was something beyond looks.

Most lizards, when they get to a truck stop like the Oasis, they go to one of three places. There is the kind who sits at the restaurant, not bad looking, revealing leg and cleavage under those bright fluorescents. She is eating something light if she's alone, a salad or whatnot. The second kind is a little older, a little heavier, or a little skinnier, always a little too something, and these ladies hang around the bar, where the lighting is lower and the men are drunker. The third type is much more random. You could never predict what they would look like. These are the ones the truck-stop owners like the least, because they almost never buy anything if they can get away with it. The owners pretend these women are invisible. Running the ladies off would be bad for business.

These always come in, order a water, and not that bottled water, just the tap water they give you in the little round juice glasses. They ask where the ladies' room is, knowing the ladies' room and gents' are generally down the hall that leads to the "truckers only" area, with the lounge and courtesy showers. The showers are never a courtesy for everyone and you have to show your license and some rig ID before they give you a key to a shower stall. It's not a bad deal, six bucks usually, or they give you one free if you fill up your rig using their preferred customer cards. These ladies, they'll do almost anything for a hot shower, anything, or so I hear. They try to make their way down that hall unnoticed and go to knocking on doors, or just try them to see if any's unlocked.

This lady did not fit any of those three categories, so my eye was up in a different way immediately. It ain't often you pull into the big back lot reserved for rigs and see a woman wandering around the landfill just beyond the bar ditch, particularly not in the November snows of North Dakota. She was looking for something, and since I was running a little ahead of schedule, was just gonna catch some tube or maybe even a shower, I figured I'd help her out. Maybe with two sets of eyes, we would find whatever it was, just a little quicker, and get her out of that relentless wind.

Out there, the state, or whoever, highway department, maybe, tries to hide the fact that they build landfills around the truck stops. Guess they figure no one is going to notice the smell seeping from them in all the diesel clouds. They try to beautify the fills, planting trees and such toward the edge of the lot. These get used for more than beautifying in the warmer months, but that day, the wind was way too sharp for any two people to be thinking about dropping their drawers for some connecting time, no matter how big an urge they might have. Most prefer the back of the sleeper cab in general, but I've seen them in the bushes often enough to know it happens.

That poor lady and I were the only ones there, among the exhaust tubes jutting from the landscaped hill, sending nastiness in invisible sheets. Her tracks were like the small, hard deer prints I'd seen in New York, all those years ago when I used to spend some regular time in the northern climes. Her tracks came and went in all directions, sometimes crossing each other, sometimes stopping abruptly and heading in another direction.

"Uh, miss? Ma'am?" She didn't hear me, the wind being what it was. If the snow had not thawed and refrozen a couple of times before that day, her tracks would have all but disappeared from behind her, even as she made them.

"Ma'am?" She turned, hearing my shout this time. She was Asian, Japanese, as you know from the news, but at the time I wasn't sure exactly which variation. I could tell people who were Vietnamese, even half-Vietnamese and half-American, right off, but I always had trouble with others. I could spot differences if you lined some up, but couldn't say which was which. I can't even do this at home.

Now, the wife says she can tell which Texans are Scottish, which ones are Irish and such, and even claims she can tell who is whose daddy and who ain't but all that's bullshit. There's some children she's looked right at and not recognized who their real daddy is but maybe that's selective on her part—hard to say with the wife. Liza Jean McMorsey likes to see things just the way she does.

She's always been that way. Whenever she demands I cut the damned lawn because of mosquitoes, she says I scared all the birds away with my noisy engine afterward. She suggests we need an ass-kicking push mower, the kind with rotating blades that eat around like really sharp teeth. When I tell her the birds leave because the mosquitoes were their food, she laughs, drinks another Big Red, and goes back into the house to watch for birds from her big old picture window.

So wouldn't it just kill her to see the exotic bird I found in the winter dusk of a North Dakota night? The wife was the one who sent me there in the first place, in a manner of speaking. Usually, I do the short haul, local runs only, Big Antler to Lubbock, Lubbock to Amarillo, and the like. Every now and then, she says I'm getting on her nerves again and lets me know it's time for me to accept one of the over-the-road runs. So this time, things worked out for both of us. She got a break from me and it was the time of year I go out for a few days by myself, anyway. Where I wind up depends on the night skies, so this was just as well. I always try to bring her back something nice. For the longest time, it was those Lladró porcelain figurines that she loved so dearly and put in the china cabinet as soon as I gave them to her but those only dredge up bad memories now, things I do not want to bring back at all.

I put in for an extended haul with several suggested cities and got an assignment immediately. Who else wants to go up to Bismarck in November? I wanted a vacation from her anyway, so I was glad to let her think she had come up with the idea of me taking the load. She even packed my bag, looking to make sure there weren't any rubbers in my shaving kit, like they weren't available in every drugstore and rest area john along the way. Even the idea of someone else looking at me in my boxers gets her crabby and cross-eyed, though she hasn't had a look for me in them for over ten years.

Anyway, when I spoke that second time, this lady came on over, opening up this rucksack thing she carried on her back, pulling out a sheet of notebook paper, like the kind you rip from a spiral-bound, raggedy teeth blowing in the wind. The sheet might have flown from her hand, but she kept a firm grip on it. There wasn't a damn thing on it except for a straight line and something that might have been a tree or a stick of some sort, both drawn in pencil. Inside that bag, she was pretty well stocked with cash, though, and that was about when it was clear she was not American.

"Miss? You might want to keep that there bag closed," I said, not wanting to reach for it, but if she kept flashing that stack around the Oasis, she was not long to have it. I won't try to repeat the things she said to me, not because they were outrageous, or anything like that. Well, they were outrageous, but not in a nasty way. She just did not seem to have a very good grasp of English, you would say. Her peculiar version of the language sounded almost like she maybe got it from watching movies on TV through bad reception. It seemed logical, considering all that eventually happened.

I assumed I didn't understand what she was saying because the idea was so darned way-out-there. I was sure she was joking on me, like *Candid Camera* was hiding in those trees at the landfill's edge, just to see what I would say to an Asian lady who could barely speak English telling me she was looking for the ransom buried by some character in a movie. Well, I showed them.

"First," I said, "you ain't even in the right town. Why don't you come on in, with me, get a little warmed up, have something hot to drink, and we'll go from there." I reached for her hand but she acted like I wanted her map and pulled away, just enough to let me know she was not being led anywhere.

I was wishing Fred Howkowski was with me. He would have known the ins and outs of whatever she was talking about, even with only her passing snag of English. I remember the story of *Fargo*, but just barely. I must have been missing something awfully important that this girl saw. Fred would have been able to tell me right off what I lacked. He knew all the movies, used to talk about them, compare everything we did together to movies. How he saw that damned many is anyone's guess.

o o o o

A lot of shows, he watched silent from the back fences of the drive-in movie places where he grew up. He'd hitch a ride out from the reservation to those neighborhoods when he was young, get dropped off at a gas station or whatever, then wander around. When it was dark enough, he'd make his way over to the Star-lite, or the Auto-vue, and watch them play out through holes he had carved, himself. I asked him how come he never just jumped the fence and watched from the concession stand where they had speakers mounted on the outside walls.

He liked it better speaking his own dialogue, making up the stories to suit the things he saw up on the screen. Sometimes he would do this after we'd gotten to know each other in Vietnam, when we were back to Camp Hockmuth near Phu Bai once a month at the rear. In the mess hall of an evening, they mostly showed us wholesome-type, inspirational movies. Who needed that nonsense with the things we were witnessing and participating in daily?

Those jokers inside the hall would be eating that bullshit up, Doris Day and all. Fred and I would be outside the back windows, sparking a joint if no one else happened to be around. He would make Doris say all kinds of things to her leading men, and the things they would say back, man, I was sore from laughing most nights by the time we went to bed. He was just crazy about the movies. Listening to him there, or in the nighttime fields, talking about his favorites, was sometimes all that kept me going. His voice, in those sweaty jungles, allowed me to forget things were crawling into the poncho we used for a tent when I would doze on patrol nights.

o   o   o   o

English was not an option with this girl, so I tried any kind of sign language I could conjure up. I'd thought I'd gotten somewhat handy with it in the war. I could only remember a few real phrases now, "didi-maow," "boo-coo," some others, and generally mispronounced them so bad that the locals there had no idea what I was saying. I was reduced to hand signals: "let your fingers do the walking"; "how much for this"; "do you have anything to drink"; "anything to smoke"; rubbing my hands together and blowing on them for cold—my toolbox of sign language was pretty limited. Eventually this lady recognized one of my attempts. I held an invisible cup of coffee, then pointed to the building. Finally she let me put my arm around her shoulder and we went inside. The light skeleton beneath her jacket felt on the verge of breaking apart so I lifted, floating my arm an inch above her real body. She mostly just warmed her hands with the cup of hot chocolate I bought her. My cell phone was not getting any reception inside, but I didn't dare leave her where I couldn't see her, so I called the state troopers from a pay phone.

"Uh, hello, hi, my name is Tommy Jack McMorsey, and I drive for Martin Romero shippers, out of Lubbock, Texas," I started.

"Yes sir, how may I help you?" the dispatch said, her voice flat, thinking this was just another call from a holy roller driver, complaining about the lizards. I hate those guys. They're not getting any—by their own choice, I might add—but they don't want anyone else getting any either. They're always filing formal complaints, particularly about those ladies falling in the fourth category. Those really aggressive ones tap on your passenger-side passing-mirror window and show you a little skin before they try the door to see if you'll unlock it.

"Well, you see, I'm calling from Oasis, on eastbound I-94, just out of Bismarck, and—"

"Yes, sir, I know where you're calling from, how may I help you?"

"Well there's this young lady here, and she—"

"Has she asked for money in exchange for services, sir?"

"Uh, well, no, she has her own money," I said. "Look, could you just send someone out here? I think she needs help, and I am pretty sure I'm not the one she needs it from." I gave her my tag numbers and told her I had to go, that the young lady had just wandered out the front doors and I wanted to keep an eye on her.

The odor of landfill is its own special rot, and I could smell it before I caught up to her. The only thing it reminds me of is that industrial sauerkraut they used to keep in the stainless steel flip-top buckets at the drive-in movie concession stand. The condiments were nastier than the roller-dogs, those orange hot dogs that spun and spun inside the glass case. It is truly the only smell that land-fills remind me of. That, or maybe the lingering odd smell in the air after someone sneezes and you are unlucky enough to be nearby.

This girl didn't seem to mind it, though. The nasty steam crept out of those white PVC pipes releasing gases from all that waste dissolving into who knows what below us. She pointed to these pipes and she would walk around them, shake her head, point to the presumed tree on her sheet of notebook paper, and head on off to the next pipe. I followed her to every damned one of them, try-ing to figure out what she was looking for, holding my coffee up to my nose and hoping for the best. This is the way the troopers found us when they eventually got there.

"Mr. McMorsey? Tommy Jack McMorsey?" the first trooper called, from the lot. Even in the gray, his holster hand was plain to see. It was near dark by that time, and for a minute I was not for sure who was calling my name. The girl's belief was so strong that I examined the damned exhaust pipes with her, for some discrimi-nating features, believing I could see differences in them, and I had no idea what she was even looking for as she touched their lips, rubbed their sides, studied the perimeter around them, decided against them, and moved on. I'm not saying I was deluded enough to think we were going to find that *Fargo* ransom and be set for life, but there was something about her belief that somehow the act of looking was enough to keep her going for at least one minute more. And sometimes, what more can we ask for, right?

I've seen that look a lot in my life. Out on the reservation Fred Howkowski came from, it was on practically every other face I looked at. He had that look most of the time I knew him, first along the firebases and out on patrols in the war and then home, when he'd headed out to Hollywood trying to join those movies he loved so much.

"Yes, that's me. I'm the one who called."

"This the woman you reported?" the trooper asked as he came

closer. He looked tired and wanting to get out of the cold and only in seeing his face did I realize how cold I was, how my bones ached. The time we had been out there at the fill had got by me.

"Well, I wasn't exactly reporting her, more concerned is all," I said. He stepped up between us and spoke to the girl. Her eyes opened wide when she saw the North Dakota emblems on his uniform, and she showed him the map right off, I guess not afraid he was going to take it from her.

"We'll handle it from here," he said, taking away the fact that she was a person, just like that. She was another situation, another incident. They took a statement from me, how I'd found her and such, but then they strongly suggested I go back about my business and I know what a suggestion from someone in authority means. They took her away and couldn't get much out of her either, I guess. They said they were going to look around town for someone who could speak her language. I have been around Bismarck and I have not seen too many a Chinese restaurant even, let alone one of those sushi bars like they have for the yuppies in Dallas. They dismissed me pretty clearly. Though I waited outside for a while, an eighteen-wheel rig is not an easy thing to hide and they came out, asking me to move along.

I headed back to the Oasis and sat in a window booth. It wasn't all that long before she reappeared and sat back down with me. You don't see a lot of people paying a cab to get to the stops. Even the lizards catch rides in some other way, either hitching on the entrance ramps or even walking to some of the stops, but the Oasis is pretty far out from where anyone might live. This is where the official story gets all lost, even though I was about as clear as I could be when they asked me questions. According to the troopers, they couldn't get her to change her mind in looking for the ransom, or get her to understand it was just a movie, that no money existed. She kept insisting, as I understand it, that the movie opens saying it is a true story, and she was sticking to that.

All her papers checked out, passport, visa, whatever, and they must have gone through her purse to see she had enough money to at least survive a reasonable amount of time in the country, and they did try to do her a favor, I have to give them that. They took her to the bus station and showed her how to buy a ticket to Fargo. Even as messed up as she was, she knew certain things to be true. Among them is that a Greyhound is not going to stop along the highway from Bismarck to Fargo so you can go treasure hunting, no matter how much you might ring that emergency bell. And if they did, they sure as hell wouldn't idle there long so you could dig around in the snow.

A cab couldn't have been too hard to find. There's usually a bunch of them around the bus station, taking home people who do not have loved ones to come and pick them up from wherever they've been wandering. She came right in and tried to get me to go back out with her to the landfill, but I'd had enough of her non-sense. I have had to be out on a cold night, waiting for the tire guy if I've gotten a blowout somewhere along the way. As a general rule, if you're not out there when he gets to your truck, he just moves on along to the next rig with a blowout. There's never any shortage of us around. So you stand and wait and flag him down and once he starts to working, he keeps asking you something or another, dragging your ass back out into the cold. He figures if he's got to be out there on your account, you're going to be out there keeping him company. Since I had no official business with this young woman on the fill hill, I wasn't stepping through those doors until it was time for me to get my ass back on the road.

"I'm heading on, going, driving," I said, eventually. Again, with the hand signals, I wished I had a little toy rig on the table, so I could move it from the salt shaker to the sugar canister, something like that. I settled for the invisible steering wheel and making the rumbling engine noise all boys learn when they play with toy cars. "Driving, yes, driving to Fargo," and I said this last, slowly, think-ing she might catch it. She grabbed my hand and decided it was time for us to leave. I held her for a minute and, given our sizes, she was no match. There was a story about the meteors coming up on the cable news that I wanted to see before we headed out, making sure the initial predictions had not been off the mark.

Again, you probably already know this from the final reports, and this part, they sort of got right. It was the night of the Leonid showers, those meteors that come on time every year, where you get a chance to see hundreds if you are of a mind to, are in one of the good areas of the country, and can stand the weather. I always made it a point to see them, if I could, no matter where I was, and I was usually willing to travel some distance on the night they were coming through, set an alarm clock, whatever, to see them.

"When Fred Howkowski made it out there to Hollywood," I said when we'd been on the road for a bit, startling my passenger at first, "he actually got a lot of work as an extra, pretty quickly. You know, westerns were still pretty much in demand then. I think even John Wayne was still alive and making movies, but I'm not for sure. He'd call me collect whenever he was going to be in a movie. He's the reason we're heading where we are. Well, he's the reason I'm headed where I am, Fred, not John Wayne. Keep trying to take care of one last thing." Most times, his movies never got out to our rinky-dink movie house back home, which is surprising since we're in ranch country. You would think the ranchers might like them, but maybe they see enough cowboys on the job that they don't want them for entertainment, and in Big Antler, the less said about Indians, the better.

Nothing particularly bad ever happened, I suppose, at least as far as anyone's still alive was concerned, but Indians and whites just don't mix too much down there, hardly any Indians at all, I can remember, except Fred's boy, who became mine when Fred gave him up to me. So, anyway, whenever Fred would call, I would get the Lubbock paper for a few weeks, and when his movie would come out, Liza Jean and I would take the boy into the city, get us something to eat at a nice place, and look for his daddy up on the screen. Sometimes we could see him, sometimes not, even when he told us where he was supposed to be.

"Well, he got word one time they were making a movie out of some book that was supposedly about Indians. He's like you, just loved the movies. But like most of those movies and books from what I have seen and what I've heard about, they are usually about some white guy adopted by Indians who then grows up and out-Indians the Indians, does everything they can teach him to do but only better. This one was going to be no different but Fred was happy." The girl continued staring out the rig's passenger-side window, occasionally glancing at me to let me know she was hearing my voice.

"Liza Jean was growing annoyed at all the collect calls. Back then, calling state to state was something only the rich or famous could do and we were neither of those things. So I paid those bills out of my junk-business profits to keep the peace around the house. I'd taken to garage sales since I had gotten home, have a pretty good eye, and I'd buy stuff up enough to have one of my own or do it as an estate sale or sell to antique shops and you can turn a pretty decent profit if you pick only the stuff that has some staying power." By her outfit, it looked like this girl was one of those who watched the fashion shows and made a point of getting new things when they came out. My clothes are a lot like the stuff I hunt for, old and reliable. That trendy stuff just never lasts.

Once people get bored with little under-stuffed bears, for example, you would be stuck with the samples you hoarded for at least another ten years when interest would somehow just spark up again out of nowhere. I stuck with other stuff that was pretty much guaranteed to grow and grow in scarcity, like real art deco, or art nouveau, no knockoffs, no reproductions. I didn't touch anything made after 1953, unless it had some of that signature "fabulous fifties" look that was getting bigger all the time. So with that cushion, I didn't mind paying for Fred's calls keeping us connected, and since Liza Jean never helped me with the estate sales, she never got a say in what I did with my profits from them, either.

"He got the call from central casting, and with his looks and his list of movies, they even said he had a good shot at some lines.

He had his SAG card, he said, whatever that was, and that meant he could do the lines if they offered them to him. He said the star was a young guy, making it big, and was always nice to the extras, letting them hang out in his honey wagon, signing autographs and what-not. I bet you would like that. Probably be carrying that around in your rucksack there," I said, tapping her little pink bag. At first she jumped and reached to grab it and then must have thought better, easing off and smiling at me more frequently, but only for a second or two before returning to her scan of the roadside.

"Fred kept saying he would get me an autograph that I could sell, and such, but he never did. That was the way of it with him." Even the time I visited him, he kept pretending that he was looking for that autographed picture he got for me, but we both knew it only existed in his head. Finally I said something like, well, it will surface, once we get this stuff cleaned up some, figuring maybe we could get his dump into reasonable shape, if we gave it an honest try, though I don't think it would have stayed that way for long after I had left. When he saw me off the next week, he said that he'd let me know about his speaking part, that he was supposed to hear back soon.

The road from Big Antler to Los Angeles is a long one indeed, and though the one from Bismarck to Fargo ain't even remotely as bad, it's still a haul, and I was getting drowsy. This young lady might have been from Asia, but she seemed to like the tapes I was play-ing, mostly old country standards, Hank Williams—the old one—Bob Wills, all those guys. After a while, even my old reliable music failed me and I'd found myself drifting. I started to tell her all this nonsense, in even more detail, a story I usually only tell myself on this trip every November, whenever the showers come. Through her fragments of English, it must have sounded like a hodgepodge, most of the time, a few familiar terms here and there. Maybe my voice temporarily chased away whatever ghosts had dragged her to this dreadful place.

"We met in the war, and though Liza Jean could never under-stand how that could make you stay connected to someone, I admit it's more complicated than that. It never starts out complicated. If a familiar face is all you got, that is what you go with. Fred was the only one I recognized from basic." I laughed a little and she tried to laugh, too. "I'm not for sure when we moved from being friendly to being friends, probably around the time I saved his ass, though." She was gone again. Sometimes her eyes would follow something at the roadside and if I had ever offered to stop, she would have been out there in a second, wandering in the snow.

She probably didn't need to hear this kind of stuff, anyway. I've been to the Trinity Site in New Mexico, where those first atomic tests were done, and of course have gone and found some of my buddies up on the wall in D.C., but I have always wondered what that Hiroshima museum must be like. I hear they have a watch there, a pocket watch or wristwatch, I am not for sure which, that survived the blast, but stopped ticking at that exact moment the bomb went off. Everyone should see that. I bet this lady has. Even if she hasn't been to that museum itself, she's seen it. It's the same way you can see the name of someone you knew, who never came home from Vietnam, written neatly in that black surface, you can feel the depths of those etched names under your fingers, as you run them across, even if you have never been down to see it in person, to stand in front of the wall. That is the nature of the way we lose some things in our lives.

"We're here," I said.

"Fargo? Here?" the girl asked, gathering up her little backpack.

"Yeah, you just hang on, missy. I got to find somewhere reasonable for you to stay." Fargo can be a bad scene, and that was all this girl needed, to let the wrong person see her. If she still wanted to continue her crazy search in the morning, that was her business, but for my part, I got her to safety and it was time for me to make my yearly trip to the designated wide-open skies. Fargo would have been okay for me any other night of the year but the light pollution would be too strong for my purposes that night. Coming into it, or really coming into any of the cities at night, was like flying into Phu Bai that first time. The firebases, and particularly the rear, just seemed to be begging for enemy fire, all lighted up in the dark jungles like that, but the NVA could never get it together enough to go that deep into our territory without getting caught. These hot spots in the dark Dakota winter also drew all sorts of their own trouble, with the promises of alternatives, and this girl would not be able to make it on her own, I was sure.

I know, she had made it all the way from Japan to the Twin Cities and then on to Bismarck in the first place, so who was I, telling her she couldn't make it? But like I said, Fargo is a tough place. The Mainline just off 94 was pretty decent, continental breakfast, you know, bad coffee and stale doughnuts, but it was something to eat, if you wanted it, and you could actually see the river from some of the rooms there. It would be fine for her, and besides, I really had to get a move on if I was going to make Detroit Lakes in the time I wanted. I don't know why she didn't just fly to Fargo in the first place, but she must have had her reasons for doing the things she was doing. Everyone does, whether you agree with them or not.

"You just head right in there, where it says office, o-f-f-i-c-e, see?" I said, pointing to the glowing sign above the lobby door, "and they'll take care of you. Tell them, one night." I held up my pointer finger again, this time, straight up, and tried to get her to do the same. I touched her hand and folded the other fingers under, into a fist, and then she got it.

"Come?" she asked. Actually, I only assumed she was asking, as about all of her brief sentences seemed to be questions. She might have been commanding, for all I know.

"Uh, no." I shook my head and reached over, opening her door for her. "I got things to do tonight, and I gotta get a move on, if I'm gonna make it. Now you watch your step getting out. There's a little platform for you there, watch. Don't fall." She just sat there, the cold wind blowing in and filling up my cab with the smells of Fargo, industry, greasy food, diesel, the works. I never drive with a coat on, so I reached back over her, shut the door, grabbed my jacket from behind me, and hopped out myself, climbing on up on the passenger's side and reopening the door.

We were beginning to draw some attention from inside the lobby. The night manager even lifted his remote and I assumed turned down the volume on his little television set. I guess what we were doing was more interesting than the goings-on in a black-and-white Mayberry. I had a sense it might turn out to be a good thing, later, that the night manager saw her refusing to come down from my cab. Now, when I'm alone on the drive and need to take a leak, I do what most do and just use Ziplocs until I come to a convenient service area to dump the full bags. You get agile with the trick after years of practice but I was guessing that would be a bit impolite with my passenger. I also wanted that night manager to know my passenger was with me not only willingly, but defiantly, so he'd be able to say so with certainty if authorities started asking after the circumstances of that evening. I just had a sense I was already into something a lot deeper than I had planned to be. So I went in and asked if I could use their john and gave him the quick rundown, suggesting she might be back in a cab later on.

I didn't have time for this kind of nonsense. I already had the key to the place I'd reserved for the next couple of nights, had them mail it to me when I paid in advance. It had been sitting in the upper compartment of my truck's cab for almost a month. As soon as the astronomers had made their predictions, I had picked up the phone and made a couple calls. I got lucky on the second try. Though they tend to be booked up solid for summer by mid-March, there's not a lot of winter demand for those little cabins around Detroit Lakes, and they were just the sort of thing I was looking for.

"Look, miss. I really need to get a move on. I'm running late. My load don't need to be to the Twin Cities until tomorrow, but I have got to get going, and I won't be making a stop back this way again. This here is the place you wanted to be. This is it." The coat she wore wasn't much, looked more like a spring jacket than anything else, maybe even silk, bright pink. She shivered as I stood in the door holding my hand out to her, all the time watching my dashboard clock too. I was about out of hand gestures other than the "come here" motion and to point to the ground.

"How save friend ass?" she said.

"What?" Her voice had been so quiet, the wind almost took all of it away, but I knew that she was speaking relatively coherent English. I had not imagined her fluency. She held her shoulders close, looking down into her lap. The map was gone, I guess, into her bag. I shut the door, shrugged my shoulders at the night manager through the big plate glass doors, and he shrugged his shoulders back and returned to Mayberry. I went around and climbed into my seat.

"His life. There was no donkey involved. It doesn't matter. Really. In the end, I don't guess I did a very good job of it anyway," I said, looking out in the yellow-gray night of Fargo.

"Where . . . now . . . friend?" Yeah, I know it sounds like I'm mocking her, but I remember the few words she spoke to me, clearly. She did understand English pretty well, it seemed, but the way she spoke it was in these long, long pauses, and big chunks of clumsy language. Why she didn't speak before, to me or to the troopers, I do not have an answer for.

"I have to go. Missy, I am guessing you have a pretty good idea of what I'm saying after all, and you're welcome to come with me. I'm sure there's plenty of room where I'm staying, and I promise, I will not lay a hand on you. I got other things on my mind tonight, anyways, but if you do not get out of this cab in the next minute, I am pulling out, and this will be the last you see of Fargo with me."

"Where friend?"

"He's dead. Been dead about thirty years now. As I said, I guess I didn't do too good a job of saving him in the end, or his boy for that matter." I put the rig in gear and pulled out of the parking lot. "The wife and I haven't seen the boy in over fifteen years. And that is surely my fault." I found US-10E out of town pretty easy and

Fargo disappeared in my side mirrors, the blackness of the night taking over as we made our way out to Detroit Lakes and the cabin I had reserved three weeks before, when the Leonid predictions were made public.

The drive was going to take a little less than an hour, even with creeping my speed up some, and I was about sick of Bob Wills. The radio offered not a lot up there, though I eventually found a classic rock station playing the Stones so I left that. Sometimes you hear a line and there you are, back where you thought you had left, many years in the past. I was home by the time this song came out, but I knew what they meant. Sometimes it is just a shot away.

"Ha. We used to listen to these guys in the bunkers, and I bet there was no joking about the lyrics there. I can tell you, not too many people would have been singing along in the jungle. We were definitely always looking for shelter. Well, we got out of that and came home, but he didn't just love the movies, like you. He didn't just want to chase them, he wanted to be in them. That was where I lost him, when he headed off to Hollywood.

"The last time I heard from him was a letter he'd mailed with a key to his apartment. You cold? You want me to turn up the heat?" She nodded and by this time had stopped looking out the window. "Here, put this on," I said, and that was the one and only time I shared the blanket Shirley Mounter had given to me, the last time I left her, after Fred Howkowski's funeral. Nobody else but me and the boy even knew it was there, and I wasn't talking, and these days, surely he was not talking, either. Maybe he'd even forgotten it after all these years. For me, though, every time I unlock the cab and climb on up, that blanket is the first thing I look for, to make sure it's still with me. It is the one thing I have left to remind me of the happiest period of my sorry-ass life.

Handing it over off the cab bunk just then was the only time I had let anyone else use that blanket, ever, and even at that moment, I didn't like the idea too much. But Shirley had given it to me that final time so I would have something to hang on to, and I thought that girl needed something to grab just that moment too. Probably, she looked at me instead of the window because we were no longer on the movie tour route for her, but I liked to think it was something else. I adjusted the heat and opened up my flannel. The T-shirt underneath was about fine for the temperature she liked but there was no way to get that flannel off while I was driving. You learn some talents for the road, but those that involve your safety belt and the steering wheel are too big a challenge even for a lifer like me.

o   o   o   o

"Hang on, we're here." I pulled up to the registration office and filled out some paperwork. The place was totally deserted, not a single car or foot track in the snow, but they had left all the right stuff in a drop box on the door as promised and the cabin was easy to find. It was perfect, just what I was hoping it would be.

I offered the girl the bathroom first, while I unpacked a little and made some entries into the logbook, and then I cleaned up, myself, when she was out of there and sitting by the fire I had started. We had made good time, and still had an hour before the first real wave, when we headed out to the fields. I gave her the spare coat I always keep in the cab's storage. The occasional snowmobile whined off in the distance, but even that settled down by midnight, when the first streaks started appearing across the sky. We had nearly this whole area to ourselves.

"Look! There!" I pointed, and her eyes followed my hand. "Make a wish."

"Wish," she repeated, arching her neck back, nearly being swallowed by my bulky winter coat.

"Don't tell me or it won't come true. Hell, I probably already know what your wish is, anyway, but I don't think you're gonna find that money."

"Wish . . . someone . . . hear . . . me."

"I'm near you," I said, stepping up behind her, wrapping my

arms around her tiny waist and resting my chin on her shoulder, my beard scratching against the shiny material. Even in that bulky coat, she felt like a bird.

"Hear me . . . no . . . not . . . near you . . . hear . . . me." She pulled away and ran a few yards from me.

"I hear you," I said. "I hear you." Watching the meteors always killed my neck and this was the longest-lasting patch I had seen in years, lots of ways for my wishes to ride into reality.

I lay down in the snow and watched them for a while until the wave eased up. The next big shower was scheduled to start in about four more hours, so I was going to go in, set the alarm clock, and catch some shut-eye. Just then, I remembered something and started doing those lying-down jumping jacks you can do. "Hey," I yelled to her, "watch this." The snow out there was a little stiff, not as bad as it had been in Bismarck, but also, not very dusty. No matter, it was for sure no challenge against my two hundred pounds.

"This here is called a snow angel. See? Like an angel? The wings, the robe? We used to make them when we were kids, on those rare winter snows when we got more than an inch in West Texas."

"Angel," she said and shook her head a little. I guessed they don't have angels there, where she was from.

"Uh, like a ghost, impression, imprint, something." I got up and she looked at it.

"Ghost. Hiroshima. On wall," she said, studying the shape I had made in the snow after I had crawled up from it. I'd heard about that, some people just vaporized in the blast, leaving only negatives of themselves on the walls around them. I had always thought it was, you know, made up for drama's sake.

"Here, you make one," I said, offering her the untouched snow to my right. She shook her head and began walking away. "Wait, come on, you go into the cabin. I'll stay out here, in my rig. It's fine, I do it all the time." We went in and I checked the fire, made sure it would last the night. These new cabins all have the modern conveniences anyway, so the furnace would just kick on if the fire went

out in the night. That bathroom even had a nice whirlpool in it I'd
been hoping to use that night, but it would have to wait for the
return trip.

"There you go, fire's all set. I got the alarm set in my rig, for the
next round. You want me to wake you?" She thought for a minute
and then nodded. I set the nightstand alarm for the same time I'd
be setting mine in the rig.

"What wish? Ghost friend?" she asked.

"Yeah, that would be good, wouldn't it? Fred finally getting his
speaking part, but only me getting to hear it?" I laughed. "No."

"What wish?"

"I told you, if you tell someone, it won't come true."

The rig's cab held warmth pretty well, so it was still a reasonable temperature when I climbed back in, started her up, took
my clothes off, and jumped into the sleeper. I wrapped myself in
the warmth of Shirley's Pendleton, the wool sliding up between
my legs, giving me a rise even then, scratching against my belly
as I buried my nose in the blanket and dreamt her smell was still
with me, after all these years. That was the last thing I remembered
until the alarm went off at a little after four, like I had planned. I
bundled up in the same clothes I had taken off the night before,
figuring I would change after I'd gotten myself a shower. I shut the
rig off and stepped down into the dark. Usually I just leave it running, even if I have to hit a rest area john, but out here, it was so
quiet, so removed from every part of my world that the diesel engine seemed to violate the stillness. It was just going to be me and
the meteors. No snowmobiles would be flying around that time of
night, or morning, or whatever.

Avoiding the neck cramps, I lay straight down to wait for the
shower to peak. The rig was finishing its last hisses and ticks, but
two other small noises bled through the sharp air, almost not there
at all, but constant. I couldn't place them at first, but then they
came. The fire must have gone out. The lower hum sounded like a
small house furnace and I could see a slight string of smoke dancing

out of the chimney, but the other sound should not have been going. Even if it was, I should not have been able to hear it.

The first few stars shot through and I laid my wishes on them, like horses racing across the sky, as I do every year. I had no idea if any of them would ever come true for me, but that not knowing always allowed me to wish for things I shouldn't have wished for in the first place.

That second sound kept bothering me, so I got up from the ground, dusted myself off, and followed it to the front door of the cabin, which was wide open. I ran in. The alarm I had set was buzzing away and I shut it off. Then only the sound of the furnace disturbed the early morning.

"Miss, are you in there?" I called. The bed was empty, but no sound came from the bathroom. My down coat sat at the edge of the bed. "Shit!" I ran outside and dug in my jeans for my penlight. It went half the world away with me to Vietnam and I actually still had it when I stepped off the plane back on U.S. soil. It wasn't worth a damn out there in the Minnesota winter night.

Her footprints were visible in the foot diameter the penlight offered, but it wasn't going to be much use to me. I started the rig, hit its headlights, and grabbed the Maglite from its mount on the dash. She wasn't that far away. I found her in the angel I had made, lying there in her pink satin jacket, the backpack straps around her shoulders, the pack firmly on her back, and that map gripped tight in her hand again.

I dug out the card of that trooper who took my statement. He'd given it to me in case I needed to do any follow-up or some damned thing, who knows. Maybe he knew. I was no longer in North Dakota and Minnesota would be out of his jurisdiction, but I had to start somewhere and he seemed as good a place as any. It was too late to do anything else. I sat with her for a couple hours, until my bones, and really, the rest of me, couldn't take the ache anymore. "Hi, this is Tommy Jack McMorsey," I said into my cell phone as the sun came up in her wide-open eyes.

CHAPTER TWO:

Signal Fade

o o o

"Based on a True Story . . . or Not"

(Associated Newspaper Syndicate Entertainment column, May 24, 2002, byline—William Donaldson, Syndicate TV Critic)

How many times have you heard that phrase? More than you can count, most likely. From claims of Bigfoot sightings to unauthorized and thinly veiled celebrity biographies, "based on a true story" has become a catchall for a wide array of the outlandish in contemporary culture. How much would you be willing to bet on the validity of that statement, for any document you have seen invoking it? Would you be willing to wager your life away? One young woman, Nuriko Furuta, did just that. The complexity of her actions, and the actions of those who encountered her, finally gets a network treatment this evening, not one of the big three, but a network just the same.

TZON, or the "T Zone" as the network has branded itself, has made its reputation on classic and obscure reruns combined with a parade of contemporary tabloid journalism and the boom of reality TV's popularity. In a classic case of the right time and the right place, the network jumped from a small independent station in the Dallas–Fort Worth Metroplex to a nationwide network with affiliates around the country in less than fifteen years, with this ratings-winning formula.

One of T Zone's signature shows, *Prime Hours,* uses the structure of one part taped interview, one part reenactment, and one part live interview. *Prime Hours* has been accused of soliciting the desperate for their subjects. The live interview is always stacked against the interviewee, but *Prime Hours* representatives consistently assert that all interviewees have signed releases before going on the air. While it's not quite the chair-throwing spectacles of other tabloid shows, a guest spot on *Prime Hours* is almost never a positive turn in the lives of those appearing in the hot seat. Usually, they agree for reasons of their own, believing their voices need to be heard, no matter the personal cost.

Tonight's television highlight is a belated postscript to one of last year's strangest news stories. In a year that will be remembered for the worst terrorist attacks on American soil, and the subsequent deluge of media coverage, the quiet tragedy of Ms. Furuta's passing generally got lost in the shuffle. While her name may not ring any bells for you, if you were watching news coverage late last November (and really, who in this country wasn't?), you probably remember the unusual circumstances of her death.

Ms. Furuta was the thirty-three-year-old Japanese woman who apparently took her life savings and set out alone from Nagasaki to Minneapolis and then into North Dakota, in search of the million-dollar ransom featured in the cult crime-drama/farce *Fargo,* then died of exposure, allegedly watching the Leonid meteor showers, mere yards from a group of cottages, outside Detroit Lakes, Minnesota.

When she was first discovered the day before, Ms. Furuta was wandering around a landfill behind a truck stop outside Bismarck, carrying a crudely drawn map. Authorities were unable to find anyone who could speak Japanese, and given the young woman's minimal grasp of the English language, they were also unable to convince her that the ransom did not exist. News coverage at the time claimed she was released because she had not been engaged in any illegal activities, and already overworked authorities chose not to hold her because "fuzzy thinking is not a crime in this country." She then took a bus to Fargo and hired a taxi to take her on an hour-long ride out to Detroit Lakes, where she died, surrounded by cottages.

Media sources generally would have tended to eat this story up, for all of its inherently ironic nature, but last November, we were not very receptive to irony. Though a number of unsettling questions presented themselves at the time the story broke, this strange set of events received little airtime and then quietly disappeared, much like the young woman herself.

The live segment of tonight's episode of *Prime Hours* (Channel 33, 10:00 EST) is dedicated exclusively to these events, where we get the first in-depth interview with Tommy Jack McMorsey. You have not likely ever heard his name before, either, even if you had paid attention to the story as it unfolded. Mr. McMorsey is the truck driver from Lubbock, Texas, who initially reported the woman to authorities in North Dakota and who was also, later, the last person to see the young woman alive.

Among the segments, *Prime Hours* will recap the original November news coverage of Ms. Furuta's death, and the brief period in which Mr. McMorsey was considered a potential suspect in the case, before authorities ruled the young woman's passing a "death by misadventure." Following that, Peter Haskell interviews Mr. McMorsey, who makes the claim that the news reports from the time were inaccurate. Authorities who interacted with Ms. Furuta are also interviewed and asked to address the truck driver's claims. The last segment includes further responses, from the news media sources local to the story, whose assertions Mr. McMorsey is refuting.

Is this story a stinging indictment of the way in which our news sources handle the smaller tragedies of our world, further dehumanizing us, or is it merely a continuation of exploitation disguised as probing news? Either way, it should make for interesting and engaging television. Be sure to tune in.

Annie Boans

Before Commencement, my regalia still cloaked in a garment bag for another year, I stopped by my office mailbox where a new inter-office mailer held the morning paper's back section. An article was circled in red marker, a note attached to the upper corner with a paper clip. The rigid, formal, and stiff penmanship was my former mother-in-law's. It was a note of very few words, each one count-ing, as if letters were being rationed and Martha Boans were down to her last few.

My world changed in that moment, within her oddly consti-pated script, as if I had donned glasses for the first time, or had been suddenly fitted for a hearing aid after years of reading lips and deciphering the intended meaning of dull consonants and vowels. The vague whispers I had heard perpetually throughout the reservation suddenly came into sharp, piercing distilled sounds, like swords drawn. For years, I had been so close to knowing the information held on this scrap of paper, and even as close as I'd come, my mother never flinched, answering my questions with the nonchalance of telling someone what was for dinner. I should have followed my usual rule.

Every year, I purposefully avoid my campus mailbox on this day. I don't want to be tempted to bring work with me to Commencement, sneaking glances at letters, calls for proposals, invitations, as the kids walk across the stage. Instead, I daydream my way through Commencement. You can only hear so many "It's a Big World Out There, but if You Are Determined, You Can Make a Difference" speeches and still be moved by them. I turn the volume down on the Potential Futures of Our Graduates speech, drowning it with future lectures, grocery shopping lists, favorite songs, harvested from memory.

I always try to appear attentive and smile at the graduates I had known. Any time I think of using a sick day for Commencement, I remember walking across the stage, seeing professors who had made a difference in my life. I have little faith that I've changed students' lives, but this was the only chance for some. Entering, they had been one step away from fast-food franchise assistant manager and they still might take my next Value Meal order.

My own time in college was spent nearly leaving those halls for good, almost every day. The only thing keeping me there for the first year was my mother's potential daily glower if I had stopped going. That I studied art merely attenuated her stares. She still scantly believes I talk about art every day and receive a two-week paycheck she wouldn't have seen over the course of two to three months in any given year. My students' faces share the same will to stare down doubting parents, and that kept me at Commencement while colleagues had already switched over to gin and sailboats and "good books."

Though my grades were in a week before, I've continued inhabiting my office even beyond finals week. Some nights my apartment seemed emptier than others. Most evenings, I enjoyed coming home to clean silence. Up to a year ago, before my husband and I separated, every night would have been my ex-mother-in-law's combination of *Jeopardy* and smoky haze. During finals week, in past years, Doug would make my favorite dishes, have a bath waiting, and a good film from the little rental place a half-hour drive away. It was the only place you could get decent films without computer-generated explosions or surgically altered couples falling predictably in love, awash in a Top 40 sound track.

This year, finals week was pizza or Chinese delivery "for one"

and whatever was on cable. Once Commencement is over, I want
to be anywhere with people, though I frankly have no idea where.
My old socializing was with Doug and our families. My colleagues
had gradually stopped inviting us to their parties a few years ago.
As much as I'd wanted my own space, lately the apartment offered
only sterile discomfort. Maybe T.J. Howkowski, sitting next to me
on the stage, would want to do something, I had thought through
the ceremony.

I had helped him get his foot in the door, almost eight years
ago when he'd come home to the reservation for good, and now we
were at the only junior college in all of New York with two faculty
members who could legitimately check the "American Indian" box
on the human resources form, an improbable situation at best and
thus frequently problematic. Though my scholarship research spe-
cialized in Indians in American film, every time I admired beadwork
for its beauty and craft, the artists thought I was working on a way
to turn it into a lecture and make millions talking to fascinated
white audiences about their work. The life this reservation has in-
vented for me is far more glamorous than the one I have in reality.

They never see lectures where the honorarium doesn't cover
costs or see conference presentations where the panel is relieved
that there are more people in the audience than there are on the
stage. They also don't see that I'm working at a very small college
where there are no courses specializing in media studies or popular
culture or even American studies. I am the art historian, period.
I can do the research I want, but in the classroom, I had better
represent the Renaissance through postmodernism, or it is poor-
evaluation time for me. The luxury of a large University, where I
could really devote my time to the study of Fred Howkowski and his
impact on the roles of Indians in film, is really more a dream than
anything else, a way to not make myself crazy repeating over and
over again the significance of the first Italian perspective painters
or Pablo Picasso's break with form, or Cindy Sherman's own ironic
take on Hollywood.

T.J. at least got some response as the chief in *Cuckoo's Nest* around the country in the summers, if not from his students. Half the time I'm not sure the audience listens as I lecture through a slide show, the only ways of documenting our culture that I have. He's also got the advantage of being a poster boy for Indian men in America—slick braids, hawk nose, thick sensuous lips, and the stoic look that just won't quit. I'm not sure he would get the same stares with a flattop or even a regular haircut but those braids are unstoppable.

Those same looks drive the Indian men around here as crazy as they do the women. That he is part white and raised by a white couple seventeen hundred miles away doesn't stop their wives and girlfriends commenting anytime they see him. Even Doug, when we lived together, carried on a running monologue about everything wrong with T.J. whenever someone mentioned him. When T.J. had a small speaking part last year on *Justice Scales,* Doug was insufferable. He'd even brought home one of the countdown calendars Mason Rollins had printed, with T.J.'s face, but not to mark the days until the broadcast. Doug's El Marko had given my colleague a pirate's eye patch, missing teeth, warts, the works.

I wonder if Doug still has it. He probably took it down last spring when I moved back to the city—the only home I had ever known. I'm convinced Doug had put it up, trying to brew tension, as if his mother's seven-year presence with us hadn't been enough. The whole time I'd lived on the reservation, people whispered behind my back, though about what, I never knew exactly. I thought maybe it would stop when I left, but they blamed the breakup on me, the city-Indian woman with the degrees, and not on the hardworking smoke-shop-clerking rez-born and -bred husband, and certainly not on the chain-smoking, soap opera–game show watching, invasive and pervasive mother-in-law who had lived with us since we moved to that trailer.

It hadn't been my fault her house burned down, and after seven years, I couldn't take one more day of that life, not knowing how much longer it would go on. I thought I'd be rid of her for the most part after I moved out. I felt safe living back in the city while she remained in my old trailer on the reservation. It was strange at first not to wake up to Doug snoring, and I had been surprised to discover that in the time I was on the reservation, I had acclimated to its otherwise quiet nights. I guess I missed the place.

"Did you know about this?" I whispered to T.J., as the students began their march across the stage. I revealed the article from the sleeve of my regalia, passing him the newspaper. He'd glanced, nodded, and handed it back to me. "It's not every day your stepfather gets on national TV. How come you never mentioned it?"

"Adoptive father. I don't know, didn't think it would be all that interesting to you. You know how that show is. I don't know what he's thinking. And besides, it's not like he's going to be talking about your favorite subject." Some days T.J. was willing to talk for hours about his real father's brief time home and then in Hollywood before he committed suicide, and some days he wasn't. Fred Howkowski's career was the major thematic core of my research, but I had to deal with my source material on its own terms, and that meant waiting a lot of the time for people to feel right about their relationships to him. I like to think that the slight reservation animosity to T.J. is what brought me to befriend him. When he showed back up here, he was so desperately looking for a community, and most people would have little to do with him. So, I did what I could, became his friend, helped him get a job, but he's also bright enough to know that part of my interest is his connection to Fred. I wish I could say it was different, but we both know the truth of that reality, and we just don't explore the topic unless he's had enough prodding. Then he reminds me in no uncertain terms.

"It's only about that Japanese woman. Didn't you read the article?"

"Yeah, what happened with all that, anyway? Did he ever say?" A colleague sitting in front of us turned and gave us the shut-up frown, so we waited for the students to move their tassels and get on with their lives. As we recessed from the auditorium, T.J. vanished, but then reappeared in my door a little while later.

"You all set?" he said. We walked to the lot in silence, the warm spring breeze rolling across the nearly empty lot. As we reached my Blazer, he said, "I'm thinking about going down there."

"Really? When?"

"I don't know, soon. It's been a while. Why?"

"I'd like to go with you." I could not believe those words had come out of my mouth. I panicked and then he offered the perfect recovery.

"Yeah, he might have a lot of useful information for you, and it would be nice to have some company," he said, staring at me from the passenger's seat. "When do you think you can go?"

"As of ten minutes ago, I am free for three months. Why don't we leave tonight?" I laughed and started the Blazer.

"Are you serious?" I wasn't sure myself if I were really committing to this idea. Maybe I was serious. So much had changed since this morning and it was true—I was free for three months. I had three lonely months of that apartment staring me down.

"Well, I should let my family know, so they don't worry," I said, finally.

"Okay, I don't have anything holding me here, and I've been meaning to make this trip for a long time. If we can get ready by five, we could make Cleveland before the TV show comes on."

"It means you have to come to my mom's with me, so I can let her know I'll be gone for a while, and I want to stop and get gas at Royal's shop, too."

"Your momma's all right."

When we arrived, my mother's eyes passed over us, trying to decide if I were really going to ask her the things I intended with T.J. in the room. This was the way she dealt with confrontation, a posh salesperson—politely and discreetly showing you the price of your desire. You might not have the necessary down payment, and she waited, wondering if you could hear the question being asked.

She was wrong this time. I'd come with enough to pay in full and to answer forcefully and clearly.

"Your TV working, Ma?" I asked.

"About as good as it ever does," she said. "Depends on the wind, season, trees, whatever." That was also part of her translation key. She could complain without ever technically doing so.

"T.J., why don't you climb up on her roof, see if the antenna is secure. Maybe it's just some loose connections or wires exposed on the line in," I said. He clearly hadn't any idea how he might implement such changes. So much for the improv skills of this professional actor. How had he ever managed to get even off-Broadway roles? "Here, I'll show you where the ladder and the duct tape are." I walked him out to the shed behind my brother Royal's trailer. "There's plenty of things that might need addressing on that roof."

"Uh, okay. Annie?" he said, puzzled.

"I'll call you when we need to get going," I said.

"Ma, let's go in your room," I said inside, my eyes adjusting to the shadowy midday light.

"No one else is here," she said. "He can't hear." She kept the blinds drawn and the curtains half-drawn, as she always had when we lived in the city. There, it had been for privacy. If you left any blind open in our old place, you were bound to catch some old pervert sitting at his window in the next building over, waiting to catch a glimpse of anything we might be up to. It didn't matter if it were washing dishes or vacuuming. You could see the fantasies they were cooking up, even as they watched you sweat across the alley. Back here on the rez, my mother no longer needed the privacy. Her nearest neighbors would need to have Superman's eyes or a really decent set of binoculars to catch her at her quilt-making but she was taking no chances or merely had grown accustomed to her darker life. T.J.'s shadow floated by us, just beyond the living room window.

"Come on," I said, sitting in the plush chair near her bed. She turned on the television, sat on the bed, and skipped though the few channels her antenna received.

"See, it works fine. Those are all the channels you get without cable or one of those dishes like they have the next trailer over. How much does the dish cost?" On the screen, images phased in and out like the badly spliced educational films they showed in high school, the sixteen-millimeter projector whirring and clacking from the back of the room, all but obscuring anything the people on the screen said.

"Ma, today, Martha left this morning's paper in my mailbox at work," I said. My mother would not make eye contact with me, staring instead at the people arguing on her television, ghosts of them crossing one another in T.J.'s adjustments.

"Well, that was nice of her, wasn't it? She probably had to hire one of her kids to drive her all the way out to the college, to get you that newspaper. What are you complaining about?" she said, finally, pretending she had no idea what I was talking about, or perhaps just hoping that I had no idea what was really in the morning paper. Surely she must have known what would cause her best friend and my ex-mother-in-law to make that special trip, but my mother would never resent Martha for anything, always looking the other way. What kept those two together was the meanness they inflicted on one another over sixty years, keeping each other going, pushing every day forward with new bitterness.

"She left a note with the paper, too. That was how I knew it was from her. I recognized her handwriting. Have you seen it?"

"The paper? Early this morning, probably before you were even up," she said. I tossed the entertainment section across the room to her. It fell about a foot short. She didn't bother to pick it up.

"The note was clipped to an article about that show *Prime Hours* tonight. Did you see it?"

"I don't watch that show, or that channel even," she said, waving her hand as if she were being bothered by a fly. "I never went in for the *The Twilight Zone* or the *The Outer Limits* or *In Search of . . .* like you kids did. And that show? What they do to people is just pitiful. If I want to see people behaving badly, I'll just walk down to Moon Road. I don't need to see it on my TV."

"You wanna know what the note said?" I took it out of my purse and read it aloud in my best Martha Boans snippy fashion: "'You might want to watch this show tonight, if you want to see your real father.'" I flashed the note in front of my mother so she could also see that, indeed, it was Martha's handwriting, and then folded it back into my purse. We both knew that the reservation was consistently very closed-mouth about suspicious parentage, but only to the child in question. Otherwise, everyone was gossipy as hell with each other. I've known of other people who reached adulthood confident in their parents' marriage, only to discover at the age of thirty or so that they are not exactly who they thought they were. I just never suspected I might be one of those people, but I don't imagine any of those who'd been zapped before me did, either.

"You know, I had always heard people talking, making vague suggestions just within earshot, at Community Fair, the Feast, Culture Night, National Picnic, all those places, but you know how people gossip, and they never offered anything other than innuendo." People on the reservation have also talked nonsense and believed it as truth forever—aspects of the culture that outside scholars tag as cute or charming or quaint. Those scholars have never had to convince an adult that a Tin Man, like that character in *The Wizard of Oz*, did not live below the hill, lurking around the picnic grove at night. When I became the subject of gossip, myself, I should have been thankful for the Tin Man, but he must have moved on, replaced by the smart girl who could not add two and two.

"What's that, innuendo?" she asked. She was a whiz at crosswords, keeping a dictionary by her bed, but she never remembered the words for longer than it took to box them in to Five Down, or Four Across.

"Vague words, with double meanings, suggesting something without really saying it. So I went to see Royal at the pumps, and I asked him to tell me the truth. I had asked him a long time ago, years ago, in fact, and back then, he said he didn't know anything, had no idea what I was talking about." If I had gotten a useful answer, I might not have left out that I had gotten him drunk to do it.

"Oh," my mother said.

"So when I asked him today, do you know what he said?"

"I don't know what you asked him."

"I asked him if Dad thought I had a different father from the rest of the kids. If that was why he left. You know what he said?" The fear in her face, as she grimaced and stared at the TV, told me she had no idea what he said. Maybe he truly didn't know anything about that hazy period.

"He said, 'If you need an answer to that question, then you better go ask Ma.' So, here I am. Am I the reason Dad left for good all those years ago?" There, it was out, the one question I had practiced in front of mirrors, on dark roads, on top of the dike, anytime I was alone, for years. Even the cat I left behind with Doug was tired of hearing that one, usually glancing at me for a second before returning to grooming itself in the sun.

"He was never at home much," she said. Royal had mentioned that sometimes our father would live in other cities for a year at a time—Detroit, Cleveland, New York—wherever they needed buildings erected. "Even before you. I don't know why he would leave. We gave him all the freedom he wanted, and the kids adored him. He just wasn't a happy person, I suppose. I tried dragging him out of other women's apartments, at first, but then he would just leave, altogether, for longer periods."

"He used to come back, every now and then, before I was born. But whenever I saw him anywhere, he always looked through me like I was glass. How come?"

"I don't know. He just did."

"When he died, I was the only one who went with Royal, none of the others, to go clean up that little apartment he kept down in Buffalo. I found his address book and calendar. You know all the birthdays and anniversaries, and all that, they were all neatly entered, as recent as Joanie's kids, and one of them hadn't had a birthday yet. But one date was missing, Ma. My birthday. Any idea why that was?"

"I bet my birthday wasn't in there, either, was it?" She stopped me dead, there. I hadn't looked, had randomly flipped through the pages, and judged it to be otherwise complete. "I went to that apartment before you and Royal went. I saw that book first, and I put it back. I knew you would look for your own birthday. You know what? I considered writing it in there. I knew how to forge his handwriting, had to learn to years before, just so I could get some money to feed you kids out of that account he kept. I figured if you wanted to look in that book for answers, though, you deserved to find them." She frowned at me, there in the dark, her face nearly disappearing in the shadows for a minute, reappearing when T.J. would move something on the roof, then her features softened.

"It's okay. I knew you wouldn't look for my birthday," she repeated, for emphasis. "You weren't the only one who became invisible to him, and there, you got off lucky. When we were first married, in the winter, I would get up before him, warm his clothes on top of the kerosene heater, and cook him a big breakfast, eggs, bacon, toast, coffee, everything. I'd call him to get up when the table was set and the clothes were warm, and he would come down, already dressed in a different set of clothes, tell me he didn't want any of that *Oo(t)-gweh-rheh,* and go out the door, sometimes until after work, sometimes until a week or more had gone by. I didn't cook breakfast for him long."

"Why was he that way?"

"I don't know, I told you. He just was. His ma and dad spoiled him, told him he was better than me, and I guess he believed it, but I don't know why he wanted to get married in the first place, if he thought that."

"But he always came back in those days."

"Yes, eventually. I would wake up sometimes in the middle of the night, startled, because he had climbed in and was snoring next to me, and sometimes I just found him in the morning, drinking coffee in front of the stove, like he had just slipped from our bed before I had stirred, to surprise me with a fresh pot."

"So why did he stop coming back after I was born? Why did he disown me?" We were getting to it, then, the harder questions, the real ones. My siblings always said our dad was never around, but more and more, I was getting the feeling that was only partially true. I had continued to hope that if I had primed my mother, used Socratic teaching method, she would begin freely discussing this forbidden topic, but she was like my students, fighting me all the way with silence and misdirection. I was prepared, though, had trained a very long time, as I had for my orals to complete my dissertation.

"He just did," she said again.

"Did he think I was someone else's kid?"

"He was just an unhappy man, I told you. He always thought funny things about people."

"Did he have reason to believe I might not be his?" Would she confirm here that he really did treat me differently than he did the rest of the kids? I held my breath for a moment, waiting it out, this time, asking it without asking it, that tightrope.

"He was coming around less and less in those days. There was a man, a very nice man, and almost everyone out here liked him," she said.

"Am I this man's child?" I asked, finally.

"He was a very nice man," she repeated, "but also very free. I thought by that time the old man wasn't coming back, and I figured, since he had been around so much with who knows who all, my keeping company with this man wouldn't do anyone any harm. The man lived in Texas, anyway, and it wasn't like he would be back much. He used to joke, said if we ever had kids . . ." She stopped, changed direction, slightly. "We both had red hair, but his was lighter than mine."

"Am I?" I repeated. It was surprisingly hard to repeat the entire question.

"I don't know. It's possible. Dad's shit-ass sister talked him into forcing me to get a blood test when it was clear I was pregnant. She was always convinced I was trying to get at his money. Hah! What money? I had this man's dog tags, he had given them to me one of the last times I had seen him, but he and Dad had the same blood type. The same you have. The only ones who knew were the three of us, and Martha. She was the one who took me. Back then, the agencies didn't chase for support like they do now. I think that's why your friend T.J.'s mother eventually just handed him over to someone else. The bother for her wasn't worth it."

"Am I really yours?" I had to ask. If everything I had ever believed was now up in the air, why not that, too? It seemed like everything was possible, even that Tin Man, lurking just out of sight all these years, hiding in the picnic grove restrooms during rainstorms to avoid rust.

"Of course you're really mine. When Dad said he wasn't going to claim you, the last thing I said to him when he went out the door that final time, was, 'Okay, she'll always be my baby.' And the rest of the kids, they didn't treat you any different, you were everybody's baby. Especially Royal, he took you everywhere with him."

"I remember," I said, which was why I had believed if anyone were going to tell me the truth, it would have been him. "Didn't you think I was ever going to ask?"

"I was hoping you wouldn't. I was hoping it wouldn't matter to you, hoping we had loved you enough that it wouldn't matter."

"It isn't a matter of love, Ma."

"It's always a matter of love. I thought you would have at least learned that by now."

"What's the man's name?"

"Do I have to tell you?"

"Don't you think I deserve to know? Is that him in this morning's paper? Is he the man you used to talk about, sometimes, when we were all little kids?"

"Yes, that's him. He's a very nice man. Could make me laugh

so hard, was so free, willing to be goofy, but the real man, the one
inside the goofy one, well, he was shy, sweet, and had the most
beautiful ears. I still don't know for certain which one is your father, could be either. You're as dark as the rest of us and that man
was very fair-skinned, but you do have such pretty ears, too." She
reached over to touch my ear. I moved away, just an inch. It was
enough, and she lowered her hand. "It doesn't surprise me to know
he was trying to save that woman from Japan. That's how he was."

"He didn't seem to help you too much," I said.

"He doesn't know. When the tests came back with no clear
answer, Dad and your aunt never pushed it. I suppose they could
nowadays, but Dad's dead, and your aunt, thank goodness, is still
busy chasing money somewhere else."

"So he has no idea I even exist? He didn't bother to find out?"

"He wondered. The last time I saw him. He asked if there was
anything in my life he should know about. I told him no. He had
married that woman by then, so there was no sense in stirring up
things that couldn't be. He wasn't going to leave and come up here,
and I wasn't going to leave and go down there, so we decided to
love each other one last night, and leave it at that."

"When was that?"

"The last time we were together. Fred Howkowski's funeral.
When he brought the boy back, your friend out there on the roof.
We had that one night, while you and the rest of the kids and that
little boy slept in the back bedroom. We took all you kids to the
drive-in that night, hoping to tire you out so we could have a few
hours together, some awful Bigfoot movie, as I recall. You wouldn't
remember. You were just a baby, then. After we put you all to bed,
we tried to get a lifetime's worth of loving into one night and hoped
we could make it last."

"But you can't just decide to stop loving someone, suddenly
one day. It's a gradual thing, or it doesn't happen at all." For me, it
had been a gradual thing with Doug. Perhaps something still lingered there, something I could find when I would run into him at

the National Picnic, or even at the grocery store, but it wasn't much and it faded fast as soon as I pictured Martha still smoking and sewing and spreading and smoothing her criticism like a quilt.

"Don't you think I know that now?"

"Which part?" I asked.

"You decide," she said.

"So I'm half white. My whole career has been a lie."

"Our life together, here, there, in the city, wherever—it's not a lie. You're my baby, the baby of all of us. You are who you are."

"I'm going with T.J. I'm going to meet him." I had made the decision the second T.J. seemed even remotely interested, but I had to come here first, ask that question before I set out on the road. The idea of that other man, that other possibility, had long lived in my mind, growing, becoming more real, but the face was always a blank, like those fake life-size cutouts you can stick your head through and become Santa Claus, Scarlett O'Hara, or a bathing beauty, but as soon as you step out from behind the plywood, you are yourself again, and that body is empty, waiting for the next identity. This man, though, living somewhere in West Texas, trying to save random delusional Japanese women, he was real, made of bones, muscle, hair, teeth, tissue, and deeper—and more importantly—DNA. Blood tests might have been inconclusive back then, but that was no longer the case. I could find a more definitive answer for myself, though it would take more than dog tags to do it.

"Well, you do what you want. Don't be so sure this place will be the same when you get back. Things change, people eventually fill in those rips that get made in their lives—Dougie, for example. I don't know what you hope to gain from doing this," she said, having always had this strange attachment to my husband, perhaps because he treats her better than her own sons do, but who could say with her, what she thinks being treated well and not so well are, where she makes those distinctions?

"Have you filled your rips in?" I turned and walked out of the

room. "T.J.? You ready?" I asked out the window, gathering my
purse.

"Yeah, just about," he said, climbing down. "You had a couple
frays on the wire, Mrs. Mounter, where it had rubbed up against the
aluminum over the years. There are some parts where the roofing's
coming loose too. I covered the bare wires and I taped the whole
connector wire in place, so that shouldn't happen anymore in the
future. I hope that'll work. But that roof, you should get someone to
look at it pretty quick. I taped it for now, but that won't last. Maybe
Floyd Page will be willing to do a side job, off the books." He shrugged
his shoulders.

"I'll be back, eventually, Ma," I said.

"When?" she asked, never a fan of vague words except when
she was the one using them to shroud some information.

"Eventually," I repeated, and we neared the door. That was
when she tried to draw me back in.

"Does he know you're coming—" was the final thing my mother
asked. She's always been this way. She knows the kind of small
phrase to use regardless of the occasion that once it is out of her
mouth it grows, and continues on, spreading out from inches to
miles across our lives.

"He will, soon enough," I said. "Besides, I have got to get away
from here for a bit," I said.

"So you said." My mother picked up her needle and threaded
the eye, letting me know our conversation was coming to a close.

"You have no idea."

"I think I might. Just that some of us can't pick up and leave
whenever we feel like it. We have to deal with what's in front of us."
She reached for her glasses. She was supposed to wear them all the
time but only picked them up for delicate work, maybe preferring
the world fuzzier around the edges, as if everyone she eyed had
halos or auras. Perhaps she just had no fondness for clarity.

"It's probably just for a couple weeks, maybe less," T.J. said.
He eyed the newspaper, making us appear guilty of something in

which we were definitely not engaged. He always looked this way when we appeared together in front of my mother or anyone else from the reservation for that matter. I think he liked the idea. "I have some things to take care of down there," he added and for a second I was nearly certain I had been the one to speak.

"I bet," my mother said. As we headed for the door, my mother went back into her bedroom. "Annie?" she called from her screen door a few seconds later. I sat in the driver's seat, letting her know I was not changing my mind.

"Come and get this." I got out and walked up the steps to her porch, where she reached a hand out the screen's frame, holding a letter. "I always keep copies, anyway. This one came back. You can read it, if you want, but I want you to give it to him." I didn't know what it was, at the time, but I had an idea. The RETURN TO SENDER stamp was smudged but clear enough, and the address was a post office box in Big Antler, Texas. I set it in the glove compartment. I didn't want to read anything that would potentially change my mind. The letter could be safely read once we were on the road, once we had committed to the destination.

T.J. and I left the reservation long before the sun went down. As the reservation disappeared in my rearview mirror, I noticed my ears, to which honestly I have rarely given a second look, except to try on earrings. These ears I had inherited apparently had little functionality. Who did I inherit that selective hearing loss from? I had asked for amplification and clarification at my mother's place. All the while, I wandered around this community, harboring only a vague suspicion of what others no doubt openly mocked me for. I was waiting for someone to creep the volume up on me, rather than turning the dial myself. Waiting for a clearer signal.

CHAPTER THREE:

Bit Part

o o o o

October 31, 1967

Dear Tommy Jack,

I am writing to you between the kids coming for tricks-or-treats. Their costumes are always the cutest little things you ever did see. Some of the little boys, though, they are dressed up like soldiers, and if I see them coming down the drive, I ask Momma to give them their candy. It makes me too sad to see them. One of them had a little burnt cork mustache, and after you said you'd grown one now because your face is breaking out there, well, that little boy especially made me think of you, over there, fighting for us. I'm glad to hear your memory skills are being put to work and that being the radioman makes you a little bit safer than the others. You didn't mention what a "Romeo Sierra" or a "Whisky India Alpha" is, but I suspicion you're not supposed to tell me anyway. Your description of Lubbock from the sky, like a giant patchwork quilt, well, I don't know if I'll ever see that. I don't think I was made to be the flying sort. I'll have to take your word for it.

I know I should have told you this in person, when you were home, but I didn't want you spending your last free time at home upset. It wouldn't have changed anything between us anyway, so I thought this was better. This maybe is just me, trying to make things up for not having been able to tell you in person, but I'm telling you now. I am sorry, Tommy Jack, for any bad feelings I have caused for you, or disappointments. Part of it is my daddy's doing. When you got that draft notice, I know he went down to the draft board with you and your daddy to try to get you a hardship deferment, but at the same time he went looking for other suitors for me. I guess he didn't want to see his little girl a spinster or a widow. Those are his words, Tommy Jack, not mine. You know I would never say anything like that.

But I have to tell you, because I always want to be honest with you, that after he said those words to me, they got me to thinking, and I sure didn't think I could bear that heartache at the age of twenty-four. I know it's nothing compared to what you are going through and I am not trying to make that heartache any smaller by saying that, just speaking my mind, the way you and I always have, over a vanilla shake or a Coke float. You know, it was funny, no matter what I ordered, I always wanted what you ordered as soon as we got it, and you were so sweet, always letting me have some, or even switching with me, whatever I wanted. I always thought that was darling of you, Tommy Jack.

Daddy says the war might be over soon, and you'll be back safe and sound, and will be able to get on with your life. He even thought he could possibly swing a job for you when you come home, teaching history at the junior college, what with your high school teaching experience, if you make some agreement that you'll finish your master's in a year. But he said that's future thinking and we need to concentrate on the present and those things that are best for us. Which brings me to why I am writing you, now.

I am sorry I couldn't take that ring, Tommy Jack. I did think it was pretty, if that's any help. Well, that shouldn't be a surprise. Even though you didn't present it, you would have had to be an idiot to not know which one I liked, since I pointed it out any time we walked by the jewelry store display. I know it was the one you would have offered if I'd given you the chance. I could tell by the look on your face that you had not even thought I'd leave my finger

unadorned that night, and I could understand your disappoint-
ment, but Daddy says I have to look to my future, as well.

I'm glad you have found a friend there. An Indian from New
York. Who would have imagined such? And what is this business
about you saving his life? Did that really happen? It is good to have
people to talk to when difficult things come your way. I have a new
very good friend, too. His name is Paul Montgomery. Maybe you
remember him. He is a very nice man, and I bet the two of you will
be fast friends when you come home. He's supposed to be the gym
teacher at Big Antler Elementary, but really he's varsity football
coach, so the boosters make his life a little better. We might be
going to state this year. He drops off lesson plans for his "helper,"
the real gym teacher, and then he drops by my office when he is on
his free period. He's been awfully good to me, making sure I didn't
get lonely while you were away, keeping my mind off those terrible
things they report on the news each night, going to evening prayer
service where we pray for your safety, and the safety of all of our
other boys who are with you overseas.

I imagine you know what I am leading up to here, and you
have always complimented me on being plainspoken, so here goes.
Paul has asked me to marry him and I have accepted his proposal. I
have tried to write this letter in many different ways, Tommy Jack.
I have even used up most of this year's stationery but it is coming
close to the holiday season, so I want to make sure my momma has
reason to give me this gift. It is not so dear, so her savings account
won't suffer so greatly, and it is something I use. Our church has
given us the names of other GIs who might want letters, that the
Red Cross had given them (I guess not everybody has someone at
home to write to them), and there is a big letter-writing campaign
throughout the school. Isn't that the most darling? Maybe someone in your grouping or platoon or whatever it is will get a letter
from one of our little boys or girls, and you can tell them all about
life in Big Antler, Texas. Won't that be a hoot? I am writing some
letters too, but I wanted to write this one to you first.

I am looking forward to your coming home and us all being the best of friends. I am sure it will all work out. I won't write to you again while you are over there. I suppose there is the possibility that you won't want to be hearing from me for a while, anyway, and don't you worry, I am not mad at that. I can understand it perfectly. I guess I will sign off here, as there is school tomorrow, and October is the beginning of flu season, and that means the beginning of the busy season for the school nurse. Please look me up when you get home, Tommy Jack. I am not sure where we'll be living, but definitely it will be somewhere in Big Antler and we will be in the telephone book, Mr. and Mrs. Paul Montgomery. Just give us a ring to let us know when you'll be coming a-calling, it will be so good to see you. Well, here comes one of those little kids from the school. This one is dressed up like Batman.

Best to you,
Liza Jean

Tommy Jack McMorsey

Yes, that was the letter that started it all. Funny that when I got home from North Dakota and the *Big Antler Daily* would run that story on me and the Japanese girl, I would be getting the same kind of looks around town I got when I returned from Vietnam thirty-three years ago to see my high school and college sweetheart married to someone else. I could have let it go with those original newspaper stories, where my name wasn't even mentioned in the syndicated story, but some old boy down at the *Big Antler Daily* had to read a little more carefully and recognized my name in the full wire service report.

This time, it wasn't just "Guess who your girl is married to, Tommy Jack?" or "What kinds of things did you see and do over there, Tommy Jack?" their looks were saying at me. This time, the Morse code they were blinking at me with their eyes, even as I bought my quick picks and my dailies and my weeklies, had a different feel, similar, but just different enough. "How come you didn't save that girl, Tommy Jack?" "Was she another one of those ladies you make time with on the road, Tommy Jack?" "Did you do something you didn't want her talking about, Tommy Jack?" That last one was probably the one that got me the most. So I just wanted to get it all out in the open, that I tried to save that poor young woman, but then that stupid article got this whole other ball rolling.

Who would have ever thought anyone read the *Big Antler Daily* besides the folks living in this pissant town, anyway? I never realized the larger syndicate works both ways, and once a story gets out there, well, it carries on. All I wanted to do was stop those people looking and whispering again, like they had over thirty years ago. A small town like this, it has got one big and long memory. I've never totally been the shy type, generally willing to do whatever it is that needs getting done, but I have also never gone much out of my way to draw attention, either, and those stares were working my nerves, all over again.

You know how it is, they knew you probably killed some people in the war, and they just applied that knowledge onto you all the way around, even though they weren't remotely involved. They never had to do and see the things I did and saw. They were sitting back home, watching the TV, maybe some of them even writing to me, because some of them did, hi-how-you-doing-get-back-safe kind of stuff, but what did they really think we were doing in the jungle, throwing mud balls? Pushing each other in the water? Maybe punching someone in the head if things were particularly bad? They were all well and nice when I made it home, even invited me to the occasional party they were having, once they realized I was back, but the looks were there. Did I do some of those things that were being hinted at in the newspapers and magazines, cutting off ears and wearing them as necklaces? The answer is no, but they thought what they wanted, anyway. Soon enough, this country will be at war again, with that crazy new president. Lord, did he have to come from this state? Seems like he's trying to drag Iraq in, but no matter where it is he wages war, those young men and women are going to come home to some of those same looks, and I do not envy them one bit. The draft might be gone these days, but I don't imagine any rich man's son is eagerly signing up for the military right now, and anyone signing up now, you know that bastard has no other options.

I returned to U.S. soil the very night I zeroed out, left the jungles, arrived back into the shipping depot in Oakland sometime later but it's hard to remember those things—not because they were terrible or anything, just the opposite, but a jolt is still a jolt, however you cut it. The day before we zeroed, we had been out on patrol, and had been for a month. I had nearly forgotten I was scheduled to be coming home. This was unlike me, as I had been a day counter from day one. That was one of the last times I ever participated in a Fireball game and it was for sure the last time Fred did. He declined to play when I went to visit him at his reservation in New York. Though he didn't think I noticed, I always pay attention to stuff like that. Just like I could remember everything that happened with the Japanese girl and was getting ready to tell it all and stop these looks around town.

"Tommy Jack, they're gonna be here soon. Are you dressed? I left a shirt and tie out for you, on the bed," Liza Jean said the morning the TV crew was scheduled to arrive, coming from her bathroom, where she had checked her makeup for the thirtieth time since she put it on an hour or so before. That bathroom's off our bedroom, but I was banished to use the one down the hall, years ago, because of splash concerns and poor aim. But in the hall bathroom, I can leave out my floss and sunblock and whatever magazines I want, and if there's a little splash now and then, I don't care. It cleans up.

"A tie? What the hell for?" I asked, tying it anyway, knowing this was another argument I would lose if I chose to engage it.

"Well, why are you doing this in the first place? I mean, Tommy Jack, if you want people to just go on believing something happened to you out there in Minnesota, then you might as well just call up those reporters and cancel this altogether, and we can get going to Cascabel now."

"And you're thinking this here tie is going to change minds in ways that my speaking the truth doesn't?"

"Well, is it going to kill you to wear a tie?"

"I've got it on." She came back through, straightened it, kissed me on the cheek, then licked a paper towel and wiped her kiss from me. She ran through the living room, fluffing pillows, moving figurines an inch or two to the left or right, or forward or back-ward. I had no idea what she was doing, while I stuffed into jeans and tied up a nice pair of brown Rockports with both of the laces matching. She sat on the sofa, going through five or six positions, locking her knees, tucking her legs under, crossing them, leaning one arm on the sofa pillows, one over the cushion, watching her own reflection on the big-screen TV, imagining what she would look like when they finally broadcast this here interview. She was going to break a sweat before they even set up if she didn't watch out, and it was likely to be hot enough under those lights without doing somersaults on the sofa.

She has been arranging and rearranging the furniture, even the pictures on the wall, ever since that TV news show called me up about a month ago to see if they could interview me about that Japanese girl. I had to tell Liza Jean to relax when she started in about getting new curtains, just for the show. She could act like it was the Home and Garden channel coming to visit us all she wanted, but that was not about to change the fact that this concerned Detroit Lakes and nothing else. I wasn't for sure why they thought it was interesting enough, but TV makes things way more real for some people than a newspaper clipping, so I understood a way to stop the clucking hens of Big Antler. And yes, secretly, I hoped the boy would be watch-ing, and yes, even more secretly, I wished Shirley Mounter would, as well.

"They're here, Tommy Jack, are you ready?" Liza Jean said, looking out a side window as this van with a big satellite dish on top of it came down the road. One nice thing about living here—there are no ways for a sneak approach, not like those jungles where you might meet a bullet around the next set of bushes. West Texas is about as flat and wide open as you can get, like God just decided to iron this big patch in the middle of the country. They were still two roads over, riding the grid to the house, but they kicked up a rooster tail of dust that was visible for miles. They wanted to come a day early for preliminary work, which I nearly knew meant that they were up to something, but I agreed anyway. I had come this far, I might as well go the whole of it and see what we would see. "Do you think they're gonna want some sweet tea?"

"I don't think it matters much to them," I said. "They've probably got their own, but it might be nice to offer."

"Well, why didn't you say so before?" she said, heading into the kitchen with one of those Tommy-Jack-you-are-using-up-my-patience sighs she gave me more and more often as the years got on.

"Well, then, don't. I don't give a shit," I said. And I really didn't. I thought she wanted to make the sweet tea and was looking for some kind of agreement. Damn, I never get this right.

They knocked on the front door a few minutes later, though I thought it was clear from all the potted plants out front, crowding the stoop, that we generally only used the back door. Maybe that was only clear to those who knew us. They shook hands all around and the reporter took some tea while the technical people set up equipment and started testing places, asking if it was okay to use outlets or if we needed them to use their generator, asking where outlets were when I said it was fine to use them—that kind of stuff. The enormous lights heated the house up fast when they tested them for a few minutes before we started.

Fred Howkowski always said the worst part of being before the cameras was sweating under the lights, knowing your makeup was washing off and they would be coming around to touch you up again, just before filming. He said the makeup was thick and heavy, like the air during a Vietnam monsoon season. When it wasn't raining but still about a hundred degrees, the sultry air was like a woolen blanket around you. Some guys wore as little as was safe, it was so nasty. Flak jacket, fatigues cut to shorts, boots. Being from here, I could wear a full set of standard issue and be okay, but the heat always troubled Fred.

I wondered if these interviewers were going to make us up, or if that was just for the stars and not for someone you are trying to get dirt on. They could try all they wanted. I've got nothing to hide. That girl didn't want to get saved. It's just that way with some people. Fred tried saving our squad one time with Fireball, toward the end, but they turned it around on him. I can still see the look on his face when he realized what they'd done that last time. They'd taken his medicine game and turned it into something else.

o   o   o   o

We pulled bunker guard duty on Firebase Tomahawk, so it was just us around. This could be the most boring part. Toward cycle's end, some guys would get antsy, looking for any kind of distraction they could find. You went crazy sometimes looking into the thick brush, seeing nothing, but trying just the same. You could see movement where there wasn't any, or watch plants change into men in the right wind. By the few seconds it took you to get your M-16 up, the potential sniper had become an elephant's ear plant again. You could not watch passionately for that long and not start inventing something to see.

"Howkowski," Reggie Hughes said, leaning against some sand-bags and lighting a cigarette, "you must feel pretty at home, here on Tomahawk, huh? I mean, being an Indian and all, right? What kind of Indian name is Howkowski, anyway?" Hughes knew the answer but some guys liked to break up the boredom with hassling other guys, forcing them to be the entertainment. Donut Dollies, USO, and EM clubs being so scarce out this far, we had to make our own entertainment. That day was Fred's day to provide it.

"It ain't," he said. "My dad's white. Doesn't matter, though, no-body from home has those ridiculous names you hear in the mov-ies. Mounter, Page, Waterson, Boans, Natcha, Gunderson, Tunny, Martin, those are the kinds of names we have."

"Don't sound very Indian. I bet you're making that whole Indian stuff up," Hughes continued. More guys gradually drifted over, hop-ing for a fight. It was a slow day. "Show me one thing that's Indian."

"Go get that propellant over there and let's see who's gonna donate some rags," Fred said, sitting up.

"Here, use these," someone said, tossing Fred a bunch of old sandbags that had seen better days. They were supposed to go back for repair the next time I radioed Romeo Sierra, but these bags would not be making resupply. Fred knotted and tied a few in a bundle and then tossed it and other bags to someone else, who had to add to it.

"What are we doing?" Hughes asked as he added to the wad.

"You've got eyes. Use them. Join in or step aside," Fred said, taking Hughes's wind out. We were being introduced to the game called Fireball that Fred tried to save us with. It was funny to see him get more involved in the squad. Usually, sharing was limited to one or two buddies, and in our case, it was the two of us.

We had an exchange, kept each other alive. There are all kinds of ways of doing that. Splitting C rations, sharing anything that might come from home, one keeping an eye out while the other slept, all through the night, knowing that sometimes guys pulling night patrol duty got a little lazy on the job. Fred and me, while we did all those things, we also had something else. Neither could take charity but we knew exchange really well.

At the rear, you got your fatigues washed and cleaned, nice and neat, they were yours, and my shirt had *McMorsey* embroidered onto a patch sewn on the right breast pocket, but in the jungle, on patrol, you just took whatever was dropped from the chopper. When we'd get the call, we'd run to the closest spot that resembled a clearing, given the day's firing patterns. They would fly in, dump for our squad, and in the twenty minutes after they resupplied the other squads, they swung back to pick up whatever we sent.

The drops were clean clothes, ammunition, C rations, big rubber jugs of fresh water that we had to chase down the hillsides so they wouldn't bounce beyond our reach, and firearms replacements if we had asked for some. In the time before the chopper got back, we'd strip down and stuff every stitch of dirty clothes into those bags we'd just pulled the clean ones from. I pitied whoever was washing those things. Sometimes we'd been wearing a set for two weeks straight. Then we'd grab whatever clothes might fit us okay and put them on. You don't want to be standing naked on a hilltop all pink-skinned and sweating, glistening in the sun, begging a sniper to pick you off. Some weeks your clothes fit better than others.

We'd send back misfiring machine guns, anything that weighed us down, and if we'd caught the good company clerk, we'd be sending money back too. In that drop we'd just gotten, there would have been a case of cold Coca-Colas that he'd fronted us if we promised him the money. You might think he would have been stiffed a lot, but he never was. He let you know, he'd do it for any squad if he got the call when you made it. If you ever shorted him, though, your squad was never getting even one bottle dropped from that point on, and he'd let you know why. Everyone always paid up. There is nothing like a chilled Coca-Cola in a 110-degree jungle.

We would hold those icy bottles to our cheeks for a few seconds, snap those caps off, and guzzle them down as fast as they'd pour from the neck. A warm Coca-Cola is nobody's friend. Cold this way, it was a brief taste of home. For that moment it slid down your throat, you might have been sitting at the picnic tables under a drive-in restaurant's neon, sharing a frosted glass with your girl, listening to the crickets ticking off the hours until you had to take her home. That company clerk never got stiffed, as far as I know, the whole time I was in country.

As sacred as a Coca-Cola out there was, it compared not at all to mail from home. Everything else was flat-out ignored when it came to mail. It didn't matter how hungry we were, there wasn't a man among us who opened C rations before he opened a letter with the red, white, and blue striping along the envelope edges. And if there was some news from home, your best friend heard it before anyone else. You might eventually show pictures and whatnot and maybe even read selected passages to everyone, if you were feeling generous, but you shared the whole thing with your best friend first. And that was how Fred Howkowski came to find out that Liza

Jean, the woman who all these years later sat beside me before the cameras, left me for a while, ditched me for that flat-footed nitwit in Big Antler.

"'Best to you, Liza Jean.' Best to you, how do you like that? Best to you," I said, and folded up the letter.

"Coke?" Fred said, still holding the bottle out to me. I shook my head. Fred got some fry bread in the mail one day and this stuff was hard as a rock by the time it got over across the globe. I could hardly see its appeal until I tried Shirley Mounter's, after we'd gotten home. I was swallowing something harder than stale fry bread and no amount of Coca-Cola was going to wash its jagged edges down any smoother.

"Still got my own," I said. "Was too eager to see what Liza Jean had written." I had skipped the Coca-Cola for a few minutes to open the letter, but I had wished that envelope had somehow gotten lost across the thousands of miles it had traveled to find its way to me there in the bush.

o   o   o   o

"Mr. McMorsey, do you want your wife to be here with you for the interview?" the reporter asked, while a technician clipped a small microphone to me and ran back to some portable machinery it was plugged into.

"Well, yeah, I imagine so," I said. I should have known at that point they weren't planning to stick to just the whole Fargo thing. Something in the way he said it suggested he was trying to let me know that was maybe not such a good idea, but Liza Jean had gone to the beauty shop the day before and had slept with her head all wrapped that night, so she would look good on TV. All of her friends would be watching, so I couldn't let her down, couldn't tell her to forget it after all that preparation. Hell, she even picked out my shirt and tie so they would be some kind of match with her outfit. I couldn't see it personally, but I trusted she could. "Right here, you can fit us both in if we sit here on the sofa, right?"

"Mrs. McMorsey?"

"Just call me Liza, everyone does."

"Okay, Liza, would you like a microphone, too?" That technician looked up and started running another line toward us, but
Liza Jean held her hand up in front of her and waved it in the air.

"No, I wasn't there, so I don't know what I could add."

"Well, why don't we put one on you, just in case," the reporter
said. The technician went back and forth across the room, carrying
that little line around with him, trying to figure out whose lead to
follow. He eventually clipped it to her collar as the reporter assured
her it was a standard procedure for anyone on camera.

They tested lighting arrangements and Liza Jean held her
hand onto mine the whole time. It was the first time, I think, since
before I had left for basic, that she held on that tight. When I came
home for those few days, between basic and advanced, she was
different already. Since I had been assigned to Fort Ord, it pretty
much guaranteed I was going over. Almost nobody made it out of
Ord and got a stateside assignment.

So I shouldn't have been surprised when I got that letter in
the mail drop while we were out on patrol. When I read that line, "I
know I should have told you this in person, when you were home," I
didn't have to bother reading the rest, but I did, anyway. I even read
it out loud to Fred and he just nodded and didn't say too much.

"Too bad you couldn't teach seventh-grade math," he said finally, as we set up the ponchos for sleeping that night.

"Ain't that the truth," I said. Though we hadn't talked at all
on the way over, too scared, I guess, Fred had been on the same
flight as me, shipping out. Funny, we had seen each other from the
first, having gone through basic together at Fort Ord and then in
the limo to Oakland. He was one of the idiots I went in with, paying a limousine to take us into Oakland. All those weeks later on
the transport, we still had not really talked again, but his face was
familiar. The engines were all running and the doors had already
been sealed for our flight to Asia when they let a couple of guys on.

They were civilian workers, by their look, their suits. One asked if any of us had a master's degree and could teach seventh-grade geometry.

I was one semester away from finishing my master's, but I didn't know shit about math, had not really passed it myself. I took Math in Modern Living in college, where I learned, for fifteen weeks, how to balance a checkbook and manage a monthly budget.

"I taught a year of high school just before I was drafted," I said, hopeful.

"I'm pretty good in math," some guy a few seats away from me jumped in.

"Master's?"

"Yes sir, in sociology."

"Step off the plane with us, please," the officials said.

"I've already taught in a high school," I repeated, louder. They hesitated for a second and one asked, abruptly, what subject. "History," I said.

"Sorry, pal," he said, as they kept escorting that other guy off the plane. All the way to Vietnam, I tried to remember the rhombus, the parallelogram, and I traced all those shapes on the ground as we flew higher and higher, disappearing above the clouds and eventually the ocean. In the waves, I could see triangles: right, isosceles, acute, and obtuse, and by the time we got close to Da Nang, I had even remembered what pi had to do with circles, but it was too late, anyway, and all the history I had filled my head with instead of math was not going to keep me from those dangerous line segments dividing up Vietnam. Maybe that was what I got for studying all these other people dying in wars for someone else. I realized only years later that it had all been a setup and there were no magic words I could have said. They were waiting for that guy to say something, anything, so they could escort him off. Someone had pulled strings for him and he hadn't even known it.

"Well, maybe it just wasn't meant to be, Tom." Fred would not call me Tommy Jack, unless he was trying to get my attention. He said it was a kid's name and we were not kids anymore, by any stretch. "Take this friend of mine from home, Shirley Mounter," he said. It was the first time I had ever heard her name. "She's got kids with this man, and he seems all right enough, as a guy, but he doesn't treat her right. They just don't belong together." The night was growing dark in the quick way it did over there, so we bedded down as fast as we could in the little remaining light. "Give me that letter," he said in the dark.

"What for?"

"I don't want you wasting the batteries in your penlight on that nonsense. You'll have plenty of time to read it over while we're here. You don't need to keep reading it now."

"I won't read it."

"Give it here."

What could I do? You almost never get unreasonable requests from your best friend, and when you do, maybe sometimes you just give in because he holds that funny place in your heart. I handed it over and slid the penlight back in my pocket. He knew I'd had it out.

"Now Shirley Mounter, she would never write a letter like that," he said. "She would write, 'Dear Tom,' and she would call you Tom because she would know you weren't a kid, too. So she would write, 'Dear Tom, I hear things aren't so well over there, but I want you to know that me and my kids, we're thinking about you. We're not the praying kind, as I'm sure you remember, but we think good things about you. We dream you into our nights, bring you home that way, so if sometimes you feel like you've been home, when you wake up suddenly over there, you have been. You've been wandering around in our heads and in our hearts.' That's what she would write."

"And how do you know that's what she would write? Who is this, anyway, your girlfriend?"

"Nope, just someone I know, a very good friend. I know

that's what she would write because that is the kind of letter I get from her."

"You never read a letter like that to me."

"You only ever wanted to hear the ones from my ma and my girl, so that was what I read to you." He rolled over in his poncho and I could see him smile a little, in that last light.

"You never told me you got any other kind."

"You never asked."

"So what else would she say to me?"

"She wouldn't say any of these things," he said, "but she'd write them." He smiled and lit a joint, passing it over once he got the spark going. So that was the way I got to know Shirley Mounter first, under the stars across the world, in that funny half world you live in after the first couple tokes, before the cotton mouth and the paranoia set in, when you are a part of the world, instead of apart from it. The only thing keeping me there, in the tall grass, was Fred's voice and the first ways I imagined Shirley must look.

At first, she looked kind of like that Land O'Lakes girl, you know, the kneeling butter girl, you can cut her off the package and fold her around to make her look like she's grabbing her boobs? Her. She was the only Indian lady I had ever seen on a regular basis. After a while, her looks changed for me. Sometimes she was Doris Day, sometimes she was Faye Dunaway, and sometimes Anne Bancroft. I was James Garner, Warren Beatty, Dustin Hoffman. What changed? Whenever we would make it to the rear for those three-day stand-downs to do a thorough resupply, Fred's made-up dialogue for the mess hall movies grew into the continuing story of Shirley Mounter and me. Though I liked being Warren Beatty, all smooth and well dressed in that double-breasted suit and white fedora, a wooden matchstick dangling from my mouth, I usually walked away from Fred's stories long before I would get all shot up on a country road in East Texas. There wasn't a single way he could make getting fifty bullets in me seem like a good story. For his part, Fred mostly filled the holes left in my heart by Liza Jean's letter with a new life for me where he came from, with this woman I had never met.

Every night, he would give me a new bit of information about Shirley. I came to think of this as S rations. She was somewhere, sleeping quietly with her kids, in New York, having no idea I existed, but for me, getting back there, to meet her, kept me from going back to that letter, reading how Liza Jean had already concluded I was dead, even before I had lost out on teaching geometry to a bunch of kids going fuzznuts.

From long before the time Fred and I were on that plane back to the States, Shirley Mounter had taken firm root in my head and had filled a lot of those holes. Fred had even gotten his momma to send him over a few pictures of Shirley, guess he was too shy to personally ask, but he got them, all right. When I would get to my lowest, when I would reach for that letter from Liza Jean again, he would pass me one of those pictures to look at for a little while. So she was no longer just the voice of Fred, over the face of some beautiful woman skipping across the mess hall screen. I knew what she looked like, could make up my own scenes by then, where I didn't have to be some leading man in a pin-striped suit, and I could just be me.

He had even gotten her pictures laminated somewhere, maybe when he was out on R & R, who knows, but there she was, sealed in plastic, safe from all our day-to-day nastiness. He never once let me keep any of the pictures, always asking for them back as soon as my penlight was off, and in that way he kept her a mystery to me, but one I was going to solve.

When I got there, to New York, a week after being home, I saw her that first night. I pretended I didn't know who she was, didn't want her to know we had been keeping company all that time I was in country—just didn't seem right—and I allowed myself to be introduced to her and danced with her that night like I have never danced with anyone in my life. She was wearing those stretch pants women wore all the time in those days, the kind that show a little calf. She was soft but muscled, in those flat shoes. She was not the kind who would wear high heels, would never allow any man to catch her off balance like that. The shirt she had on, it was homemade but not in a bad way, more in the way you could see it had been measured, cut, and stitched to fit her body and hers alone. When we danced, I reached around and she let me touch her back, leaned into me, and I smelled her hair, almost the same shade of red as mine. In that hair, there was the scent of rainwater, some basic shampoo, nothing fancy, and a slight hint of a vinegar rinse. She washed her hair like a country girl, as I had known she would, and I did not want to let go, that whole night.

Any song could have come on the jukebox, but I had put on "The Name Game." She thought it was so I could goof on her name and I never corrected her but back in those dark jungle nights, her name was the line, the connection to home that made me want to keep going. Fred had that little boy's picture but all I had were glimpses of this woman and the rhythmic way my tongue moved, mouthing her name over and over until I fell asleep for a few hours.

∘ ∘ ∘ ∘

"Okay, great, Mr. McMorsey, what we'd like to do is conduct some establishing shots here, maybe have you take us around the house, the backyard. This is a fascinating place you've got here, like some of those buildings out back. Our audience might be interested in those kinds of things," the reporter said, once he'd gotten the nod from some of the technicians.

"Well, those buildings—" I started.

"Wait, sir. What we'd like to do is get some of this footage and transmit it back to the station today where they'll edit it, neaten it up for the broadcast tomorrow night, to use as an introduction of sorts. But what we'd really like to do, I'm sure you've seen our show—"

"On occasion."

"Yes, well, we'd like to do the real interview live, right from your living room, tomorrow night. It's one of our hallmarks, as you know. If that's all right with you," the reporter said. I didn't know, never did watch that much TV, but this seemed like the right idea to me, everything live, no chance for these guys to change and rearrange the things I say, since as soon as they leave my lips, my words will head on out across America.

"Sure, that's totally live? As I say it, it goes out?"

"There's a brief signal delay, a few seconds' transmission from here to the network and then transmission back out across the country, but yes, other than that, totally live, sir."

"Okay, and what is it you want to do today, then?"

"We'd like you to walk around the grounds here, we'll shoot you, walking around your property, you and me talking. We'll use some audio here, but mostly, these shots are just to give our viewers a context for who you are, so they'll be ready to receive what you have to say with a minimum of introduction tomorrow night and then we can get right to the story America is going to want to hear. Would you mind if we started outside?" They all stood up without waiting for an answer. Apparently they learned the same kinds of questions Liza Jean knew so well. What could I do? I went outside with them but this time I guided them through the back door, the proper way.

Someone who called himself the segment director yelled out instructions to the people scurrying around with all this equipment. Every time I looked up at them, the segment director would yell out to me to act natural, just pretend they weren't even there, as the reporter and I walked out through the back deck, the little pond I had built the year before. How are you supposed to act natural with a cord tied to you, running down the inside of your pant leg and several folks swarming you armed with electronics and screens and lights?

"You have a really nice place here, Mr. McMorsey. Peaceful."

"That was my goal. I like to meditate, not in any kind of fancy way, just be alone sometimes. I sit here by the pond a lot. There's fish in there, but the water's too murky to see them. These plants are supposed to clean it up some but I don't care if I can't see them. I know they're in there. You make the best of where you are. That's pretty much what I have always tried to do, anyway. A lesson I learned from my best friend a long, long time ago." The reporter walked the little bridge over the pond with me, and I wondered how those cameramen were keeping their reflections out of what they were shooting.

"You've constructed most of these buildings yourself?" the reporter asked, gesturing to the outbuildings on the property, the pump house, the Yorkston house, the seed barn, the others.

"Me? No, I've had them built. I don't have the time or skill to do this work. This is the work of some very good local laborers. Sad to say, there's a lot of underemployed men in this town, so their labor rates are competitive. It's a good gig. These guys do the backbusting work for me that I don't have the time or body for anymore, and some of these families around here, they get to put better food on their tables. I probably couldn't fund it on my paycheck leftovers, but estate sales, and now those online auctions? I have turned a lot of junk into a lot of cash over the years."

"He has one very good eye," Liza Jean said, stepping forward.

"Two decent eyes is more like it," I said. "When I don't have trips, sometimes there are some slow periods in driving a rig, I do the interiors, some, and smaller restorations, furniture and such."

"Tommy Jack, this is not their work," Liza Jean added. "It's yours. These are your ideas. They just do what you instruct them. You should take credit where the credit is yours." Then she turned directly to the camera, waited for it to focus on her, and said, "He's had the idea to build this place up to look like it might have a hundred years ago, when the first settlers arrived here."

"You started these places from scratch?" the reporter asked, as one of the cameramen crossed his lenses over all the outbuildings.

"Well, no, this here house was called a saltbox style, because it resembled the old-timey salt boxes, which would be obvious if you ever saw one. This was out in a cotton field, a few miles from here and families of hands lived in it over the years, but it had been abandoned by about the time I was a little boy. The family that owned it, the Yorkstons, ended up owing my daddy money right up to the day he died, and they offered me the house, I guess, as sort of settling old debts of their conscience. And since Liza Jean and I have been collecting antiques for so long, and running out of room in the house to put them—"

"And not wanting to part with anything," she added.

"I thought this might be a nice way to store and display our collection. So we looked into how much it would cost to move the building, and saw it was feasible, and we did it. The interior restoration took about three months of straight work, and most of the replacement boards came from other old buildings of the era, to make it as authentic as I could, and, and, why am I telling you this? What has this got to do with anything?" I finally asked. Funny, sometimes, we get schoolkids out here on field trips to check out the old buildings and I do this routine with them and here I was, rattling it off for these cameras, almost forgetting they were there.

"Please, this is very interesting, Mr. McMorsey. I'm not sure what they'll use and what they'll leave out, but who knows, there might be enough here for two stories. A human interest story on your hobby, pursuit, here seems like a natural. Now, what about this burned-out foundation? Do you have plans for that?" he asked, as we got closer to a patch of my life I try not to see too much.

"No, no plans. An old cook shed used to be there, but it's long gone."

"No desire to rebuild or use the slab as a foundation for something else?"

"Nope, no desire. Now, this building here, next to the pump house, this is what they called a granary, or seed barn, where a farmer would keep cottonseed for the next yield, oats for the horses, cattle feed, and—"

"What is Fireball, Mr. McMorsey?" the reporter asked, acting all innocent, bringing me back not to Vietnam, because I really do not like to think about the last game there, but instead back to the time in New York. Liza Jean knew I'd broken my nose in a Fireball game, and that I never got it fixed, but she didn't know why, and she didn't like to talk about it much either.

o o o o

"Come on," Shirley Mounter said, that summer. After that first evening at the bar, somehow we had made it back to her apartment. Okay, yeah, I had a part in persuading her we should go back there for coffee to sober me up before I drove back to Fred's place on the reservation. The one thing I had hoped for had led to another, and suddenly, it was months later and we were deep into a routine of encounters, falling in love along the way. I had already begun to fall for her over in the jungles, so really these times were her catching up to where I was.

Oh, it was always early of a morning when she would wake me. I'm a pretty early riser, in general, but she was dragging my ass out long before the sun come up. I think there were still crickets chirping it was so early. This time was to be one of the last encounters I would ever have with her, but we got a lot of experience fit into a few short months, here and there. Every morning was like this one. She would shag me out and I would make it back to Fred's momma's place for a while, catch another couple hours of sleep before he got up, and then we'd be off, doing something or another. "I'll see you tonight, at Fireball," Shirley said, kissing me in the dawn.

"Okay," I said, and she seemed all disappointed that I didn't ask what it was, but I already knew. I was for sure it would be different from the way we played it at the firebases but did not realize how different it would be until that night.

"Wait," she said, reaching around my neck. I thought she was going to hug me, but she grabbed the chain of my dog tags and lifted them off of me. "Can I keep these, until tonight?" She reached down the front of my shirt to get the tags themselves, her fingers running through the hair there. I wanted nothing more than to go back into her apartment for just a little while longer but that was definitely out, as far as she was concerned.

"Yeah, I guess I know who I am, if I get lost," I said. "And there's less chance of a sniper out here." I felt naked and missing something once they were gone, kept reaching for them in the few months following, but eventually, I guess you grow into the feeling of absence and I have never since worn anything around my neck.

That first year I saw real experts playing it, shortly after Fred and I got back from Vietnam, I just watched. The parking lot lamps around the field were switched off and the only light we got was from the flaming ball and goalposts. With Shirley guiding me, my sideline commentator, I studied the dark field filled with men chasing this blazing clump of rags across the grass toward opposite goalposts. Some picked it up with gloves and threw it, some didn't even bother with gloves, some jumped to block a shot with their chests, heads—the crazier the man, the louder the cheering. At the firebase, we had played it like a friendly game of soccer. These men were in it for keeps, as if their lives depended on what they were doing out there in the dew and kerosene smoke.

That next year was a different story. Shirley and I had spent a lot of time together by then. I had gone back to Texas in the middle of the summer, got my truck-driving-school certification, and started taking the long hauls, from Texas to New York—that was my standard route for that whole year. It was a year for me to get used to living back out in the flats, the barren areas around home, where the only trees were the pecans and mesquite around the place my daddy had set aside for me, while I was over. In his own way, he was trying to believe I would come on back. I was also trying to get used to another idea Fred sprung on me one night while we were lying out by a bonfire in his momma's backyard, drinking and watching the stars, our usual habit. He fired up a joint and passed it to me, just like we used to do on patrol. That night, it was just the two of us. For whatever reason, everyone else was busy, and Fred had told me when I pulled in that Shirley's old man was back in town.

"Hey," he said, after throwing down another log. The sparks shot up and disappeared among the stars.

"What?"

"I want to ask you something."

"How come I can take a bigger toke than you?" I laughed.

"No, I'm serious," he said.

"Then you shouldn't have passed this," I said, laughed again, and drew another big lungful, watching the embers creep closer to my fingertips. He didn't laugh. "Okay, okay, I'm serious, too. What?"

"The kiddo? I want you to take him. Not right away, maybe next year, this time, when we're both on our feet. You and me."

"Take him? Like to come visit me in the summers or some shit like that? The road is probably not such a good life for a little kid like that, and I think he would get bored and wanna come home after a week of hanging around my momma's place. There is not a lot to do in the flatlands of West Texas. Why do you think I'm here?" I propped up and looked at him across the fire, trying to see what he was getting at. His face was blank, like it got sometimes in the jungles when he saw things he didn't want to sink through the surface.

"No, I mean take him, period. I'm getting out of here. I had to come back for something, some purpose, Tom. And this is what I think it is. I'm going to Hollywood. All those Indians die on the screen up there. If I could survive Vietnam, I can surely survive Hollywood. It's the one thing I've wanted to do, in my whole life."

"Yeah, okay, pack the boy's bags and throw them in the rig right now. Come on, Fred, what the hell kind of talk is this?"

"This is the kind. If I stay here, I'm going to be dead, five years, tops. Man, I just can't do this. My liver's going to be shot. I get up in the morning, every morning, with a hangover. I don't remember what it feels like to not have one."

"Well, then don't drink every night, simple as that," I said, though I knew for sure it was not nearly as simple as that. The thing keeping me sober was the road. I didn't have to look at those faces from home asking me how I could kill someone, even in wartime, and then come home and eat a hamburger at the drive-in, big as life, as if I had never shot someone in the head. I never did, as far as I know, but it's possible. You get shot at, you shoot back, and eventually, the person shooting at you, he stops. Either you got him, or he's moved on. I nearly know someone is dead on my account, probably a lot of someones. We found bodies at times, others not, and who could ever say whose bullet had blasted the top of some VC's head off like a popped piece of bubblegum?

The road was free. I could sit in a truck-stop diner anywhere in the country and eat in peace, no one looking at me and seeing the history he had decided I owned. There was something awfully powerful in that, in being just another grubby-faced long-haul driver with a cup of coffee and a greasy cap. And there was always Shirley to think about too. That seventeen hundred miles disappeared when I knew she was waiting on the other end of things, warming up a place for me in her Pendleton blanket. I knew if I lost my license drinking on the road, my days of seeing her on any kind of regular basis would be at an end and that kept me in line, so I guess I knew the attractions of hangovers as a way of life, too. I just had better incentives than to keep that up.

"You know how I found him, when I got home? Nadine, his ma, was living over at Bertha Monterney's house, where all those dancers live? I don't know. Bertha has a good reputation for keeping her dancers, but maybe they've had a rough year, I can't say."

"Dancers? I'm not for sure I know what you're talking about here, Fred. We don't have such in parts where I come from, I guess. Like the striptease we saw at that burlesque house at China Beach?"

"No! Of course not!"

"Well, I don't know. Why don't you tell me what you're talking about, then? Remember, I am not from around these parts."

"Sorry, Tom. Bertha, she runs kind of a house for castoffs, people who don't fit so well with their families anymore but who still want to be part of the reservation. She takes them in, teaches them traditional dancing, and they have to perform at exhibitions and competitions, mostly Indian Villages at state and county fairs. The prize money helps keep the house afloat. But you know, you can't change everyone overnight and Nadine, she's kind of a tough one. When I got to the house, my boy was sitting there, under the kitchen table, eating a bowl of cereal with water, wearing nothing but a diaper he had shit in, a long time before I had gotten there, maybe even the day before."

"Shat."

"What?"

"Shat, a diaper he had shat in. It's the past tense of shit."

"Are you even listening to me, Tommy Jack?"

"Yeah, I'm listening," I said, but I didn't want to. I had seen enough nasty things over there. I didn't need to hear of things just as dreadful on the home front.

"Anyway, my ma is getting too old to take care of a little guy like that. He's a handful and her patience is thin. Bertha talked Nadine into giving him to me, or else she was going to throw her out of the dance group. Now Nadine, she's one of Bertha's good dancers, steady prizewinner." He paused, then ducked his head and said, "She does other things well, too, but not that you can get paid for—"

"You can get paid for those things. Shit, I've paid for it."

"Well, either way, that's what's going to happen to this kid if you don't take him. If I stay here, I'm going to wind up dead, and he'll wind up with her. And if I leave, he's going to wind up there with her. Unless you take him. I checked into it, already. Since my name is on the birth certificate, I can appoint you his guardian, simple as that. Nadine isn't going to contest it. As I was trying to say, she's got enough of a problem keeping herself fed, let alone dealing with a kid."

"For the record, I haven't really ever paid for it." I laughed, but it was a fake laugh, and he knew it. He waited me out and finally, I agreed to do it, probably for all the wrong reasons. It wasn't to save Fred, and that's a good thing, since you can see how that came out, but he needed something to hang on to and I guess that thing for him was Hollywood. For me, it was something else. I had fixed up a life for myself, all nice and neat in my head. I was going to take Shirley Mounter away from that place, her cramped little apartment in the city, and make a home for her with me out on the plains. The boy seemed fond of her when she came around, and I could picture us all living together: me, Shirley, the boy, even her kids, when I found out about all of them. It was going to be okay, and what was one more kid? And the boy would have some folks from home, too, so that would be good for him. I figured I had a year to work on this before I asked her to unplant herself and move with me to Big Antler. In the meantime, I would get to know this little boy who I guess was going to share my life as well as my name.

A year goes by remarkably fast sometimes, for sure, and suddenly, I'd been home a year and it was the next July and there I was, lying on Shirley Mounter's floor, where I had just about taken up residence for a part of most months that whole year. We had gone to the National Picnic together that second year. The first year, I had gone with Fred and had only met up with Shirley at the Fireball game that night, just before the lights had been cut. I don't know what we were thinking the second year.

There were some white folks who came out to the reservation for the picnic but not too many and mostly they stuck together and did not socialize with any Indians. It was clear they had not really known any and had just come down to see what there was to see, buy some beadwork or feathered headdresses for the kids, stuff like that. Kind of like the Indian zoo, I suppose. Fred and I had stuck out that first year, hanging around together. Their world on the reservation was not unlike the small towns of West Texas, everyone knowing everyone else, but there were differences. Their kids seemed vastly more independent than the kids in Big Antler, wandering free at very young ages like every adult in their imme- diate area was looking out for their well-being. Another strange thing was the way they interacted with adults, as if their opinions counted with the same level of believability, and as I watched the adults respond, that seemed to be true enough. The whole reserva- tion moved back and forth between a place I could easily recognize and one almost as alien as Vietnam had been.

That second year, I had mostly gotten used to the way things operated on the reservation but maybe had just turned a blind eye to the ways I didn't fit in, wanting to fit anywhere as desperately as I had. While I only had eyes for Shirley that second year at the pic- nic and probably didn't notice the stares and glares we must have gotten, we for sure must have stuck out even more obviously than Fred and I had. She and I paraded around the picnic grove filled with carnival booths on Friday night like any other couple who had come down to share the weekend together. We'd done the penny pitch and the tomahawk throw, had some cotton candy, fry bread, that weird corn soup they serve, and were about full to the point of busting a button, and had watched the Fireball game for the sec- ond time, as played by the experts.

"Do you think you could play?" Shirley asked, that Friday night, laying her head on my chest. Her hair still smelled of the kerosene smoke that filled the air, long after that ball had died out and the parking lot lights came back on and everyone pretended we didn't live in a world where people we knew died left and right, all around us, one day, and the next day, we saw men proving their strength by picking up a flaming ball and heaving it across the night sky. Those changes in the places I lived were not that fast, I know, but it seemed like it. Shirley put up with a lot that year, as I would wake up almost every night at least once, jumping from her floor, shouting after my M-16 for a few minutes until I saw her,

lying there, drowsy, pulled awake by my leaping, and I made my
way back to this place. But that night, I just lay awake and thought
of her question.

"I played, already," I said finally, toward morning, and she
roused some. I guess she had finally dozed, waiting on my answer.
"Over there. Fred showed us how, told us that it was a medicine game,
that it would get us through the night. Funny, no one knew we were
playing since we did it at a firebase. The bases were supposed to be
hidden, so the snipers and launchers couldn't get a clear bead on our
location. Fires were, of course, frowned upon, and we must have put
ourselves and others in danger, but the funny thing was—"

"No one ever saw your game fires, did they? Aside from the
people playing and the people who were supposed to be watching?"

"Well, I don't know about that, but we never once were fired on,
any of the times we played, except for that very last time, and, well,
that was a different circumstance, I think. Things had changed."

"That's part of the medicine. Only those who are using it right
get to see it, get to be a part of it. Sometimes, people have invited
others, you know, like you, white people, out here to watch the
games, and they must not be intended to be a part of it."

"The players just don't play if the wrong people are there? That
seems, well, a little odd, don't you think?"

"No, the games always go on. But something happens. No
one knows what, could be they need to get back to a babysitter, or
someone needs to use the bathroom and they don't want to use
the roughing-it kind we have here, but I've heard there have been
people who've tried to watch the Fireball game for years and it
never, ever happens."

"You don't believe that hoodoo, do you?"

"Hoodoo do you?" she mocked me, in a fakey West Texas accent, and we laughed silently for a minute in the dark of her apartment. She felt so sweet, her body bumping just light and warm
against mine, like she was knocking on the door to my heart, you
know, and I was running for the door as fast as I could. We were

silent for a minute, then she brought her face up to mine and smiled, those white teeth picking up any light in that darkened room. "So what happened, then, that last time?"

"Nothing important," I said.

"You're lying to me, Tommy Jack."

"I never claimed otherwise," I said, and switched positions, climbing back on top of her, gently, letting my belly rest against hers but keeping my knees on the floor, so I wouldn't squash her with my weight.

"I think you're ready to play here," she said and craned her neck up, like she was going to lick on my ear and I confess, I lowered my head a little to give her a better angle but all she did was whisper. "Tonight, you have to play," she said.

"What makes you think so?"

"You saw the game last night. It's time."

"I saw it last year too."

"Then you're overdue," she said as her hips rose to meet mine and we didn't say anything more for quite a while, probably not until the sun came up and I got my clothes all gathered up and headed back to Fred's house.

So that night I played, there, on the reservation, for the first time. There were no real rules about who got to play, other than the side you were on, Young Men if you had no kids and Old Men if you did, but there was that unspoken rule about only men from the reservation or who had some real connection with it being able to play. Shirley and I had waited on the sidelines until the lights had been cut and then she pulled a pair of gloves and a bandanna from her purse, putting them on me to protect my hands and hide my hair. This seemed pointless to me since there was not one other person on the field with a red beard and I would be visible even in the minimal light offered by the flaming ball, but if this was what she wanted, I would do it.

I ran out and joined the Young Men's team since I didn't have any kids. I kept looking for Fred on the playing field but he disappeared when the field went dark. He should have been on the other team and I still thought, long into the game, that he might have been there, it being so dark and all. About midway through, I was out of the game, anyway. I ran with the best of them, kicking the ball when I could, getting kicked by other players, getting tripped, these guys all played for keeps but I was okay with that. I knew how to trip someone up too, if need be, so I was holding my own until I ran afoul of two men who disappeared right back into the black night of shifting legs and arms.

One of them dropped under me and his ribs connected with my kneecaps as I tumbled straight on over him. My face met the chest of someone else standing right behind that guy. He took my head, wrenched it sideways, and gave me three direct knuckle punches to the nose, wham, wham, wham, then he helped me straight along in my free fall, shoving my head into the grass. The world was spinning around me. I was as visible as I suspected, even there in the minimal light.

By the time I got up, most of the game had passed me by. I wandered off to the sidelines and waited to get my vision straightened out. I pulled up the belly of my T-shirt and held it to my nose. My mustache was already matted with blood and it wasn't showing any signs of stopping. I tried holding my head back to stop it but that just kept me choking on the coppery taste of blood sliding down my throat. I pinched my nose shut and saw some of the brightest stars I ever have seen. It felt wrong, like one of those noses they attach to the glasses with the funny eyebrows but I could not bear to move it.

The lights eventually came up and Fred found me, took me back to his place, and got me cleaned up.

"I guess some of Harris's cousins must have been playing. Maybe I should have warned you but you seemed to really need to play again and I didn't think it was my place to stop you," he said, wiping a warm washcloth through my mustache and beard, then rinsing it out, turning the water a dull pink.

"Harris?"

"Harris Mounter, Shirley's husband. I told her she shouldn't bring you to the picnic, that you should have come with me, but that was the way she wanted it."

"Husband?" I asked.

"Yeah, he's gone right now, but that doesn't mean he don't have eyes here. And fists, from the looks of things. We better get you to the hospital. I'm pretty sure that's broken," he said, touching my nose a little. I jumped back, couldn't help it, it hurt so bad, and he just nodded away. "Come on, they'll fix you up."

"Husband?" I repeated.

"You're not telling me you didn't know. Where did you think all those kids came from, the stork?"

"Well, everyone always just called him her old man—you, even. Man, what do you think, I would just . . ." It was the same feeling I had when Liza Jean had left me with nothing but neatly looped cursive letters on that stationery her mother always gave her for Christmas. I suppose I must have known they were married, but after all that had happened in the war, I had gotten pretty good at telling myself lies. You had to, in Vietnam, or sometimes you would just go crazy. Some of that shit was not meant for humans to do or see.

"Like I said, they never were a good fit. Remember? How many times have you been here when he's even been around, twice?" I nodded. I always called before I showed up, and once, one of those kids answered the phone and asked their dad when their mom was coming home, so I hung up the phone quick. The second time, he answered. It was funny to hear his voice. He became real in that moment, not real enough to keep me away but real enough to keep me cautious. I know, some people would say I only got what I deserved, but there's more to it than that, and somehow, knowing this was not just someone she had grown comfortable with, but instead someone she had walked down a church aisle with, someone she had shared a honeymoon with, all those things I had never done and had dreamed of doing with her, it was all gone when I found out Mounter was her married name.

"Doesn't change anything," Fred said.

"It changes everything," I said. "When are you leaving for California?"

"I could anytime, I guess. Was kind of waiting until you were ready to take the kiddo."

"That should for sure not have been your biggest deciding factor. What if I changed my mind?"

"You wouldn't have. Even if I left, you'd be back here for him in a little while, on your next trip to see Shirley."

"Well, this is it. I'm leaving tomorrow, and I'll take him with me then. If you want, you can come along and we'll take you as far west as Big Antler. Might be kind of nice for you to help the boy settle in with me, but if you can't do it by tomorrow, you're gonna have to do this yourself. I won't be back."

And so that was how we left, without much of a word to anyone. When I had last seen Shirley, I pictured her single with that bunch of kids. At that time, I didn't want to see her again, knowing I would remember her face as a married face instead. I am sure that doesn't make any sense to anyone, but to me, right then and there, it did. That feeling faded in time but things were different when I eventually saw her, those couple years later. She did have a married face then but so did I. We were somehow equal in what we were up to then.

So Fred and the boy, they climbed up into my cab that morning as I hurried so as to not break down and go see Shirley anyway. We said good-bye to Fred's momma and she gave us a bunch of fresh fry bread for the trip. We got on the road and I never looked back, until I had to. Fred stayed at my place for almost a month with the boy. I got him a job lifting down at the Tractor and Feed, and he saved enough to cushion himself when he got out to California, and the boy and I saw him off from Lubbock by the end of summer. I got my route switched to do the locals only, so I was always home for a late supper.

My momma had grown accustomed to watching the boy some when I was on the road during the day and she seemed to really like his company. He didn't laugh a lot at first but my momma was always a crackerjack talent with filling the time of little kids, and soon she and the boy were doing all kinds of things together. That show on the public television for kids was just coming on in those days, with all those puppets, and she picked up some puppet like-nesses of them for the boy. He would put on shows for hours on end for her and her lady friends. They thought that boy just hung the moon, as Liza Jean would come to, for a while.

For my part, I worked hard on trying to forget the sound of Shirley Mounter's voice, the feel of her skin next to mine, the fry bread she fed me, in little tears from the piece, licking the butter from my mustache and kissing me, the way she would rub my back just a little when I walked by, that feel from her fingertips to the middle of my back—there was nothing like it. Did I ever success-fully forget it? No. Not one bit.

Even after Liza Jean came back into my life, things were not the same. We walked down the aisle and all, but she had already done it, before me, with someone else. You think that doesn't make a difference, though I can tell you, it surely does. She finally took the ring I had for her, which was admittedly not as nice as the one the Giant had given her and she has worn it since that day but my memories never left.

o   o   o   o

"My wife here, she don't like to talk about Fireball, too much," I said, as we stood out in the backyard. "That burnt-out foundation you were pointing at, back there? That happened the only time the game was ever played here, so you can see why she's not so partial."

"That was what we were curious about, Mr. McMorsey. A sig-nificant number of residents of Big Antler thought Fireball was something we should ask you about."

"Nosy fuckers. Sorry, guess you can edit that out, though."

"Not a problem, sir. Now, about this Fireball?"

"Most of those nosy . . . nosy buggers probably weren't even living here then but the old-timers, they got nothing better to do than sit around the coffee shops and gas stations and tell old stories and that is one of the stories they tell. Why don't you save me some trouble and tell me what you've already heard for yourself and then I can fill in the gaps for you."

"That's not the way interviews work, sir. If you'd rather not go into it, Mr. McMorsey, that's fine, but we'll probably have to note your reticence in the segment."

"My what?"

"The way you are not answering the questions, Tommy Jack. Laws, you would think someone with almost a master's degree would have a better vocabulary," Liza Jean said, giving me her favorite eye roll.

"There's no almost. I got the degree," I said. She didn't count it, because I did it by correspondence at an extension site and transferred it in, just to be done with the damned thing.

"Well, there was this boy I adopted, my best friend's boy, and I raised him as my own, at first, and then, when Liza Jean and I married, we raised him together. He was from, I guess what they call now, a different subculture. See, I do know some of those more sophisticated words, and anyway, Fireball was from his world. I was trying to give him a taste of his heritage, but that game, it's a funny thing. Some people from that part of the world, they say only those who need it, and who are supposed to see it, can be involved in it, at the time."

"And do you believe that, Mr. McMorsey?"

"Does it matter what I believe?" I was beginning to think it really didn't anymore, and hadn't, since I got that letter saying I was supposed to go get Fred's stuff, the letter telling me he was dead. I had believed, right up to the moment I opened that envelope, that he was going to really make it, and he would come back for the boy, then, and they would have a good life together. I would miss the boy something terrible, mind you, but a boy should be with his daddy, after all.

"Tommy Jack, you are not playing that game here, again," Liza Jean said, as I unhooked that microphone and slid it out of my pant leg. She ran back to the house, flipped the switches on the secondary pumps, and started hooking up hoses, figuring I was going to screw up something. She was never all that hot on the way I did things on my own, which stands to reason, given my past.

"The last time I did this," I said, "was when I brought my best friend's clothes back, after he died. I brought them here, made a ball with them, and it was a big one, I can tell you for sure. I soaked it to high heaven and dragged it out here into the yard. It was time to teach the boy we both claimed as a son about the medicine game of Fireball. I don't know what the boy was thinking I was gonna do, he was only a little guy at the time, you know, but it was for sure he didn't know I was gonna do what I did. I sparked the ball the way we used to, back in the jungles. I had a couple of tokes off a joint, I know you're thinking I shouldn't have been doing that in front of the boy, bad role model and all, but he couldn't tell any difference. I used to smoke hand-rolled cigarettes, anyway. So I got the tip hot and touched it to the ball, and it went up like the well-made fireball it was. I kicked it to the boy and told him to kick it right on back." I had to stop there for a minute. Liza Jean never much particularly cared for this part, but she watched me tell it.

"He was crying, screaming. He could see his real daddy's shirts as they disappeared into that black smoke, and he let it go right on by and then he started to chasing it. I don't know what I was thinking. I guess I had kicked it a lot harder than I had thought and it rolled right on over into that cook shed I had made it in, straight through the open door, and I must have left the lid off the gas can, 'cause a few seconds later a big rumbling fireball pushed its way out that door and then the can exploded, and, well, I had to tackle the boy to keep him from trying to go in there to get those clothes.

"It was the wrong medicine for him, or the wrong time, or something. I fu . . . I messed up. He wasn't hurt, any."

"You mean he wasn't burnt, any, Tommy Jack," Liza Jean said. They saved that in the interview, I am sure.

"Yeah, that's what I mean," I said. I didn't say anything for a while and none of them did, either, but their tape machine was still whispering on the uptake spool. "You might as well shut that off," I said to the cameraman. "The only people who can ever see this are the ones who need it. You can try, but when you watch your tape, all you'll get is static and snow." They all looked at each other like, who is this crackpot? I could read that one, easy.

"So," I said, after some prep, lighting my first fireball in about three decades, "who's ready for some medicine? Who needs some healing?" I kicked the ball hard the other day and the sparks flew up into the darkening sky to join the stars just coming out. The ball rolled out across the dusty yard and I waited to see who was brave enough to admit on national television they needed medicine and what that segment editor might see when he chose to run this tape through. They watched that ball arc out across my backyard, not a one of them daring to admit what I asked them to. Their feet hesitated. I could see in their eyes that they had done things wrong in their lives, maybe crossed people they'd loved, said things they shouldn't have, walked away when they knew they should have stayed and tried to work things out. Each of them twitched just a little as the ball rolled by, heading toward invisible goals. This time, the sun was still up and not a one of them was willing to admit there what they might have admitted, had I waited until the shadows ate up our past mistakes. We all watched my one lonely kick and got ready for the live interview that was to come, not even remotely aware of these lost opportunities. They were, well, really, we all were, deeply unprepared for what would eventually arrive.

ACT TWO:

Camera

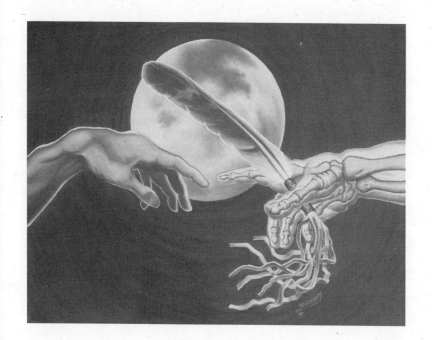

CHAPTER FOUR:

Sound Track

o o o

IF THE TELEPHONE ON THIS TABLE RINGS, ANSWER IT. IT WILL BE HIS WIFE ON THE OTHER END OF THE LINE. SHE WANTS YOU TO KNOW IT IS STILL POSSIBLE TO TOUCH SOMEONE WITH A RANDOM ACT OF KINDNESS.

—Artist's statement placard,
John Lennon Exhibit, 2000
Rock and Roll Hall of Fame,
Cleveland, Ohio

Annie Boans

T.J. wanted to hit Cleveland before the news program went on the air at ten, so we had plenty of time. We passed out of Niagara County and merged with the interstate that would take us all the way there, a straight shot once we were outside of Buffalo. The dead and decaying steel plants gave way to anonymous highways, surrounded by equally anonymous dense tree lines.

Though I hadn't wanted to, we went on the section of the thruway running straight through another local reservation, our most direct route. Off to one side, an enormous wooden statue of an Indian wearing a Lakota headdress, his skin painted nearly fuchsia, was the only indication we were within an Indian nation. My new life was mapped out, literally, on the landscape—an Indian history abruptly split by two concrete ribbons, asphalt, white dotted lines. Only clichéd codas gave any indication of the lives beyond the thick wild growth. I tried to ignore this display and watched, the markers and occasional green signs announcing the number of miles to Erie and then to Cleveland and the implied places after. Those implications weighed heavily, though T.J. had the good sense not to ask about my silence. Usually, we had no trouble filling our time with discussions of his father, or with laughter or academic discussions, sometimes all three at once.

"What do you make of that?" he asked, crossing into Pennsylvania, pointing to one of those interstate information signs. The sky, that vague yellow of an old bruise, would soon fully bloom in orange and purple hues on its way to darkness but it was stuck on that sickly yellow. "What can that possibly be?" One of the restaurant options was something called the Quaker Steak & Lube. "Do you get fine dining while your oil's being changed somewhere else in the building?"

"The sign says restaurant," I said. "Here's the exit. We have time." I didn't want to engage in a lot of small talk in the motel room before the program started and was hoping to get checked in only minutes before. The topic of fathers would bring us both discomfort, though he had no idea about my potential unpleasant associations waiting ahead. I have no way of knowing definitively if Tommy Jack is my father or not, but my mother's reaction put it a lot closer to probable than I had anticipated. T.J. didn't need to know this potential, though. Maybe after I could say for certain one way or another, I'd tell him. But until that time, what would be the point?

We imagined so much more than the restaurant truly was. Even when it came into view, it had so much potential. The owners had made the place to look like a garage. We dreamed up tables in pits, where hydraulic chairs lowered diners to table height. The waiters of our imaginations wore dark-blue, ill-fitting coveralls as they took your orders on parts invoices. They wiped dirty hands with oily rags, fingernails hopelessly blackened, their names embroidered on small, oval-shaped chest patches. The salad bar would have thick hoses hanging from the ceiling, labeled bleu cheese, ranch, French, Italian, instead of 10W-30, 10W-40, synthetic, blend, and when you pressed the trigger, an air compressor would pump measured amounts of dressing onto your salad.

"Not bad," T.J. said as we ate, and he was right. We'd had the right idea, just a bit too elaborate. The tables and booths were nondescript but there were metal lifts, holding restored classic cars above you as you dined. Random antique gasoline pumps littered the room, with small televisions embedded in their innards, airing a baseball game.

The place fell into that bar and grill category, emphasis on the bar. Rowdier patrons reminded us, screeching and yelling and slapping at each other's shoulders and backs over the game's score. The menu had clever, automotive-sounding names for items, beers listed as "lubricants," but I felt absurd ordering a hubcap of anything.

We studied the menu and came to the same conclusion. It would be a while before we tasted food from home again. Though it was risky to be a hundred miles from Buffalo and order chicken wings, we did. Most places away from home do a dreadful job, in the same way I imagine a Philly cheesesteak in Philadelphia is likely quite different from the mall food court versions back home.

"O-ring?" T.J. offered when our order came, lifting one from the plate. A small aerial mounted at its center held the stack of battered onions. He wanted me to bite the onion ring he held, to have his fingers so close to my mouth, to be intimate in ways that only long-involved couples are. The gesture was not the high school crush version of offering your date some food, the implied new sexuality of orifice and extremity. It was the gesture of someone knowing everything there was to know about another's body, tactile memory. These were definitely memories we did not share, and I had no intention of ever becoming involved with him. It would be inappropriate to encourage T.J. in his belief that we might.

"No thanks," I said. "I'm good with the wings." He silently ate what he had offered. These wings were decent. We were at the exact outer edge of appropriate wing territory, where they still called them chicken wings, instead of needing to add "Buffalo" as a modifier. Though I'd never been to Texas, I suspected nobody from there had ever heard of a Texas Red-Hot.

"What are you thinking so profoundly about?" T.J. asked.

"Texas Red-Hots," I said, laughing.

"What's that?" he asked. "Sounds obscene."

"It's not, don't worry. I was just thinking, no, never mind, it's stupid. Doug used to hate when I would rattle on about stuff like the names for things," I said.

"I'm not Doug," he said, looking right at me and nodding.

"We should go," I said and I grabbed the check. He said he had to stop at the men's room and would meet me at the car.

We got into Cleveland far ahead of schedule and decided to get a motel on the city's perimeter, rather than paying downtown tourist prices. A bed is a bed, and as long as the TV had decent reception, I really didn't care, otherwise. T.J. suggested we share a room, dual queen-size beds, and I agreed, if that were available. I didn't know how long we would be gone, truly; my finances were not limitless, and I was certain his weren't, either.

The room was reasonable, and I kept my things on my side, even in the bathroom, setting lines of demarcation clearly for T.J. He would not succumb to the belief everyone else had about us. We've had a certain kind of intimacy, a professional intimacy if there is such a thing, sharing the same strange life of the Indian academic, but that was all it was and all it ever would be. T.J. wanted more but I took great pains to make sure he never got any encouragement. To do anything less only would have been cruel.

"Anything you want to do?" he asked. It was still three hours until the program started, and he seemed agitated about seeing Tommy Jack McMorsey again, even as an image shot from a cathode ray gun.

"Let's go to the Rock and Roll Hall of Fame. I think that Lennon exhibit is still up, and I really did want to see it," I said. "It's still hard to believe he's been dead over twenty years, now." We parked in front of the strange contemporary glass pyramid in less than ten minutes.

"For a while there, I played *Imagine* almost every day. My daddy always loved his music," T.J. said, paying our admission. My family had immersed me in it with almost no awareness on my part. I gradually understood the specifics of artists with their art while I was still young. With songs I loved on the radio, I asked someone older whose song it was, and the answer, almost invariably, had been the Beatles or one of them individually after it was over. When I began buying albums, my first were theirs, and Royal, when he moved out, took his favorites from his collection and left me the rest. Naturally, he took *Revolver* and *Abbey Road*, but he left me all of the early stuff and *Rubber Soul* and *Let It Be*.

My mother and I had been watching *M*A*S*H* on late-night TV, after the news, when we heard of the shooting. I was nearing junior high school age, and New York City was an imaginary landscape I had formed from years of films, television shows, and news stories. It was a place where you might get murdered, turning any street corner, or you might run into a celebrity, turning the next, instead. The odds encouraged certain inevitabilities.

The TV news that night didn't show much—police cars outside the Dakota building, lights flashing, people standing around, crying. At first, I wanted to believe he'd been wounded, that he would have a long recuperation period, where thousands of people would send him flowers and cards, and we'd all be aware of the precious thing we'd almost lost and we'd cherish him from then on, though he would never acknowledge anything had ever happened. He would continue to walk in Central Park, still have his picture taken with fans, the only difference being the bodyguards who would stick closer to him than they had before. All those people crying, singing his songs, lighting candles in that cold December night told us differently, though, and my mother had shut the TV off, mid–laugh track, once the show resumed.

The museum was sparsely populated when we arrived and we headed up to the main exhibit, not bothering to look around. Other opportunities to visit the museum would present themselves at some later date. At the entrance to the exhibit, two things caught my eye, though I initially refused to look at one of them. It would have to wait until I was ready.

A white telephone with no dial sat atop a small white table, next to a stylistically identical white chair. The phone appeared to be live, as a white wire trailed off into the wall. A small wall-mounted description informed us that if the phone were to ring, we should pick it up, as it would be his wife, widow, on the other

end of the line. I thought this was a fairly interesting and provoca-
tive installation and it did keep my mind away from what I knew I
would find in that other small exhibit case a few feet away.

It seemed strange that the table was not roped off, like so
many other parts of the show, and I wondered how many people
had picked up the phone to hear if indeed there were a dial tone.
Two men about my age, maybe a little older, stood just out of reaching distance the whole time we walked through the rest of the exhibit. One looked bored but attentive to the other, who, it was clear,
desperately hoped that phone would ring. The slouched posture of
the one suggested they'd been loitering there a while. They were
plainly best friends, standing as close as they were, trading quiet,
reverent stories—best friends, at least.

Were people looking at us the same way? I supposed they
were. We probably even looked like stronger candidates for couple-
hood than those two keeping vigil. In fact, to anyone who didn't
know us, we probably looked more like a couple than I ever had
with Doug, even before we had separated. The real reason my ex-
husband and I had stopped going to others' parties was not so
much dedication to our families, but that we had each grown tired
of the other's friends wondering what we'd ever had in common
enough to bring us together. My colleagues wondered what I was
doing with a factory worker, would even go so far as to ask what
we could possibly talk about when we were alone. They wondered
if I were reduced to fishing stories and stock-car races, laughing
dismissively and shaking their heads, asserting that it must be
love. Doug's friends, I'm certain, asked each other over endless ten
o'clock coffee breaks what he saw in that bitch who always needed
to be right and who could never use a regular word if there were an
awkward and secret one handy.

What Doug and I had shared for so many years was something
T.J. and I had little of: a communal history. A thousand things kept
us different from our non-Indian friends, the same thousand that
had held us together for so long. Those same thousand things had

eventually driven us apart as well. It seems odd to be legally separated. Almost no one on the reservation went the formal route.
They just quit living together, but few filed the papers. Even as
close to the broader world as we were, we knew the difference they
never would. It's easier to forget minority differences when you
are part of the majority. Aside from T.J., I was the only Indian at
the college, and Doug had been the only Indian at the plant before
getting a job at the smoke shop.

We crossed into mirror worlds every day, where everything was
the opposite. Our colleagues laughed about drugging aging parents
and checking them into nursing homes while they were addled.
They would never laugh during that same parent's funeral, as we
would, resurrecting a joke the deceased had famously told, cele-
brating their ability to make us laugh, even in our sadness. So we
spent years laughing with our co-workers, knowing that we would
not laugh about those things at home. We stifled giggles when our
colleagues carried stern or grave expressions, knowing we would be
in hysterics if the same situation occurred at home. I suspected T.J.
did not laugh at all during his grandmother's funeral and was probably puzzled when so many people did, in the outer lobby.

Doug knew the fear of a fire siren that rang eleven times the
same way I did, the sound of a reservation call. T.J. was startled
by the firehouse's noon siren every day, saying it sounded identical
to the tornado warning siren that sounded in Big Antler. When
he'd told me that the first time, I asked him if he had not been able
to look out the window and see the blue skies. He'd said his eyes
knew that, but his nervous system was something else. It jumped
alive with that sound, ready to work his body as fast as it could go
to any shelter.

I couldn't really imagine storms like that, coming on suddenly
out of the sky and ripping lives apart, with little or no notice. We
had storms that killed, blizzards, but they did it slowly, freezing
you to death if you had been unwise enough to be on the road as
the storm gradually got worse, or inducing heart attacks, if you

hadn't paced your driveway shoveling to your own health. Both of these kinds of death occurred only out of stubbornness or ignorance, but if a tornado crossed your path, there was little you could do. Either you would survive its impact or not, with little indication, ever, as to which outcome would be yours.

Walking past the two men one last time on our way out of the show, I approached the small Plexiglas container, and looked in at what I knew I would find there. Even after all these years, the dried stain across the broken pair of glasses was still very evidently blood. I imagined that the final things on earth he'd seen—doorman, wife, floor—all had a red cast to them before everything went black for the last time. Next to the glasses was a brown patient's belongings bag with clothing inside, and his name handwritten on it, left exactly the way his widow had received it, after the autopsy. T.J. kept his distance, stood near those other two men until I walked away from the exhibit.

"I can't see that," was all he said and I respected his decision. I didn't think Fred Howkowski had worn glasses, but he certainly must have left red stains that eventually dried to rust on some things, and perhaps a bag with his clothing in it lay somewhere before us. We walked away, assured the two men would tend to the phone if it rang, and headed back to the motel, with less than a half hour to go before showtime.

"Think I'm gonna grab a shower," T.J. said, taking his shirt off, after we locked the room's door, "unless you want to go first."

"No, I'll do that later, after the program. Go ahead." I watched the television, not looking up, as he began undressing before entering the bathroom. He turned on the showerhead and left the door open, and I only hoped he would not attempt what he had during that first conference we had attended in New York City, the first time I had ever been there.

"Let's go out tonight," he said then, after the first day's sessions. "I lived here for a while, in the early nineties, and it can't have changed that much." I was terrified and excited in equal measure.

"I'll take you around the Dakota. As close as we lowlies can get, anyway." I had always wanted to see it and that was the tipping point. "All right, why don't you go get ready and come up to my room. I'll leave the door unlocked, just come on in." When I entered a little while later, he casually left the bathroom, toweling off nude, as if nothing were amiss. I looked out the window.

"No big deal," he said. "I had to do a few nude scenes while I was working here. *Hair, Oh! Calcutta!* Even a really experimental version of *Cuckoo's Nest,* where we all had to wear hospital johnnies that only came down to your navel. Like scrubs, but only the tops. Not for sure what that was all about, probably just another way to sell tickets. But anyway, once you've stood naked in front of a Manhattan audience for six nights a week with two matinees, it's kind of like an immodesty inoculation. The novelty of embarrassment wears off for good." He had looked, though, from under that towel, to see if my glance had lingered, even surreptitiously, on him. He stood behind me, even as I looked out at the Empire State Building, watching our reflections in the glass as he dried himself. In retrospect, the scene had some humorous phallic relationship, but at the time, I was not laughing. He eventually gathered his clothes, and dressed on his bed. "Would you braid my hair?" he asked, tying his shoes.

"You know how to braid your own hair, quite well," I said. That was that and we saw the Dakota and its gated entryway, and in the years since then, neither of us has mentioned it, even in teasing.

Now, when he went under the spraying water, I pulled out the letter my mother had given me. She had said I was welcome to read it. I neatly opened it and there was nothing magic in it, no doorway for me to this other life, to this stranger who would be my father. It was more of a doorway into my mother's life.

I kept trying but could never hear her voice right in my head. I only heard the alternately stern and critical or closed and protected voice I usually received. If I could reconstruct the voice she'd used when I had confronted her this afternoon, I might get the tone of this letter, but I had almost never heard that voice. It was hard to maintain it in my head, having so few words in it stored. The voice kept reverting back to the one with which I was most familiar—the one she used in trying to persuade me of something. It didn't matter what: that I should grow my hair back; get a summer job with Doug at the shop; stop talking about dead people in public; and most frequently, that I should stop this city nonsense and come home.

The woman who had written this letter knew how to risk everything. The one I knew risked almost nothing in her life unless she had five backup plans. This was a woman who had harbored possibilities for many years, who dreamed of a different life, knowing it was not possible but still investing in it. This was a woman I had never glimpsed in my mother, even once. This unfamiliar woman was a stranger in love with a man who was even more of a stranger.

In a few minutes, I would see the man who had found this woman hiding inside of my mother. This man had magic that caused her willingly to endure a thirty-year mockery, to disregard her whole community, and to lie for my entire life, for his sake. There was more to this story than I'd ever glimpse, but the next doorway I would get to that world was about to open and I had the key in my hand, the small black plastic remote control unit to this motel television set.

A part of me wanted to shut the television off and close that door before it opened even a crack. What kind of wind was going to blast through it? Would I hear an evacuation siren over his voice filling my ears for the first time? Would I find shelter? I had given up the possibility of tossing that key in the trash, though, when I agreed to accompany T.J., knowing he would not miss this broadcast for anything. What could this man possibly have that would invoke such dedication from three people who should have no affinity with him whatsoever?

The shower stopped a minute before the program with Tommy

Jack McMorsey began and as T.J. stepped back into the room, he wore a T-shirt and a pair of gym shorts, and he squeezed his hair in his towel, then efficiently braided it and sat on his bed. I stayed on mine and watched the television while the opening credits scrolled. I held on to the remote in one hand and the bedpost in the other, wondering if I were ready for what might come abruptly for me over the air.

CHAPTER FIVE:

Live Feed

o o o o

Dear Tom,

When are you gonna come back down? Or is it up from Big Antler to L.A.? I had to get rid of my compass a while back. Or I thought I did, but it wasn't really the compass talking to me. I only realized after I had already dismantled it to see if there was a secret Army device inside trying to send me home, and all I saw was what I guess you're supposed to find inside a compass. But since I didn't know how you were supposed to put it back together again, I decided to get rid of it. Don't worry, it won't be telling anyone else any of the things we saw over there in the jungles. I was very careful to collect all the pieces and put them in a plastic bag with scraps from other things, a couple old alarm clocks, even little tubes from inside my TV that didn't seem to affect it too much, and then I filled the rest of the bag with dirt, and buried it in the undergrowth in a park a few miles from here, so even if someone digs it up and tries to put it back together, they'll be thrown off wondering where all those extra parts go. Pretty good idea, huh? Just like what we used to do in the jungles when we got some of those nasty C rations nobody wanted. Remember ham and claymores? What was that shit? Lima beans? Oh man, gives me the shivers now, even to think. I never got hungry enough to eat that nastiness, and remember: "nobody eat the apricots." That sad motherfucker Hughes ate the apricots and bought it not ten minutes later. Never eat the apricots, Tom, no matter what you do, never eat them. I bet maybe the bear was looking for apricots. As bad luck for bears as for us, those apricots were. Also remember, you have to puncture the cans when you leave them behind because even though you don't want to eat them, you also never want to feed the enemy. They can try if they want, but the punctured cans in that heat, mm mm good, isn't that what the Campbell's Soup kids say? I think it is. Okay, anyway, I better get going here.

                              Not eating the apricots in L.A.,
                              Fred Howkowski

Tommy Jack McMorsey

That letter has never left me. It stayed in the back of my head all the time. Even there, on live national television, it continued to play, as it always did when things stress on me. Like the Japanese woman, the letter from Fred was a constant reminder of my failures in life, so there I was, thinking about Fred and talking about that young woman, again. The interview was going fairly routine, about as I expected but how do you describe someone going insane on you? It's a gradual process and one day, the person you used to spend every waking hour with is saying the craziest of things, and you are left trying to carry on a conversation with him in this world when he has clearly moved on to another. It's a little hard to notice when there is the language difference between English and Japanese, but even in English, just a thousand miles' distance can change the sharpness of observation until it is too late. When I received Fred's letter, I thought he was joking, a way to goof and get me to come back.

Fred was always asking me to come on down and visit him, and the one time I switched routes with one of the other drivers and did just that, I knew for sure that I would never want to get myself back there again. Some people like that kind of driving, but me, I'll stay in the countryside. Small towns are, for the most part, good enough for me. I don't mind the long hauls, but those eight lanes of freeway are just dangerous, plain and simple.

"Hey, let's go out and catch the high tide," Fred said, as soon as I had got myself situated at his place. He decided we should do this after I'd given him the eye about some of the really odd junk he had crowding in his little room at that housing project where he was living. I mean, I liked junk and all, made a pretty good side living off it, all this time, buying, selling, trading, auctioning, but what he had was real junk, the kind of stuff you'd pass right on by at the curbside, because you knew nobody in his right mind would want it, no matter what kind of price tag you might tie to it. Lined up on one shelf was a lunch box thermos with no cap, the overflow plate from a terra-cotta pot, an old grape Nehi bottle with a chipped lip, the filter half of an old coffeepot, a shuttlecock without the weighted rubber head, crazy shit like that.

"Remember that R & R we took at China Beach? I had to borrow some boxers from George just so I could swim," Fred said, as we walked the beach here. The sun was setting and his ribs were showing in the new shadows. He'd lost a lot of weight since he'd left Texas.

"I didn't care a thing about swimming. I just took that blanket from the hooch and didn't want anything more than to catch some sleep and not worry about getting shot," I said.

"The water was nice, nicer than this. It never really gets all that warm here, no matter how warm the air is. Back there at China Beach, I could swim for hours," he said, walking along close to the water so it brushed up against our bare feet, swallowing our prints as we made our way.

"As I recall, you did."

"Yup, man, I almost lost everything. That tide crept in on my stuff and before I knew it, my things were passing me by in the surf. Had to move quick to get it back. I got almost all my belongings, but I lost a few things to the tide that day." He picked up something that washed ashore before us and stuffed it into his shorts pocket.

"What was that?" He looked at me like he had no idea what I was asking of him, like I had not just seen him pick up a piece of trash and put it in his pocket.

"I always try to learn from the world, Tom, and the tide and the moon taught me to be more aware." I could never quite understand some of the things he said, and on those occasions I would nod and let him believe whatever he wanted.

"The tide here washes all this stuff in and you have to look at it as a gift from the man in the moon. It still kills me, the way the moon makes people nuts once a month and pulls something as powerful as all the earth's oceans, by doing nothing but hanging in its rightful place in the sky. This is an astronomy lesson, Tom. First we check out what the moon offers us, and then, the other heavenly bodies." I thought he meant we were going to hook up with some of those fine Hollywood women you always see on the TV and in the movies, but instead, after touring the trash-strewn beach, we walked on down in front of that movie palace where all the stars are in the sidewalk.

"This is the one, man," he said.

"The one what?"

"The one that's gonna have my name on it. Soon, man, very soon. I can feel it."

"Have you gotten that speaking part yet?" I asked.

"I'm working on it, man. They're supposed to let me know any day now, any day now."

"Maybe you'd get a speaking part faster if you got your teeth fixed." He ignored my comment and kept walking. "So how are you losing them, anyway?" I asked after a couple blocks.

"It happens."

"What do you mean it happens? Teeth don't just fall out of a man's head."

"Sometimes they do. They've been bothering me, anyway."

"Well, get to a dentist. You need some money to get you to one?"

"No, that won't help matters."

"You want me to track down old Jangle and get you some of those he picked up along the way?" I joked, bringing the war back into our lives, and he wanted no part of that. Not even one joke from the guy he shared a poncho and a hooch with for almost the whole year we were involved in that predicament.

Jangle Kirby kept a tiny pair of pliers with him and some little steel rod that came off of something or another, at all times. And any time we came across a dead VC we'd shot, or mined, or that had died in some other ways, Jangle would stick the rod in his mouth, open it wide, and look for the glint of a gold tooth. If there was one in there, he would yank it and drop it into his shirt pocket—said he was going to have a necklace made when he got stateside again. "The older ones are the best. Heads just full of treasure," he'd say when he came across one. He was skillful with those pliers, if you want to call that activity a skill. He was able to pull the gold tooth out, leaving the old rotted roots of the real tooth behind in the corpse's jaw. He was proud of showing off his fistful of gold teeth, with not one speck of real tooth still attached.

He trusted no one, ever, and figured we would all steal his old teeth the second he turned his back, so he even slept with his shirt on and those teeth in the breast pocket, no matter how hot and sweaty the evening got. Every night about a quarter after twelve, if there wasn't a lot of cross fire going on, and the moon wasn't so full, you could hear those teeth clanking away from his poncho tent as he took care of his own business. He was a man of regular habits.

I never had the desire too much when we were there, worrying too much about dying to think about being horny. Some of those guys were shameless. They would take care of business in the fire-base latrines, which only had a partition wall that came up chest high when you were on the pot, so all you had to do was take one look at them to know what they were up to. Most times, you just pretended they were invisible. When we would go back to the rear once a month, and get a break from the jungles and the firebases, watching some movies and having some beers, maybe then I'd get the urge and sneak out behind the hooch for a few minutes by my-self. Kind of private, I am.

Some guys in my unit got it taken care of by *ville* girls, but I was never one for that kind of thing. I have never paid, and never will. But the place in the ville I used to go to get my hair cut, well, I guess they were kind of what you might call a full-service barber. I would be getting a trim in one chair and in the chair next to me the guy would be getting a trim and getting his pipes cleaned at the same time. I wouldn't have even gone there, but all the places that cut hair offered the same services and there was always some guy in the next chair with his fatigues around his ankles and a ville girl's face in his lap anywhere you went. Kirby must have never gone for that kind of thing either, and it got him sent home. He was jangling one night and some sniper with good ears got a bead on him by sound, and his right knee was shattered before he finished the job.

He got sent stateside to finish out his time at a desk job, shuffling papers. They were always calling those jobs "dick jobs," and I'm not for sure where that title came from, as I would have done almost anything to not be on DMZ patrol all the time, but that was just all the desk jobs were ever called. We loved having a different reason for calling it that when Jangle got that kind of job. You had to find what you could to laugh at in that time. Laughter was darn scarce in the jungles. I thought Jangle would get a laugh out of Fred, but it was not to be.

"What you could laugh at when you know there's a gun looking down on you all the time, and what you can laugh about when you're where you think you should be, those were different things, Tom. You should always remember that." We kept walking, talked out, so we headed back to the little rent-controlled place he had gotten himself.

I agreed, but I always sort of wanted to know what happened to Jangle—never enough to investigate, mind you, but curious just the same. I had to wonder, after the years, if he would be hobbling along with a cane, telling his grandkids about that odd-looking necklace he wore, and how he got wounded in the war. I know he was from somewhere in Iowa, have even probably driven a haul through his town—have done the plains quite a bit—but never bothered to look him up. Not for sure what I would say. Fred was the only one I was ever going to visit but I felt, even as I left him that weekend, that I would probably not be visiting again. I guess he made a liar out of me after all but at such a cost.

You can say I should have known by the way things had gone, or been able to tell from those letters, that something was wrong, but it's not always true. The vision is not so clear from the inside, which is sort of what I was trying to get through to this interviewer and the rest of the country we were sending this signal out to.

I told these television people the same things I told that woman from the *Big Antler Daily*. It was almost becoming a script for me. I wondered how many more times I had to tell it, but I could also see in Liza Jean's eyes, as she listened and held on to my hand, that she was lining up all the elements, to make sure I didn't mess up even one little thing. She would never say anything in the middle of the interview of course, had she heard something, but I would be getting myself an earful later.

I can't blame her. I bet she suspects I was up to something with this girl, but I for sure wasn't. I imagine the medical examiner checked things out just for the record. Maybe for one of the only times in my life, I tried to do something totally for someone else, and this was what I got. The girl was dead, my wife was studying every damned word I said like I was the cryptogram game from the *Big Antler Daily* "Fun Page," and I was sweating my ass off on live national television under those blazing lights, and in a tie, no less. I should have kept my mouth shut and let the papers say what they wanted about her, but I just couldn't do that.

Some of that stuff about Fireball they brought up the other day was kind of a sudden jab though I sort of expected it. I figured they had probably gone around town asking questions before they got to our house. Any smart news crew would. I've seen those shows where they burst into the guy's office and he has no idea what to say and runs on out into his car while they chase him with the cameras. Well, no chases were going to occur here. They were going to ask their questions, I was going to deliver my answers, and then Liza Jean and I would watch them leave down the grid and maybe we'd watch the tape we were recording of ourselves that very minute before we headed off to Cascabel in the morning.

"Mr. McMorsey, your usual driving route takes you through the southwest—Texas, New Mexico, Arizona. How did you happen to get the route through Bismarck that night?" The reporter kept smiling, and was watching me as carefully as could be, trying to see if he was getting himself a big scoop, but there was nothing to tell.

"I put in for it. I do the long hauls from time to time," I said.

"Yes, we noticed that. Your manifests going back a number of years suggest there's some sort of pattern here. Mid to late November, that seems to be the consistent 'from time to time' that you mention."

"Yes, that's right," I said. "My manifests?"

"And the records from the place you stayed in Detroit Lakes, Kwitchurbeliakin Cabins, a virtually abandoned set of summer resort accommodations in the middle of nowhere, clearly document that you made your reservation weeks in advance. This was obviously not a last-minute decision. Why did you want to be isolated? Did you plan to pick someone up to join you? Anyone in particular or didn't it really matter?"

"I'm sorry, what are you asking?" I said. Liza Jean was still holding my hand, but her nails were beginning to dig into my palm. This picture the reporter was making, cutting up pieces of the truth and moving them around, was one she was already willing to believe herself. She was just waiting for someone else to tell her the pieces. Other than her nails, though, she said nothing, just kept on sitting there. I tried to gently pull away, but she dug deeper for a minute, letting me know she wasn't letting go, no matter what.

"Mr. McMorsey, you went to the newspapers, and the police, with a story that had enormous holes in it. You couldn't really agree to an interview and not expect to be asked questions about these significant gaps, could you?" This was another one of those questions that aren't questions, I could tell. "Why don't you tell us what really happened with Miss Furuta that night. You obviously had some need to tell it to the public or you would not have agreed to this interview in the first place. So, shall we?"

"I went to the newspapers because they got it wrong before, and I didn't think this poor girl should have been made out to be even more troubled than she obviously was. You've done your investigation. Don't the things I am telling you match up with the police reports and not the news stories?" I said.

"About those trips, sir. Comment?"

"I go out to see the meteors," I said, "once a year, when they come, in the early winter."

"The meteors?"

"Yes, the Leonid meteors. I thought with y'all's crackerjack research team, you would have known that."

"Actually, we did. But why all this . . . ritual? You'll forgive me, Mr. McMorsey, but you don't seem like the stargazer type."

"Well, I guess you don't know everything, then, do you?"

"That's why we're here, sir. Now, back to the meteors and this young woman. Did you purposefully take her to see them?"

"She went with me. Like I said to the papers, I was giving her a ride to Fargo, 'cause that was where she said she'd wanted to go, then when we got there, she wouldn't leave, wouldn't get out of my rig. That's all in the statement I made and it was all confirmed by the statement they later took from the night manager on duty at the Mainline Motor Inn that night." She wanted to hear all about Fred Howkowski, but even then, talking to someone I was sure I would never see again, I still couldn't tell it all. Maybe if I had done with her what Fred had taught us to do that night at the firebase, things would have been different. She and I could have soaked a ball of rags, all those things she had brought with her from half the world away, into some diesel or gasoline, sparked it up, kicked that flaming ball

all over those frozen fields, melting paths as we went, but aside from teaching the boy, and the time just yesterday, I never played since that time on Fred's reservation, when I got my nose busted.

"Why do you travel all those distances every year, Mr. McMorsey? Why is it so important to you to see an astronomical event?" The reporter was certain he was going to get something here. He leaned forward, nearly ready to fall off the chair Liza Jean had offered him. The answer I was going to give him wouldn't amount to much, I suspect, but this was as good a time as any, since it seemed like my plan was never going to work out the way I wanted it to, every year, anyway.

"I wish on those meteors, those falling stars," I said. "Figure if I wish on enough of them, maybe my wishes will come true."

"And what do you wish for?"

"If you tell, the wishes never come true." Does no one know this ritual? Where have these people grown up, anyway? "I never took much stock in that belief until I was in the war. In Vietnam, we didn't see them so often, the stars, I mean. The skies were foggy, clouded over, most nights. We'd be mortared all night long, sleeping under those ponchos and staring up at the stars, knowing our people at home would be looking at different stars. Between mortar fire, things would be so dark a lot of those nights that you could only tell where the jungle ended and the sky opened above you, in those patches where you could see a few bright spots, millions of light years away. Some of the darker nights were so filled with those red flares the NVA shot off, hoping to expose us in the light, those fireworks were like a thousand dangerous falling stars coming our way, so you got to cherish the few real ones you ever got to see.

"I was used to the skies here, which, as you saw last night, are as wide open as can be, nothing but stars and the moon, as far as you might want to look in any direction. Back then, every falling-star wish I had was the same, and it ain't too hard to know what that wish was. I wanted to go home so bad, sleep in a dry bed, hell, sleeping without my boots would have been a treat, almost anywhere. I wasn't wishing for much, just to make it home alive, and maybe my wishes came true. Maybe they added up, finally. I made it back, relatively intact. A lot of guys didn't."

"And a lot of our boys who made it back were changed," Liza Jean said out of nowhere. "Why, one of the men from Tommy Jack's unit told me himself in this very living room that he has tasted the barrel of his own gun a time or two, and Tommy Jack's best friend made it back here only to go and kill himself a few years later, and you had to go and deal with that mess too," she continued, turning to me at the very end, like I had somehow forgotten that had happened. The second cameraman, who had been looking bored most of this time, was suddenly up and zeroing in on her.

"Liza Jean, that is no one's concern," I said.

"This is the second alleged suicide you've been involved with, Mr. McMorsey?" the reporter asked. "The odds of that seem rather unusual."

"Yes, the second suicide," I said.

o   o   o   o

This guy Liza mentioned, George, and of course Fred, those were about the only two from my squad I kept in touch with, after I got back. Man, I thought I was a redneck, but George was about as big a cracker as you would find anywhere. He came and stayed with us for a couple months a number of years back, stayed in what used to be the boy's room, and he and Liza Jean got on just about as good as you can, and when she told him to make himself at home, he surely did. At night, we'd be watching the TV, and he would come on out in his white skivvies and a T-shirt and make himself a sandwich and sit down on our couch, just like that, to watch the TV shows.

I thought Liza Jean would pitch a shit fit, seeing as she's always been so particular about our living room, but she never said one word except to offer him some chips to go with that sandwich. He'd come around and ride the short hauls with me, during the day, but at night, he usually talked with Liza Jean while I caught up on the logbook, and they buzzed away like a couple bees in the living room, but just below the point where I could really hear what they were saying above the action on the TV.

"Tommy Jack, what did y'all do when you were over there in the war?" she asked me one night after he'd gone to his room and we were climbing into bed, tossing to the floor the eight million pillows she kept on the bed when it was made up. I could have answered her any number of ways, that being a pretty broad question and all, but I think I got the gist of it.

"Not for sure what you're wanting to know about," I said, regardless. Lying has always come easy to me, and this one was no big one, just the same one I had been telling for years. You can't really talk about that kind of thing with someone who wasn't there.

"Well, George in the other room has been telling me he knows what a gun barrel tastes like. And while you never said how Fred Howkowski died, I can put the figures together. Do you know what a gun barrel tastes like, Tommy Jack? 'Cause if you do, you are going right on down to the VA in Lubbock, and get you some help first thing in the morning." She was lying on her side of the bed, but propped up on one elbow, like, giving me the third-degree eye she rarely gives. Ever since she gave it to our boy that one year, and got an earful of confirmation she did not want to hear, she rarely administered this look to anyone other than the knocked-up girls coming into her office at work. I could see in her eyes, even in the dark of our bedroom, that fear of being alone she has. I supposed it was time to tell her then, though I never would have dreamed she would introduce this information to the whole damned country.

o   o   o   o

How do you tell these secret parts of your life to a camera? They're not secret because you need them to be, but secret because they are the moments you share with one other person, and here on the camera everything about you is at least once removed. Their machine keeps rolling magnetic tape from one spool to another, copying your image over and over again, but they never get it right. No matter how closely they try to document your moves, they only ever get one angle, the one they've chosen for you. Though your words are not smooth when you try to talk to these others, try to record the realities, you know you fail because you see different things.

You see a woman who loved you enough to give you her virginity on a blanket in a park one summer night just before your senior year in high school, though she had never touched you beyond a handholding and a hug and a kiss, and though she had never let you touch her beyond that point, either, she had known she was in love and that you were going to marry her one day, and therefore, that night, it was finally okay. You see that same woman smiling through tears and hugging you as you prepare to leave for Fort Ord and what they called "points beyond," knowing only later that she was already deciding she couldn't marry you because she could see you dead, bloody, blown apart and fragmented, even as she holds you close that last time. You see her walking down the aisle with that other man, knowing he will discover that night he is not her first, and you see the way she will try to make him feel like he is, anyway, the way she will try to make him feel like he moved her the deepest. You can see these things, these secret things between them, because you can see her, trying to make you feel that same way, that you move her the deepest, in the dark of night, after you don't die in Vietnam, and after you come home, and after she divorces that other man, and after she later marries you, not before, only after, but you can feel his presence even then. You can see that they made love different from the way you and she had, and that in the time you were sleeping near rotting corpses across the planet, too scared to even think about jacking off, she had learned to move her body in different ways, without you, with someone else. You can see that afterward, in the dark, when you lie there awake in the bed you share with her, still trying to not reach out for your M-16 every night, like you had for that year, she falls right asleep, contented.

You can see that to her, the period between your engagement and your marriage no longer exists. You can see that for her, it is seamless, she has always loved you, you have always loved her, and you will always live together, for better or for worse. You can see she meant that only conditionally. You can see there are heavy costs when you cause the "for worse" part of the deal, but you can see the contract remains for her. You can see that she is willing to potentially get humiliated on live national television if it's revealed you were fucking around (you weren't, but she has no way of knowing that for sure, given your past) because regardless of the costs, she is your wife. You can see she will continue to love you and stay as you each get older and more peculiar with age, as everyone does. You can see one of you is going to die one day and the other will have to figure out how to go on, how to fill those silences, and if it's you who has to go on, though you of course do not wish to be the one, you know you can handle it because you have seen some things like this before and in your head, you still do see them.

You see the other woman you have loved, and still love, though you can tell no one. You see her the way you saw her that first night, filling your dreams and fantasies with her reality even better than you had ever imagined it. You see her in the dark of her apartment the first time you remove her clothes, slowly and gently, waiting to see if she is going to reach out and stop you, but she never does, she waits, instead, patiently, as you try to undo buttons on someone other than yourself, getting hung up in the reversal of movements every time. You see her as she awakens you early that first morning, licking your ear, around the edge over and over until every part of you is awake and you open your eyes because you can no longer ignore the needs you have at that moment. You see her smile as she sends you off before the sun rises, knowing you will be back after it has gone down again that night. You see her other smile, the one that is not so wide, the one she gives you when she knows you are leaving town again and won't be back for a number of days, but it's still there, because though the days will seem impossibly long to both of you, they will fade the minute her body touches yours upon your return. You see her smile through tears, but a different sort on this face, when you come back two years later, for the funeral of your best friend and to see her one last time. You see her across the grave from you, where she can't hold your hand, and you can only nod to one another, with everyone else around, and then you see her, later, at the fellowship, where all the people crowd around and tell stories about your best friend, stories you are not a part of, because you knew him in a totally different life. You see her there at a table at the far end of the room, watching you over her potato salad in the same way you watch her over your macaroni and cheese. You see her later, from the parking lot of her apartment complex, where she has been sitting in the dark, waiting for you with the curtains open, just enough to let you glimpse her in the glow of a nearby streetlight, and you see her a few minutes after that, opening the door as you reach for it, and then there you are again, standing with her, after all the kids are in bed, including the one you brought back with you across the country, and she gets that blanket out, and though you know you shouldn't even be there, because you generally wear a ring on the third finger of your left hand, you stand with her, that blanket around your ankles, and you see her smile open, just a little, as you reach over and undo that top button, and have the same trouble you always have. You see her after it's all over, and you are packing up the few things you brought with you, and you see clearly her lack of a smile, because that absence looks so unfamiliar to you, but you know the reason she wears her mouth just that way when you leave that time is because she knows you aren't coming back.

You see your best friend days earlier, lying in shit and plastic, half his head coloring the walls of a low-income apartment, wearing only a revolver, a blanket, a dirty pair of white briefs, and socks that had no elastic in them. You see his neighbors eyeing you up, knowing he's dead and that you have the key, wondering what it might take for you to let them in and have a look-see at the

furniture before the super comes to clean his stuff out. You see him
before that, always making sure you were treated right by those
around the two of you. You see him that first time at the Oakland
shipping depot, where you and he didn't know any better and were
conned into taking a limousine from the depot barracks to the air-
strip, each throwing in ten dollars, and facing the laughter of all
the others who were smart enough to wait for the shuttle bus. You
see him smile at the little plastic hula girl dancing on the limo's
dashboard, and at the dingleberries swinging from the window
frames. You see his dark skin grow pale and know yours must be
nearly glowing, it is so white, when the two of you get your orders
in Da Nang, and the men stationed there say things like: "Phu
Bai, you fuckers better have some good life insurance because you
are as good as dead" and "Man, who did you guys piss off? You sad
fuckers are right on the DMZ." You see him close his eyes as you
are all loaded onto a chopper and taken out to what you think
is exactly the place the others described, the demilitarized zone,
but you only see this for a little while because you close your eyes,
too. You find out you're not as close to the DMZ as those guys
claimed, but you're close enough, closer than you want to be. You
see him light a ball of rags and make some magic that keeps you
both alive long enough to see your zero day in country. You see
someone who had walked with you through jungles full of mines
and snakes and little people wanting to kill you all the time, and
who had made it back safely with you, and who had decided to
become a movie star, and who had made it into the movies, even
a little, someone who had been able to find all those paths, but
just could not find that path back home.

And then, you see her, and no matter what you have seen before, you have seen nothing like her, and you have nothing to compare to the way she pleads in silence with you. You cannot see her
life, only things you have imagined badly for her. You cannot see the
family that doesn't recognize her ideas are just not right. You cannot
see that they think a good therapist and some new antidepressants

are going to work just fine, so fine in fact that they take her to the airport, themselves, because she has made so much progress in her stability. You cannot see that they think this is the right thing to do for their daughter because they love her and they want to fulfill her dreams. You cannot see that her family loves American movies like she does and that they've maybe even vacationed here, themselves, visiting Snoqualmie, Washington, where *Twin Peaks* was filmed, or maybe they looked for Anarene, Texas, where they think *The Last Picture Show* was supposed to take place, not finding it because it is really called Archer City, but they do not realize what Fargo is to their girl, and you cannot see how they let her leave, not to visit the city but to find the ransom. You cannot see how they could not think this was like going to Devils Tower, Wyoming, hoping to find a giant spaceship. You can see, though, the way she was willing to deal with terrible environments to get those things she dreamed of. You can see it was not really about money, at all, because though she didn't have a million, she had plenty enough to be comfortable. You can see she didn't want that last criminal to get out of prison and get it, and you can see she didn't want the cheating husband to get it, either. You can see she thought she had a better plan for it, maybe a school, maybe a trust fund, maybe a museum; these are things you cannot see. You can see that, for her, the phrase "based on a true story" absolutely meant something else, and that there was something imperative in that pronouncement, a responsibility for her to do something noble with that million dollars, for her, a great disservice to humanity—perhaps if she'd had the million dollars, she could go back in time and visit those scientists at Los Alamos and tell them they should stop working on the atomic bomb, encourage them to give it up, and if she offered them the cool million to do that, to walk away and retire somewhere warm and beautiful, maybe they would have, and we would not be here right now.

You can think all these things, in the space between someone clipping a microphone to you and the record heads engaging on the tape machines as the lights are fired before you, but you think these things in images, sounds, smells, full moments reconstruct-ing themselves in your head, quilting themselves together with the thread of your lifeline, but when you open your mouth, you are still a redneck from West Texas with a correspondence course master's degree and a lifetime of memories, and the vocabulary of a pretty sharp seventh grader, and this is what they record, because they can only record what you give them, maybe even something less, but certainly nothing more. They can only see the face you make when you remember these things that are forever burned into the back of your head like so many frayed patches of clothes that had seen better days.

"I don't know why she did those things. Maybe she was, you know, plain and simple, just nuts," you hear yourself saying. "She didn't say, and I understand she was on medication." Even as those words come out of your mouth, the image of her flat wide-open eyes drying out in Minnesota's November winds begins to fade from your brain. Maybe, if you say these things enough and to enough people, you can stop thinking them. Maybe, then, they will erase themselves from your brain and you can stop seeing the things you do not want to see anymore, the way Liza Jean turns away when she smells an unfamiliar perfume on you, the look on Shirley's face as she helps you empty some things from your suitcase so you can take the blan-ket you always make love to her on, when you leave for the last time, the way Fred's face stopped mid-forehead the last time you saw him, or the thing you saw roll out of that last fireball someone made when you were back in Vietnam and the dubious things that object said about all of you there, and that was how I arrived at the end of the interview, standing in my living room, telling my wife things I had always thought, but had never said, on live national television.

o o o o

"Yes, the second suicide," I repeated to the reporter, a couple sec-onds after the first time I said it.

"Some people, you just can't save," Liza Jean went on. "Tommy

Jack even went so far as to raise this fellow's boy as his own. Well, we both did, eventually, but it was Tommy Jack at first. Gave him every opportunity in the world and he just threw—"

"That is none of your concern, either, Liza Jean," I said. Only I didn't just say it, I shouted it. "And if you hadn't been saying I wasn't home when Fred would call us collect, when I was only outside in the yard, he might still be alive today. You didn't think I knew you did those things? You know, not everyone who calls this house calls for you. I know you have the need to think that, but it just ain't so. Mostly I can overlook some of the shit you've done, but you leave my best friend out of your little story of how much better you are than a lot of others!"

"Tommy Jack, we are on the TV, what in lands sakes are you thinking?" she said, starting to get up off the couch, upset, but I didn't care, anymore. "What is everyone going to think?"

"What is everyone going to think? Is that what you said? They're gonna think the same thing about us that they think about anyone else they see on these kinds of TV shows. You don't think they're looking for hard news now, do you? They're gonna think, 'Look at those sad fuckers. Aren't we lucky our lives are so much better than theirs?' And just why are you on TV? You haven't tried to save a single person in your life, except for yourself. That wasn't me who ran off and got married to that flat-footed nitwit while I was in Vietnam. That was you, not me, Liza Jean, you, not me. You just better look in your own hamper before you start to digging in mine." This time it was me who held on, and I didn't need manicured nails to keep our hands locked together.

"You know what?" I said, turning back to that reporter. "My wife here wanted to redecorate this room, just so you fuckers would be impressed. How fucking sad is that?"

"Mr. McMorsey, please," that reporter said, but I could tell this was what he'd come for.

"Please what? You wanted a freak show, or you wouldn't have come out to this shit hole in the first place. Don't fuck around with me! You sniffed around for a story, and now you've got one. The story of an idiot. She wanted me to move this here curio cabinet out of the living room because she thought it suddenly didn't go anymore. That it would look bad on TV because it had clearly been something else at one time and I made it into a curio. It was a grocery store humidor, yes, I know it was a humidor! No matter how you cut it, that was what it started off as, but sometimes things change permanently, and they are never going to be what they were before, and you have to fucking recognize that! This curio saved my life, have you forgotten that, Liza Jean? Saved my life. You asked me one time if I knew what the barrel of a gun tasted like." I stopped for a second and she stared into my eyes, waiting for the answer she had never gotten before, no matter how much she had tried to weasel it out of me for years.

"Well, you know what? I don't! Because restoring this curio, stripping off all the abuse people had committed on it for years, that was how I filled my time when I first got back from Vietnam, while you were off getting fucked every night as Mrs. Paul Montgomery in your first marriage bed, all the while waving to me like we were strangers if we happened to run into each other in town. That was what kept me from the taste of a gun barrel. But you want to know what else? This was the last thing in this house that was truly mine, anymore, and you have made it pretty clear just what you think of it. Maybe other options wouldn't be so bad." She broke loose from me at that point and tripped on her microphone wire, bumping into one of those big lights.

That spindly light pole vibrated briefly then toppled, the bulbs exploding across the floor. The room went dark, filled with the sounds of sobbing and regret.

CHAPTER SIX:

Broad Cast

∘ ∘ ∘ ∘

"Rebuilding History, One Board at a Time"
(article in *Small Town Texas* special interest newspaper,
September 1986)

If you're taking a Sunday drive on the outskirts of Big Antler, Texas, and you think you've come across a very small unmarked ghost town, you're not far from the truth. You've just experienced your first glimpse of McMorseyville, as over-the-road truck driver Tommy Jack McMorsey's neighbors teasingly began calling the northern patch of Mr. McMorsey's property a little over a decade ago, when he started his unusual and delightful project.

"Tommy Jack has always been a little bit different," his wife Liza Jean said, holding on to his arm as we strolled the buildings and grounds with the charming couple who are clearly suited to one another. "That's what I have always loved about him," she said, smiling and kissing the red-bearded cheek of Mr. McMorsey, who seemed a little embarrassed at all the attention.

Mr. McMorsey, a Vietnam War veteran, said a series of converging events was the impetus for his lifelong project, constructing a group of old houses and other period buildings on the property he had inherited from his parents. He and his wife had been avid antique collectors since they were first married, and they were running out of room in their house to store their continually expanding collection.

"It seemed a shame to just pack the stuff away," he said, as they had no desire to stop collecting, nor any desire to dispose of the things they had already gathered over the years. They had learned to do small restoration projects on their own years ago, Mr. McMorsey teaching himself the skills on a magnificent general store humidor that he transformed into a lovely curio cabinet. The couple eventually branched out from furniture and tried a remodeling job on a cookhouse from an earlier era behind the family house they continue to live in, and though this was a small-scale project, they proved to themselves that they could do it.

As sometimes happens, fate stepped into their lives in the form of the Yorkston family, also from the rural community surrounding Big Antler. Knowing Mr. McMorsey's love of nineteenth- and early twentieth-century items, the adult Yorkston children donated their deceased father's abandoned house to the McMorseys, if they were willing to move it from the cotton field where it had sat empty for more than fifty years.

The McMorseys took the Yorkston children up on their generous offer and the rest, as they say, is history. They moved the house and gradually restored the dwelling to its former state and began moving period-appropriate antiques in, to furnish the home. By the time they were finished, the refurbishing bug had deeply bitten the McMorseys and they moved on immediately to doing the same kinds of work with other buildings, at times recreating whole places with only photographs, imagination, and again, period-appropriate lumber, taken from other abandoned structures around the county. The McMorseys explained that new lumber would be apparent if it were used in the construction, and they wanted the whole place to look as if the small community merely continued unchanged from the previous century. "It would be like cheating to not use the real thing," Mr. McMorsey explained simply. They have allowed for some modern modifications like electricity, but rustic still rules the day here in this little hamlet, where an outhouse sits behind a one-room schoolhouse on the northeastern corner of the property.

"It's just for show," Mrs. McMorsey said, winking, saying they have indoor plumbing and offering it if we needed to freshen up. Mr. McMorsey laughed and told us some of the migrant workers who helped him work on the structural elements were unaware it was not supposed to be a functional latrine.

When time allows, the McMorseys give group tours of their little village to school and church groups, and if you happen to catch them right, ring the doorbell and you might get your own personalized tour. They welcome guests anytime and enjoy showing their collection. We asked Mr. McMorsey when he planned to stop, and he spread his arms out across the expanse of his property and, smiling, said: "When I fill all my spaces."

"Y'all come see us again," the McMorseys offered as we pulled out of the driveway after a cool glass of sweet tea prepared by Mrs. McMorsey. We just might have to.

Annie Boans

"Well, I told the authorities, when I found her the first time, that she was an odd one, and when they just let her go, I couldn't see her trying to make it on her own, since I was going to Fargo, anyways," Tommy Jack McMorsey said, from the little speaker on the bracketed television across the room, "and these roads can be a little dangerous." I touched the arrow button on the remote control mounted by an anti-thievery umbilicus to the nightstand, and his voice rose. The hue seemed a little off, but the basic remote in the room didn't allow access to the menus that adjusted elements that technical.

"I assume he's not really that green," I said.

"In what sense?" T.J. asked. We laughed a little, but our eyes never left the screen.

The man before me on the screen was smaller, more slight than I had imagined, sitting on a sofa in a tastefully decorated living room, which was filled with antiques. An enormous curio cabinet filled one whole wall in the room, but seemed to be a natural fit, as if it had been built specifically for that space, though it clearly had come from an earlier era. A woman sat next to him, not saying much, but her hand never left his, as if he were a tethered balloon, and would float off into the atmosphere if she accidentally let go, for even a second.

I had a particular stereotype in mind when I thought of the phrase "truck driver," the sort from films or on television, or, frankly, at interstate service areas. I have certainly stopped at enough of those, on the way to or from conferences, to have seen the type. This man in a poorly fitting dress shirt and an out-of-fashion wide tie simply didn't fit that image. His beard was nearer the shade of my hair than my mother's hair is, but T.J. seemed to not even notice that. The things Tommy Jack McMorsey talked about on the screen were incidental to me, really. Instead of the words he said, I felt the sounds of his voice. He and T.J. had very similar accents, though there was a little something extra in T.J.'s that I couldn't place. It wasn't a reservation accent. I was certain of that.

"Next to him? Is that your . . ." I asked, not exactly sure what he preferred to call them.

"My adoptive mother? Liza? Yes, that's Momma. I'm kind of surprised she was willing to do this, but I guess nobody turns down a chance to be on TV."

"Why surprised?"

"Well, let's just say the history of my daddy giving women rides while he's on the road is not something either of them likes to talk about much," he said, again staring straight at the TV.

"Your daddy and other women, period, from what I hear."

"So you know? About your momma and my daddy? The thing they had for a while? I didn't know if anyone had ever told you, and didn't think it was really my place. Well, you know one side, anyway, I would guess."

"You know things I don't?" I asked.

"Probably lots. He kept a box of things he collected from her, hidden away in our pump house for years. Funny, meeting your momma as an adult for the first time, after all these years I've been back, that wasn't an accident, you know."

"No, I didn't know. What kind of stuff?"

"Stuff," he said, and his vague answer left my imagination to conjure up a highly incriminating box, probably like the one I had found in my mother's sewing closet a couple years ago, though I had assumed the men's things in that box had belonged to my dad—her husband, I mean. "You know, I would guess she mailed some of it, letters, pictures, other things, I can't remember." The image of a young Japanese woman's passport filled the screen, while a recording of Tommy Jack's initial phone call to 911 played in voice-over and a transcript of it scrolled superimposed across the woman's face.

"But she did understand English, I'm telling you," Tommy Jack told some reporter on the screen, who nodded and prodded some more. "I was telling her all about my best buddy from Vietnam. He wasn't from Vietnam, we met over there. He was American, American Indian, in fact. Anyway, I was telling her all this sh . . . stuff, just to pass the time, really telling myself more than her, I thought. And she starts asking me questions about him," he said, poking a finger on his free hand into the knee of his Levi's. "She didn't ask them well, mind you, but enough so's I could understand her. She knew what she was doing, and she knew what the police were asking. They just pretended to not get her, you know, 'cause then they might have to do something with her, or something for her. I don't know." He shrugged his shoulders and continued to talk about a variety of things. They were trying to corner him, and though I had no love for Tommy Jack McMorsey, I felt some sympathy for him because of the way they were treating him.

His wife started talking and then the interview faded rapidly out to black and stayed that way for a few seconds too long for this sequence to have been the planned progress of the show. Finally, a commercial came across the screen. I wondered what transpired in that darkness, that dead air. When the show returned, the cameras were no longer broadcasting from the McMorsey living room.

"What do you make of that?" I asked T.J. and he shrugged. It was surprising, though it shouldn't have been, that he and McMorsey shared the exact nuances of that gesture. T.J. had learned to shrug noncommittally from the man who had adopted him. What else had he learned? The show continued broadcasting from the network, the anchor claiming technical difficulties with their live feed from

Texas. They ran some footage of the McMorseys taken at some earlier point. They walked around the house, inside and out, while a narrator gave a brief biography of him, one that decidedly did not mention my mother in any capacity. They concluded with a scene of what I swear was Tommy Jack lighting a fireball. There was no commentary, just that image, fading, before the anchor came on to wrap things up. He promised that next week, they would have highlights of the lost live transmission, and segued into the concluding segment, where officials naturally denied any improprieties of procedure.

I shut the television off and we lay there in the dark while the cooling electronics ticked for a few minutes. It had been like much of that type of programming, an abundance of hype, suggesting tremendous secrets would be revealed, when in fact what you had was the mundane, ridiculously unglamorous retelling of the moments leading up to a young woman's death told by the only person who could have prevented it. So many things had come to be aligned for this young woman to die as she had, and it was obvious that, even if you had tried to orchestrate such a plan, you never could have pulled it off. The variables for that equation were so unlikely as to never be aligned again.

Had she met someone else, or had the authorities been able to find someone who could speak Japanese fluently, this would have been a different story. They should have decided the obvious, that she was not right, that she was delusional and should have been held for observation. McMorsey wanted to clear his name by claiming the newspapers had gotten it wrong when they'd reported she took a cab to Detroit Lakes. In fact, he only showed his involvement in this private disaster all that more explicitly. Had he been even a little smarter, or a little more attentive, or cared a little more, she would not have had to go through the things she had. Her delusions were another matter, I understood that, but it seemed like the whole situation was mismanaged by everyone involved.

We lay there, in our separate queen-size beds, both pretending to sleep, for about an hour, listening to the air conditioner engage and shut down, on and off, when I spoke, softly, assuming if he were asleep, he wouldn't hear and my words would just disappear into the drop-ceiling tiles.

"Do you see your mother, much?" I asked.

"No, not really," he said, immediately. "I had an idea when I came back to take care of my grams that maybe we could start something slowly. I found out where she was living and went over to see her. She poured me a cup of coffee, showed me pictures on the wall of my half siblings, then told me she had some wash to do. She asked me if I wanted to go to the Laundromat with her. I passed."

"That's it? You live one road over and you never see her?"

"Sometimes I see her, you know, grocery store, sometimes even at the Laundromat, but that's about it. I guess I've helped her fold some clothes now and then, maybe. We just don't have much to say. In a few minutes, we're reduced to talking about whatever was on TV the week before. There's just no connection. Maybe kind of like you and your daddy, before he died."

"I suppose," I said and that was the end of the conversation for a while. The air conditioner continued to cycle in the dark. "You wanna just get going, move on?" I eventually suggested.

"Sounds good," T.J. readily said, throwing off the sheet and going into the bathroom to change. We decided to drive on ahead, switch off, and sleep when we felt the urge, figuring that if we timed it correctly, stopping to put up only when rest was a necessity, it would take another twenty-four hours to make West Texas, more or less. As T.J. checked out, I grabbed a large cup of coffee and settled into the driver's seat. In the disc wallet, I found *Imagine* and put it on.

o o o o

"Those women he mentioned," I started, a couple hours later, beyond Columbus and the complicated thruway system that ran through the center of Cincinnati. "The ones who frequent the truck stops," I clarified, not sure what to call them.

"What about them?"

"They're real?"

"Oh yes, they are real, and some of them can be pretty dangerous. There was that crazy one down in Florida, one of the only female
serial killers ever caught and convicted. She would act like all the
others, but once she got you to drop your drawers in your sleeper, or
wherever, she got out this straight razor, and you became a soprano
in the boys' choir," he said, miming a quick movement with a blade
and then held himself, rolling in the seat next to me.

"You're making that up," I said, having never heard of this incident. It would have made national news, had it truly occurred.
It sounded like all those crazy stories you hear on the reservation,
just trucker style.

"Oh no, I am dead serious. You can look it up, can't remember her name, but you do a search when you get home. You'll see. I
hear someone has optioned the rights of her story for a screen-
play. Maybe there was already a show on her on, you know, the
same network we were just watching. Here, there's a rest area up
here, I saw a sign a few minutes ago, said twelve miles. You pull in
there, shut off the lights and the Blazer, and you watch." I wanted
to stop anyway, stretch my legs a bit, so when the sign came up, I
pulled over and into the lot, used the ladies' room, and did notice
the couple of women standing around the benches nearby, giving
me surly glances and smoking cigarettes with serious arcs of their
arms. I settled back in and closed my eyes while T.J. watched for
something to show me. I didn't know what it was going to be and
wasn't even sure how I felt about his knowledge of this particular
subculture.

"There," he said a short while later and I opened my eyes. He
pointed to a small car that had pulled into the truck parking section, stopped head-on in the actual lane rather than in a parking
slot. The dome light was on, the woman driving it highly visible.

"That doesn't mean anything," I said. "She's probably looking
for a map or a drink or something. It is the interstate."

"Just watch," he said, confident he had called this right. "There she goes." The woman stepped out of her car. While I grant it was over seventy-five degrees out, she wore a decidedly skimpy outfit, even for that temperature. I didn't think they made tube tops anymore but this woman sported one along with cutoff jean shorts that looked more like a thong and high heels so absurdly steep that she skidded, stepping from her car. She walked slowly around the car clockwise three times, slowing each time she entered the scope of her headlight beams, her shadow undulating across tree branches swaying in the breeze.

She got back into her car, pulled over to the standard parking spots, and shut her car off.

"And what was that all about?" I asked.

"Just wait, and keep watching the trucks," he said. "There," he pointed again, and three of the trucks turned running lights back on for a minute, and then shut them off, and each turned on cab lights. She left her car and walked toward one of the trucks, while the various cab lights went out. As she neared the passenger-side door of the truck, it opened for her from the inside and she crawled up the running boards and closed the door behind her.

"Satisfied?" he asked, and I started the car in answer, getting us back on the road. We drove a while listening to *Imagine* straight through a couple of times, and then T.J. put on *Double Fantasy*.

"Your turn," he finally said.

"For resting? No, I'm still good to drive."

"I answered about my momma. How does your momma wind up at your brother's? And how did you and Dougie wind up living with his momma? I assume he's still living in that trailer, even after you moved back to the city."

"Royal is a much easier story. After Suzy and he split, he was living alone on the reservation and my mother was living alone in that apartment we always had."

"Yeah, I remember that apartment."

"What do you mean?"

"I was there. You were there, too, of course, but you probably don't remember. You must have been about two or so."

"When was this?"

"My real daddy's funeral. We stayed with you. That was what your momma was talking about that first time you brought me over there. Remember? She said the last time she had seen me was with my daddy, my adopted one. We went to the drive-in movies and then stayed at your place."

"You remember that?"

"Well, of course. You might have been too young to remember, but I wasn't. It was, as far as I know, the last time they saw each other. They took us to the movies, I guess to make us tired enough to sleep through the night, but it backfired. We went to see *The Legend of Boggy Creek,* and man, that thing scared the shit out of me. I was just so glad we weren't staying on the reservation that night. You know, it was one of those Bigfoot movies, where the Bigfoot stayed in the woods and the swamps, and for sure, to a little kid's eyes, those woods looked just like the reservation. Even Royal was scared shitless and he must have been a teenager. He and I stayed awake much of the night, listening for Bigfoot outside the window. It didn't matter to us that we were in the middle of the city and on the second floor to boot."

"Did you know?" I asked, relieved that he seemed to have forgotten about his desire to hear my personal history.

"What, that he loved her? Sure. I don't think he's loved anyone in his life as much as he loved your momma. My daddy thinks he's a good liar, but he is as clear as rain. That was also how I knew my real daddy must have looked pretty bad when he was found. I could see it in my daddy's face when he got home."

"Well, I mean, what they were up to. Wasn't he married then?"

"Yeah. Hey, check this out," he said, flipping on the dome light and opening the map. "Fouke, Arkansas, is just the other side of Texarkana, which we have to go straight through."

"Okay, and why would I want to go to, what is it, Fouke?"

"That's where *The Legend of Boggy Creek* took place. I always wanted to stop there."

"For what?"

"You know, based on a true story. I think they filmed the whole thing right there in that little town. Maybe the same reason that woman went after the Fargo ransom, chasing a dream."

"Okay," I said. After all, wasn't that what I was doing on this trip, myself? He calculated the distance and our time, and if we put up somewhere in Tennessee—he said Milan looked like a good enough place—we would get to Texarkana late the next day, and then it would be another day to Big Antler.

"Unless of course you want to push through to Memphis and grab a quick tour of Graceland," he said, grinning.

"Milan it is," I returned and watched the dark wilderness and the things hidden within roll by.

o   o   o   o

"What did I tell you? We are making great time. We'll be in Texarkana long before dark, get some supper, relax, take it easy a bit," T.J. said, as miles and miles of giant trees passed by our windows at seventy-five to eighty miles an hour.

"We should find a place with a pool," I said. I had known it would be warm down there, but the difference from New York still surprised me.

"That should not be a problem down here. It's almost required equipment. Now, we kind of got sidetracked, and you never did tell me how you arrived at the living arrangements you finally got sick enough of to move back to the city."

"Well, let's see. I started to tell you about Royal and my mother and—"

"I was really more interested in your situation. Doug's momma, from the few times I've met her, doesn't seem like the easiest person to get along with."

"You picked up on that, eh? Let's just say I don't think I can go back. I mean, I'll go back to the reservation, I imagine, at some point in the future, but not back to that trailer. I can't live with her ever again."

"You should not make such absolute statements. They can come back to bite you in the ass."

"Not this one."

"That is what everyone says at times like these. I've made them, and been unable to keep them," he said as we pulled into the parking lot of a motel with the required pool, and we said little else for a long time, just enjoyed the water and the meal later. As T.J. got ready to doze, I told him that I was going for a little drive, that I wasn't sleepy. He couldn't believe I was willing to get back into the car after all those hours, but I wanted to do a couple things, and I wanted to do them alone.

                                   o   o   o   o

Fouke, Arkansas, was even smaller than I had imagined it, a virtually unnoticeable slow spot on US-71. Perhaps I was missing some of it, but I didn't dare wander onto those nearly unmarked side roads, disappearing deep into the wood. The map was vague at best. Fouke was barely a period-sized dot. A small convenience store wall displayed a badly painted mural—Bigfoot riding on the back of a giant pig. Already closed for the night, it still offered just what I wanted, an outdoor phone booth and a lighted parking lot. In the building's shadow, one of those cutout figures kept me company. Naturally, a Bigfoot, this one appeared to be made of metal, something more permanent than plywood. Did anyone slice his neck pushing through the Bigfoot face portal?

I leaned against the Bigfoot mural, pressed zero, and waited for the digitized operator. I instructed the computer to dial my brother's cell phone number and spoke my name into the receiver at the cue. My voice, inserted into the collect-call-request message, was transmitted to a tower at the reservation's edge.

"What time is it?" Royal asked, after telling the phone company computer that he would accept the charges.

"After eleven, I think."

"Where are you?" he asked, the question I was most hoping for. When I told him, he was silent for a minute, then he said, "Are you outside?"

"Yes, why, afraid Bigfoot is gonna get me?" I answered and laughed.

"Hey, you never know. They didn't ever find him."

"They never found him because he doesn't exist, you idiot."

"Well, just be careful, there is a lot else to be on guard for besides Bigfoot. You shouldn't be standing around outside late at night in a strange place. It ain't the reservation, you know. Where's T.J.? And what are you doing there anyway?"

"He's asleep probably, back at the hotel. We're just on our way to West Texas. So you must remember going to the movies, then. He said you were scared of that movie, and I guess if you remember the name of the stupid town where this Bigfoot is supposed to be . . ."

"Well, sure, I remember it. I couldn't sleep for weeks after that one, and forget about walking around the reservation at night from then on. Every sound I heard, shit, I was positive it was that Boggy Creek monster."

"So you remember Tommy Jack McMorsey then," I said. He was silent for a couple minutes and then he admitted it.

"You probably also were old enough to know he and Ma were not just friends, then, too," I said and waited.

"Yeah, I guess."

"What do you remember?"

"That she was a lot happier when he was around than she was when he wasn't," he eventually said. "That she was happier than when Dad was around."

"I wouldn't have that comparison."

"What do you want me to say?"

"The truth." He was silent for a while though I could hear him walking down the hall in the trailer and then the door opening and then the crickets as he stepped outside.

"I'm not sure what that is. He didn't come around for long, maybe a couple years or so, for a while, then nothing, and then that last time."

"So did you think I might, you know . . .?"

"I never really thought about it."

"Liar."

"Okay, so I thought about it, yeah, and I guess I thought that was possible. But it didn't matter to me, or to anyone else. Dad wasn't ever there when we were growing up either, so what do you want, to be ditched by two fathers? Is that what you're looking for?" I wasn't sure how to answer that. I really didn't know what I was looking for, or what I expected to find at the Big Antler exit off of Interstate 84, but it was coming fast in the next day.

"What was he like?"

"Just some guy, I never knew what she saw in him, but what did I care? I wasn't the one in love with the guy. He used to play the guitar, shitty. I remember that. We were wishing he would leave it at home, but when he came, he almost always brought it."

"Was he nice?"

"To us? Yeah, I guess. I don't remember him being especially nice, but he didn't treat us like shit, the way Dad used to. Between shitty and not shitty, I'll take not shitty, any day." While Royal was talking, a long-haul truck slowed down as it came toward the convenience store, and the driver, visible in the parking lot light, watched me. He pulled off to the side of the road across from where I stood, engaged his brake, turned on a light inside the cab, and began writing something down on a clipboard, glancing over at me every now and then. From what I could see, he looked like the typical driver type I had seen for years, dirty-billed cap propped back far on his head, short, slightly messy hair peeking out from below it, bushy mustache, couple day's growth on his cheeks, and one of those short-sleeved, striped, button-down shirts that only truck drivers and car-parts salesmen seemed to wear. He kept trying to catch my eye. I pretended to examine the Bigfoot painting, keeping my hand inside my purse, on the trigger of my pepper spray. I had left my Blazer's door open and the baseball bat that lay just behind the driver's side seat would be easy to reach after I used the spray, if need be.

"Anything else or do you just like hiking my phone bill up?" Royal asked from the other end of the line.

"It's after nine, your minutes are free," I said.

"No minutes are free."

"Why did you lie to me?"

"I don't know."

"Yes, you do, or you wouldn't have done it more than once." Now it was his turn to be silent. We stood there, listening to crickets across eleven hundred miles filling in all the spaces where we didn't tell each other things.

"It wasn't my place," he said, finally. "I imagine if Ma thought you should know, she would tell you, or you would ask her. I don't know. It wasn't any of my business. The rest of us have a very specific history together, but yours is different, yours and hers is different. Like I said, it wasn't my place. I don't think I have anything more to say on that, except . . . be careful, okay? It can be dangerous, down there."

"Bigfoot?"

"You know what I mean, just, well, that guy, Tommy Jack, he's got a different life, there, and he might not be too happy to have you show up in it. Your buddy, there, he's part of that life, and I don't know what you and him got going—"

"Nothing," I said. The truck driver switched his dome light off and opened the door, climbing down from the cab and waving to me.

"Well, none of my business, but your buddy has a place in that life. You don't. You might not like what you've gone looking for."

"Listen, I have to go," I said to Royal, and palmed the pepper spray. "I'll keep you posted." He started to say something but I couldn't hear it, as I put the handset back into the receiver and moved toward my Blazer.

"Ma'am? Miss?" the driver said, not picking up his pace any, as he approached. He was big, heavy, solid-looking, and if I couldn't get him with the spray, I might have far more on my hands than I had thought. Damn! Why hadn't I waited for the next day to go to Fouke? "Do you need some assistance?"

"Not the kind you're thinking of," I said, reaching my open Blazer, the can ready to emerge from my purse the second I needed it, the bat within reach.

"Beg your pardon?"

"Not every woman out late at night is looking to be swept off her feet into the back of an eighteen-wheeler."

"I guess I don't follow you, ma'am. You looked like you might have been calling for some help and I was gonna put up for the night in Texarkana but thought I would see that you were okay, first."

"You weren't thinking I was, you know, looking for action?"

"Action? Now, I don't know where you got your ideas about truck drivers, ma'am, but I can tell you right off, I don't go in for that sort of thing. I know that some do, and that's their business, but it seems a shame to me those ladies need to find their lives in that way." He seemed sincere, but I kept my hands on the spray can.

"Or the men. It isn't just the women who are engaged in funny behavior, now, is it? It's not like those women have access to the truck cab, themselves, now, is it?"

"I reckon you are correct there, ma'am, but as I said, I don't go in for the likes of that. My wife would about string me up by the jewels if I did, but that ain't the reason. It just ain't . . . listen, you wanna get a cup of coffee? I know a nice place in Texarkana, real easy to get to, you can just follow me. Got the most terrific cherry pies you have ever tasted. Just like that guy used to say on *Twin Peaks*, amazing cherry pie and a damn fine cup of coffee. I promise, coffee and pie is all," he said, holding his hands out in front of him, as if their emptiness illustrated that his intentions were good.

"I had better get back to my motel. I have a long day on the road tomorrow," I said.

"Yeah, me too. If you don't mind my asking, what were you doing out here? I know it's none of my business, but I know there ain't no hotels in Fouke, so I'm assuming you're staying in Texarkana and there's plenty of pay phones there."

"Just wanted to come here, see what it was like, but I had better get going."

"Afraid you might hear Bigfoot out here by yourself once the sound of my truck disappears?" he asked, smiling and walking across the road.

"Afraid I might not," I said, and he frowned a little, nodded, and got on his way. His taillights disappeared down the highway and I sat in the gravel parking lot for a while longer. This sleeping town was so much like the reservation, a place so quiet and remote that nearly any dream was possible. There might be a large hairy man living along the banks of sloughs and creeks, and there might be an Indian boy who learned to cope with life watching the movies who believed he could just wander into them, like Gumby with his magical powers to enter books. How many people in this town sleep with a window open and a bare foot exposed? Not many, I bet. Just before I started the Blazer to head back into the city and my sleeping friend, I heard some unusual sound off in the distance, but who could say what it was? I couldn't, not with any certainty.

o   o   o   o

"There, that's it," T.J. said, pulling off Interstate 84 before we reached the actual town of Big Antler, onto some road that only had letters and numbers identifying it. He pointed to a patch of growth and buildings on the horizon, silhouetted in the setting sun. By the time morning had come, he'd forgotten all about heading into Fouke, or perhaps he was just anxious to get to his old home. In any case, we'd risen early and gotten immediately on the road, even eating breakfast from a fast food drive-through window.

"Almost there," I said, and couldn't wait, my eyes fighting sleep, even with the break we took. Staying in Texarkana after that long push didn't ease the fact that we'd covered nearly seventeen hundred miles in a little over forty-eight hours.

"So why is this town named Big Antler? I haven't seen a deer since we left Tennessee." He sped up, stones and dust from the roadside kicking by us, tracing our progress.

"Oh, well, you're in Texas, where a lot of towns are named after either the white guys who killed things when they got here, or the people and things they killed. So, you got your Houston, Texas, and you got your Comanche, Texas. Big Antler got its name during the depression, from a cowboy killing the biggest mule deer on state record by a creek where the town is now located. You know the kind of story. He kills the deer and saves all the people from pellagra with the meat from this one deer, because they were all so niacin deficient they'd nearly eat rats if they could find them. A regular down-home fishes and loaves story."

"Pellagra?"

"Disease from a niacin deficiency in the diet. Pay attention, Mrs. Boans. You should have gotten that from the context."

"Dr. Boans, to you."

"Even more so, then, that you should have gotten it, doctor."

"Shut up," I said and we laughed, easily.

"Actually, you'll be interested to know that corn was originally thought to carry it, because people here in the South got sick with it, after eating a steady diet of mostly corn, and they only discovered it was not the corn by noticing that Indians didn't get pellagra. The lye method, you know, like for cooking corn soup, changes its structure. Indians knew this on some basic level, and settlers didn't."

"Colonizers, not settlers. There were already people here, remember?"

"Yes, of course," he exaggerated. "Anyway, they named him

town father and put the antlers up in the town hall when they eventually erected one. There's even a big sculpture down in the town square, based on the antlers of that mule deer. We can go by there before we leave, if you'd like." It seemed to take forever, the buildings on the flat, open space an optical illusion, remaining the same distance away no matter how long we drove, then we crossed some train tracks without any guard bars and suddenly the buildings and trees finally took on some depth, vividness, became real.

"I'll pass, thanks," I said and we laughed. "But why do you know so much about pellagra?"

"My daddy. Well versed in the history of West Texas, American history, period."

"Really?"

"Really," T.J. said. "Well, we're here," he added, flying into the driveway, a huge cloud of dust from the road and drive surrounding us. I got out and stretched, wandering over toward the furrowed fields. Their endless flatness looked like a one-point perspective drawing come to life. I had seen little like it outside of coffee-table books at the houses of various colleagues. It felt so good to use my legs again.

"This is like a compound. Who else lives here?" I asked, though I couldn't imagine anyone living in the more rustic houses on the lot.

"No one, just Daddy and Momma, and all their ghosts," he said, and that was an apt description. There was one contemporary-style house on the southernmost side of the property, the house whose carport we had pulled into, but all the others looked like they could have been reservation houses from around the time I was growing up. It was as if some small piece of my homeland had been transported out here onto this impossibly flat patch of land where the dust blew and the grass had only a saint's prayer of getting the shade of green we normally saw. It felt strangely like home and an alien planet at the same time.

The outhouse behind the furthest north building really made

me flash to home. I had always hated going back to the reservation as a kid to visit some of my mother's friends and our relatives. Whenever I knew we were going, I refused to have anything to eat or drink the whole morning before we would head out. "Please tell me this house has plumbing," I said.

"Don't be a goof! Of course, what are you talking about?" he said, then laughed. "Oh that. Yeah, Daddy likes to be authentic with his reconstructed old town. It's just for show, but feel free." He smiled and started unloading things from the Blazer as I wandered out among the buildings. I was still trying to figure out what was so unsettling about the place but it would not come, like an itch somewhere just below the skull, the kind you know you cannot scratch.

"Hey, don't go too far out that way. It's getting dark," he said, "watch where you're walking. Be careful of the *cascabel*."

"I thought that was the town in New Mexico where your adoptive parents have a cabin," I said, still not sure what I was supposed to be careful of.

"It is. The town is named after its shape, the way it lies narrow and long on the mountainside. Spanish for rattlesnake."

"Rattlesnakes? You used to live here?" What had been alien beauty to me a few minutes before was filled with invisible threats, every shadow suspect, every small noise the beginning of a fateful warning, just before I would feel the fangs and the venom.

"You get used to it," he said, taking our bags from the back of the Blazer. "You just accept the things in your life as they are, or, you know, you get bit."

"Aren't you all Creation Story philosophy," I said, thinking of all the lectures I'd given on our faith, and how pragmatism is at the heart of Haudenosaunee culture and, consequently, our art. It was always one of the hardest things for my students to get—the idea of being thankful for what you have, not waiting for a reward in heaven. I wonder how those ideas fit into Fred's scheme of thought.

"More like rattlesnake country philosophy."

"Your gram said, when I interviewed her those years ago, that was the reason your dad didn't head to Canada. She didn't say *pragmatist*, of course. Wasn't in her vocabulary, I'd imagine, but she said he accepted what he was supposed to do, when he got the letter, no matter how much others begged him to leave and go up to the Six Nations rez."

"I guess. I wish I had more answers for you about him, but I can't really see how I could possibly have learned to be like him. We really didn't spend all that much time together."

"Doesn't look like anyone's home," I said, while he peeked in through the garage's back-door window.

"Nope, the other truck's gone. They must have headed out to Cascabel right after the interview."

"Do you have a key?"

"They always keep one in the pump house, since you have to turn the well on anytime you come back, anyway." He set the bags down on a rococo park bench on the back porch, and then headed into the small building a few yards away. The building was stacked with anonymous boxes and pieces of junk lying everywhere. One of those boxes might still contain letters and other belongings of my mother's.

An old-style locksmith's key carousel sat on a countertop, and he gently spun it until he came to the peg holding a certain key that looked like all the others. He took it to the back door, and it turned the deadbolt lock, easily. He slid the key into his pocket. "Helps to know which key," he said.

"What if they'd moved it to a different peg?" I asked. I suppose it would have merely meant another hotel room.

"Well, I would have tried this one," he said, pulling a key from his wallet and inserting it in the same lock, where it also turned the bolt. "Some things never change," he said, turning it back, putting it in his wallet. He returned the other key to the pump house, flipping the power switches so the pump came to life. I suspected he would have tried that key, hidden in his wallet, at some point before we left, to see if they had changed the lock on him.

"Laundry room's over there," he said, pointing with his chin, "in case you want to do some before we head on."

I stepped into the house, looked where he pointed, and stood in the dining room while he went around, turning on water valves, adjusting the thermostat, and bringing the bags in. The decor suggested the same style I had seen from the news program, overwhelming antiques, but tastefully arranged, a larger picture emerging from the play among all the items. One of the couple had a real eye. The kitchen counter was high, kidney shaped, with bar stools surrounding it. I could almost picture T.J. eating cereal there in the mornings, all those years growing up.

The living room was larger than it had appeared in the interview, the weight everyone allegedly gains over the air. A big-screen television dominated the far corner of the room. The curio case I had seen on the broadcast indeed filled one whole wall, and other oddities engaged one another in visual dialogue through much of the space. Professionally, I was impressed with the breadth of their collection and their curatorial and presentation skills.

"This is really beautiful," I said, running my hand along the curio. I had never seen anything like it. It ran ten feet long and stood nearly eight feet tall, clearing the ceiling by maybe an inch. It was a deep rich oak, solid, not veneer, the veins of grain running identical on the inside and out of its three evenly spaced upper cabinets. The dead center section was open, and gorgeous art deco table lamps inhabited the recess, a series of figures dancing against frosted-glass full moons. The cabinets surrounding the dancers each housed other unusual deco pieces behind rippled old leaded glass doors. The items were the kind you might find in a Manhattan antique shop, if you were diligent and were a good enough customer that the proprietor would show you the back room. I had certainly never been in the preferred customer category there, but I had some friends, colleagues who were and who went to New York on buying trips.

"Daddy's therapy."

"What do you mean? Like a hobby?"

"No, really, his therapy. He's never articulated it as such, but that's what it was. When he got back from Vietnam, and things were so different here, he wandered around lost for a long time. This was all before he and your . . . this was before his trips to New York became a regular thing. He did a lot of wandering around here, Central Texas, too, wherever. He just couldn't keep still. This taught him how to keep still. He found it in pathetic shape at an old general store that was going out of business around the time the big chain food stores were making inroads, somewhere a few hours from here.

"It was a humidor and they'd left it out in the rain with just a tarp on it. He bought it and brought it back here, and started to work resurrecting it. I think it took him most of three months, stripping it down to its essence, firming its infrastructure discreetly, and then enriching its skin, saturating its surface with oils, one slow and smooth coat at a time, stripping and starting over if it didn't have the right sheen for him. He worked on it every waking hour, and one day, he looked up and it was done and he felt like he was home again." He reached into one of the drawers in the lower half and after rummaging for a few minutes, pulled out a little newspaper in a plastic sleeve. "It was probably the beginning of all this, all the outbuildings, the Yorkston house, everything. Here's an article on some of it. There's more to tell. There always is, but you'll get the essence from this."

I took the article and set it on the center open shelf in front of the dancing figures. Something else had caught my eye as T.J. had looked for that newspaper. The curio's top center shelf was barren except for two items, both of which I was very familiar with. No dust filmed the shelf, as often happened with this sort of thing, so the pieces had been lifted and set back in place not that long before we arrived.

"A Baby Snookum?" I asked. These small, rust-colored Indian baby dolls had been sold at reservation roadside stands and souvenir shops through the earlier part of the century. Wrapped in a small piece of rawhide, they usually had some simple beadwork design on the hide, and their heads were the only visible part of them. This was in pretty decent shape, though it had the problem most surviving examples had, making it less valuable on the collector's and museum markets. Supposedly, Indian women would buy or trade these small plastic dolls by the gross, and make the wrapping blanket out of scraps left over from moccasin-making, and they would do the beadwork there at the stand while they sold them, charging extra for custom work. The hair on the babies, though, was cut from their own heads, or from the heads of their children, and glued on in little patches. This was usually what was missing from these survivors. The glue was not very stable, and grew brittle, or generations of kids had pulled it off, so these dolls were usually bald and scarred. This one was no different.

"Hmm, it is still here. I wondered," he said, carrying two cardboard boxes of nearly identical size into the room and setting them on the couch. They had been in the back of the Blazer, neatly tucked away behind the cooler and backpack.

"Time to trade," he said, gently opening the curio's center glass door and pulling the other item, a plastic Indian warrior, from the shelf.

"What about this?" I asked, holding the Snookum.

"That stays. Daddy found it at some estate sale a long time ago, negotiated, got it down to a quarter, then brought it home and put it next to the other figure, and said my real daddy and I were together again."

He opened the first of the two boxes and pulled a figurine from it, the same sort that took up the other shelves. It was a groom carrying a bride in his arms. It had been broken at some point, and someone had tried to repair it, but the damage had been substantial. There were gaps in it, where the shadows within darkened it. Not even hot glue had the ability to fit all these pieces back together. He set it on the shelf next to the Snookum, took the packing outside, and wandered to the road, where a small residential Dumpster sat. I didn't ask.

Several walls in the house were jammed with photographs of strangers, some formal, some informal, some candid. T.J. was not in a single picture that I could tell. There were plenty of group shots and I scanned them closely, but he was nowhere to be found. The only picture that was a fairly decent candidate was mounted in the hallway that divided the house in half. The photo showed a much younger Tommy Jack standing in front of his truck, leaning against the grill, and a small boy standing next to him, wearing a cap that was too large for him. The foreground was darkened by the shadow of whoever was taking the picture. While I looked at the photos, T.J. walked around the front yard, touching the fence, throwing a few stones off into the mesquite trees across the road.

In the laundry room, a stack of neatly folded clothes sat on a table in the corner. I turned the washer on and went for our dirty clothes. Pulling a couple of softener sheets, I discovered the dryer was still full. I loaded its contents into a basket, all men's clothes: Levi's, T-shirts, boxer shorts, and white socks with the stripes at the top. I held up one of the shirts, a horizontal striped one, the kind Charlie Brown or Dennis the Menace might wear, and it seemed larger than I would have guessed from the images on the television. The pairs of Levi's were all thirty-six by thirties, and that seemed to fit more of what I was thinking. Doug was a forty by thirty-two, and T.J., I could see from the jeans I'd just put in the washer, was a thirty-six by thirty-four. I folded the clothes and stacked them with the others.

A baseball cap hung on a hook above the table, clearly worn, broken in. The logo BIG ANTLER TRACTOR AND FEED, BIG ANTLER, TX, was silk-screened across the front, along with an image of, I presumed, the famous antlers. This close, the scent of fake banana, cocoa, and sweat hung in the air around me—sunscreen, of course—his life soaking into the cap's band. As fair-skinned as he appeared to be, he would burn easily in this sun. He was in a lot of the photos on the walls, and in almost all of them, he wore some sort of cap, hiding his hair. His copper beard shimmered in the sun. There he was, playing a pickup game of softball, putting on a Santa Claus outfit, digging in a Dumpster, buying something at a garage sale, any number of other things. The only photo with his hair visible was the one of him and the child in front of the truck. A copy of his truck-driving-school certificate hung with the photos, along with a high school and two college diplomas.

"He went to college?" I asked, when T.J. finally returned.

"Yeah, he got the degrees. I think he either got a job teaching high school or was about to when the army decided his number was up. After he got back from the war, he said he didn't have the heart to teach kids who were lining up to get shot to death half a world away. Sometime in the same period he refurbished the curio. He disappeared on and off then too, and came to the reservation, probably other places as well. I think that was when he found he liked doing the long hauls and signed up for trucking school when he got back here."

"You're not in any of these," I said.

"I'm in some."

"Where?"

"Probably in the albums." He looked around, spreading his arms as if there were thousands of photo archives in the room. A variety of things filled the shelves, and some of them might have been photo albums, but somehow, I had my doubts.

"Is this one you?" I asked, pointing to the one in the hall.

"Yes," he said, smiling and nodding. "Well, you can sleep on the pullout here," he said, patting the sofa, "or you could stay in my old room." I had expected more about the photo from his expression, but he was not talking.

"This is fine," I said. "Where is your room?" He led and I was not especially surprised to see a room decorated like all the others: interesting antiques, tastefully arranged, contemporary bedding, and not another trace of T.J. Howkowski anywhere in that room either.

"You wanna watch some TV after your shower?" he asked when we'd stared at his room, devoid of him, for an awkward, silent moment.

"Sure, that'd be fine. Do you know how to use that thing?" I asked. The giant satellite dish in the side yard looked like it could take a pretty complicated negotiation to anyone unfamiliar with it.

"We'll see, I guess," he said as I went to shower. He opened the bathroom door and I cursed myself for not locking it, but it shut again a few seconds later. A bright green shirt sat on the counter when I got out, the Quaker Steak & Lube logo screened onto it, like the emblem I had seen on that cap a little while before. A small note resting on it said "nightshirt" in T.J.'s sprawling handwriting. The shirt billowed as I opened it. The size tag read 2X. What was with these guys that they didn't seem to know sizes at all? I put it on and it hung down past my thighs.

"You like it?" he asked. "I bought it when you went out to the Blazer. Remember? When I said I was going to the john? One of my old girlfriends in the city used to wear oversized T-shirts as night-shirts, so I thought you might like that too."

"I was wondering about the size," I said. "Thought maybe it was some weird thing with you and Tommy Jack."

"What? Oh yeah, Daddy always liked T-shirts way too big, who knows why, I guess he still does."

"It would appear. So, did you get the satellite working?"

"Well, no. I switched it on, and pressed some buttons, and the dish outside grinds and moves direction, I went out there and looked, but not much happens here. I switched over to the antenna, but this far out, all you get is snow on most channels and I think one Spanish channel from Lubbock fading in and out."

"Why don't you just call Tommy Jack and ask him? I'm sure it can't be that hard. You're probably just doing one little thing out of sequence or something," I said. He stood there and played with the box some more. The snow on the screen would turn to blackness but then nothing else. He stared into it as if that would make something appear there.

"They have no idea you're coming, do they?" I said, looking at his reflection in the dark screen. He shook his head back and forth. "How do you even know they're there?"

"I know."

"This should be an interesting day tomorrow."

"Well, there's some tapes, here," he said, squatting in front of the entertainment center. "*Fargo*?" he laughed.

"Sure, why not," I said. He turned on the VCR, ejected a tape, and inserted *Fargo*. The snow from the airwaves cut off and the digital snows of the northern United States spread across the screen along with the opening credits. He was asleep on the sofa not long after. I had forgotten there was an Indian actor in this movie, too, but he had almost as few lines as Fred Howkowski might have had in any movie he was ever in. At least this guy definitely looked Indian, which was kind of a dubious compliment. His primary role seemed to be to savagely beat someone with a leather belt. Some things don't change. I inched the volume down to nearly nothing. I could almost see Tommy Jack McMorsey, the man I had the strong sense was indeed my father, trying to help a small Japanese woman across the long anonymous stretch of snow-covered, frozen earth, in the ransom-money scene. I could almost force the pixels to change in my mind, one color dominating the other two in every small fiber of the image, creating him in small colored dots, shifting and moving across the screen before me.

I quietly got up and went to his desk in the den. It was odd, going through someone's private belongings, someone you knew of but didn't know, really, forming new opinions with every revelation. A stick of Black Jack gum, probably years old, a fingernail clipper, strips of one- and two-cent postage stamps, a pocket-size bottle of Germ-X antibacterial solution, an accumulation of used and bent staples still in the jaws of a staple remover, brassy tokens that looked like they would be used in a video game arcade, neatly cut out pictures of blankets from catalogs, a small copy of the same photo with him and a boy in front of the truck's grill, and hundreds of twist ties. What do these things add up to? Who was this man who would be my father?

I found the things I needed: a small pair of scissors and a

tube of superglue. In the bathroom, I reached to the underside of my bobbed hair, where its dense layers would afford some invisible sacrifice, and I cut a small patch, gathering it on the counter. In the living room, T.J. still slept as the VCR had run through the film, rewound, and shut off, leaving the blank airwaves to refill the screen again with shifting snow. The curio door opened quietly with the gentle lift and pull I had seen T.J. perform earlier. I removed the Snookum, took it to the bathroom, swabbed its bare head with superglue, and lay the strands of hair across it, then returned it to its place in the cabinet.

I lay down for a while on the sofa, not bothering to pull it out, my head against the padded arm where a Pendleton blanket lay. It was an old knockoff Navajo design, by the look. Eventually, I got up, went to the laundry room, took off the T-shirt, and folded it neatly. I exchanged it for one from Tommy Jack's pile of shirts and stepped outside. The cicadas sounded like a lawn full of rattlers might. I watched the ground carefully all the way to the Blazer, removed the envelope from the glove compartment, and read the letter again. Back inside, I turned on the moon dancer lamps. The Snookum and the fractured couple threw long distorted shadows on the ceiling of the nearly dark living room. By this artificial moonlight and the blue cast of the television, I read the newspaper article T.J. had shown me, over and over. Who was this eccentric man my mother claimed as the love of her life? Eventually I fell asleep in that electronic snow, contemplating Cascabel and all the things that awaited us in a few hours, beyond Interstate 84.

o   o   o   o

The six hours to the New Mexico mountain town went by surprisingly fast. Even on winding roads when we'd get stuck behind a slow-moving semi, I didn't care. I had steeled myself for the meeting in Big Antler, but now it was almost as if we'd already met somehow. To have been in that space, and then left it, changed me, though in what ways, I couldn't say. I suspected whatever I felt would be reawakened the closer we got, but at the moment, I could have perhaps left, returned home, and never spoken with him in person. T.J., in the driver's seat, said very little about the time we spent at the house. He walked around the grounds in the morning before we left his old home, and it seemed like he was perhaps taking it in, one last time, but I didn't ask.

Entering Cascabel, we passed an old A-frame that had been a restaurant named Wanda's, but it hadn't been Wanda's in a very long time. The signs advertising specials had been so sun-bleached that they looked more like watermarks on fancy stationery than actual writing. T.J. pulled into the parking lot there, peeked in the window, and then used the pay phone at the far end of the lot. After several tries he came back and sat on the hood for a bit, so I got out and stood with him. The morning chill was burning off and a nice day bloomed out of it.

"My momma hates being woken by a phone, says it scares her witless and shaves time off her heart," he said. "So for the last few years I was around, she made my daddy take it off the hook just after the news and before we all went to bed, and we couldn't put it back on until she'd had at least one bite of the toast and one sip of the tea. The recording of the operator asking if we needed assistance would come on and then that whining beep would go on for a minute and then be silent. She begrudged even this brief intrusion so we generally didn't lift it off the hook until she was already in the bedroom.

"When she first informed us of the new phone rules, Daddy used to ask, 'What if there's been some accident? What if someone's died?' She would shoot right back that they are still gonna be dead in the morning when we wake up, and there's not a damned thing we can do about it. When she gave one-sentence answers, that was pretty much the end of any dialogue."

"You could just go up there," I said.

"That over there is the Mescalero reservation. You can't tell so much until you get inside, then you see that certain roads have roadblocks. Only people who have real business can travel there," he said, as if I had not made a suggestion.

"You could—" I started.

"I gotta do it this way," he said, walking back over to the pay phone. After a few tries, he got an answer and then we headed down the street to an old department store that had been converted into a flea market. The word PRIME had been crudely painted over the old name, but done so badly that neither the new nor the old name was all that discernable. People milled about, buying, selling, but it seemed that the main currency in this store was gossip. Every single person there knew all the others, and it felt like the reservation. Maybe they were all just the dealers, passing time until potential customers came in. A little while later, a red pickup pulled in and I caught my first look in person at Tommy Jack McMorsey.

When I saw him for the first time, I didn't really even know what I was doing there. Though I'll probably never admit it to him, Royal was right. I was driven by two things in collision, my personal life and my professional life. Of course, he might offer me some real information about Fred Howkowski, but what did I think he might offer me as a father? Did I really need to connect the dots in this formal way? Self-righteous abstraction was fine, all the way here, rage and embarrassment driving me half the distance of this continent. This man, though, standing in front of me, the tangibility of him, the way his clothes fit a little funny, the arch of his aging back, the flicker of a smile mixed with anxiety, the sunburn on his pale cheeks and ears—these things defied the cardboard cutout that had ridden the two thousand miles along with me.

"Daddy," T.J. said, running up to the man, arms open, but Tommy Jack, it seemed, had a force field around him that deflected our northern world from him, defying T.J.'s embrace with a simple look. Instead, the older man held out a weathered hand and with that simple gesture, T.J. remembered where he was.

"Boy, what are you doing here?" Tommy Jack asked, almost matter-of-factly, but not quite.

"We saw you on the TV," T.J. said, as if that were sufficient explanation for erasing the gap of years between them. T.J. shifted, the cocktail-party-introduction move, and suddenly Tommy Jack noticed me. "Daddy, I want you to meet someone. This here is Annie Boans." He took my hand and shook it lightly, the way a man of an earlier generation touches an unfamiliar woman's hand. "She's from the reservation. Her momma was someone who knew you. You know, the one who—"

"We finally meet, Mr. McMorsey," I interrupted. I wanted this introduction done on my own terms. "My mother still talks about you, with some."

"With some . . ."

"People."

"Oh, some people, yes, of course," he said, embarrassed that he hadn't understood. Then the rest began to sink in. "Your mother?" Though he made it sound like a question, his gaze flickered to T.J.—a brief glint of hostility that he masked almost as soon as it had washed over him. He knew. And it seemed that among the expressions he wrestled with hiding, pleasure was one of them, pleasure that she still thought of him.

"Shirley Mounter," I clarified. "She would have been Shirley Mounter, then, too. She was married when she made your acquaintance. This is of course not to say that they ever stopped being married, right up to the point he died." Were these the things I had come all this way to say? I supposed they were.

"Daddy?" T.J. asked, maybe trying to ease the situation or totally oblivious. "You still got stuff here?" Tommy Jack nodded and T.J. smiled, oddly transformed into a boy in this man's presence. "I'm gonna go see if I can find it. I bet you a dollar I can, just by what you're selling and the prices you put on." His grammar also seemed to have been transformed by our crossing into the South. He ran into the building, leaving us alone in the parking lot, among the bargain hunters. How he expected to identify Tommy Jack's booth among all the broken Kewpie dolls and cheap glassware was beyond me, but I had bigger concerns.

"When I was younger, she used to talk about you, though only on rare occasions, like you were some sacred legend we could only hear about on special days. It took me years to realize that the special days were those when she and I were the only ones around."

"You don't know everything, missy. That was a long time ago. Probably you weren't even born then, the first time. Your momma was a wonderful woman. Full of life. How's she doing?" he asked, his voice dropping a little, as he lowered his head.

"She's fine. You know, I don't really see anything so special about your ears." I smiled, but not a real smile. I wanted him to know that I had more information than just how my mother was doing.

"Oh, there ain't." His head lowered even further, and his ears reddened. I guess there were more ways than one my mother admired his ears. Probably more information than I needed to know, but the upper hand is always useful. "A nice thing about having a beard, though, is that I don't have to worry about trimming the ear hairs all that much. They just blend in." He laughed, shuffled around, kicked a small rock from the asphalt and watched it bounce into the weeds.

"Blending in."

"Listen. You're talking about things that happened, now, almost thirty-five years ago. I don't know what you expect me to say. I got a life here. Hasn't the boy told you anything before bringing you out here?" T.J. was working his way back toward us, frowning a little, perhaps having heard us, though we stayed around whisper levels.

"T.J. is not a boy, he's an adult, a successful professor and professional actor who—"

"I only call him that 'cause his real daddy named him after me," he said, exasperated, unsteady, like he was back in that interview. "And when I got with the wife, we had to make some difference between us, so she could separate who she was calling. I guess it just stuck." He paused, noticing T.J. getting closer. "In his thirties, man alive. So, uh, he's successful, huh?"

"Successful enough," I said. How could he not know? How long had they been out of regular contact?

"Daddy, I couldn't find your stuff anywhere," T.J. said. "You switch the kinds of things you're selling? Or did the supply of war stuff finally dry up?"

"The market for war stuff sure never dries up. People change, boy. You ought to know that. My stuff is over there, lot number fifty-eight, same as my age. Guess maybe I'll be having to change lots in a little while."

"Yeah, that's one of the reasons I came back. I came to be here for your birthday, like we used to." T.J. smiled, hoping for it to be infectious, it seemed, expecting Tommy Jack to be happy about his surprise, congratulate him for being so clever, but the only response he got from the older man was a slow shake of the head.

"So, uh, are y'all staying here?" Tommy Jack asked.

"We made reservations down at the inn," T.J. said. "Thought maybe we could go and play some slots a little later, if you were interested. Never was very good at the card games, but all you need for the slot machines is correct change and I've certainly got that." T.J. slid his hands into the pockets of his jeans and rattled change. I wondered when he picked that up. It sounded like mostly quarters. "Kind of figured Momma might still not be too interested in seeing me, and I know how she is about unexpected company of any kind, but I thought it was time to clean some things up in my life, and this here place is as good as any. I assume you still have that letter from my real daddy?"

"I do, but it's at the other house," Tommy Jack said, again bowing his head. "I would have to go looking for it. I'm not for sure where it is. It's been a long time since I've had a need to read it," he finished, but we both knew he could place his hand on it in a moment's notice. It wasn't exactly the sort of thing you forgot.

"Most everything from the war's in my duffel bag, with my nasty old boots and the one set of fatigues they let us take home, that my old body will never see the fitting side of again, and all the other things from that time. But the letter . . ." he said, looking out toward the rolling mountains of the Mescalero reservation just the next rise over.

"It's been years since you read it to me. Did you read me the whole thing or were you selective, Daddy?"

"The contents of that envelope weren't addressed just to you, boy."

"Does he say in it why he gave me up to you, Daddy?" T.J. tried his hardest to say this in a casual way, but whatever acting skills he had were not active on this day. What he wanted was very clear, even as it changed. His face was like one of those magic rings we used to have, Flickers, where you looked at it from one direction and as soon as you shifted it, the image changed a bit, a surprise. He wanted to know and didn't want to know. He wanted to be able to hear it and then decide for himself if he liked what he heard or not, and if not, wanted to be able to wipe it clean, shift, forget he'd ever heard the violation. But we all knew the world doesn't work that way.

"Coming home has been a long time in the making," T.J. said. "I want to read the letter. All of it. And I want to see Momma. I have something to give her. It took me a long while to get this right but it's time. I imagine the two of you have things to talk about as well." I didn't know if he were referring to Tommy Jack and his wife, or Tommy Jack and me. Either way, he was a keen observer. "I'm getting the Blazer, and we're going to follow you back."

"So you've told him about your momma and me?" Tommy Jack asked when T.J. was out of earshot.

"Me? He knows more than I do," I said, watching him. His forehead wrinkled and his mouth pushed out a little.

"Missy, you think we're all just going to run to my place and have us a good old conversation?" he said. "Well," he added, shaking his head, kicking some more stones, and then sighed.

"I had my own business in coming here. I don't really know why I had to see you, or even what I expected. Somehow, in person you're not the creep I thought you must be, but I sure as hell don't know what my mother saw in you either."

"Like I said, before, missy—I'm sorry, what would you like me to call you? I don't want to be rude."

"Maybe you should call me 'the girl,'" I said, staring at him, watching him come to realize my eyes and his were more or less the same shade of green. I walked over to the passenger side of the Blazer as T.J. pulled up.

"What?" He didn't want to believe what I had suggested.

"Daddy, are you going to lead or follow?" T.J. said, rolling down the window. I knew it was a Southern thing, but the name T.J. chose to call Tommy Jack still bothered me. It made him seem childish, and I was embarrassed every time he used it. "Either way, we're gonna be at the cabin in under ten minutes." The air-conditioning blew out and around us, breaking up as it hit the hot noon air.

"Boy? Will you wait? Maybe tomorrow? I thought you were going to the inn and the casino. Maybe I can, you know, let her know easy that you're back, let her get used to the idea before you come barging in." He was asking to buy some time, but I had to wonder how he intended to spend it, once he got it. My guess was he might try to bolt, but where was there to go, at this point?

"It's almost noon. You have until noon tomorrow, Daddy. One way or the other, I am going to be on your doorstep this time tomorrow. So, are we going to see you tonight? Dinner and some slots? See you at the High Tide?"

"I'll get back to you. Are you already registered at the inn?"

"No, check-in isn't until one, so we'll probably go get some lunch, and then go to the desk. You want to join us for lunch? One of those awesome desserts at Wanda's?"

"Wanda's is closed," Tommy Jack said, his eyes squinting.

"Yeah, I noticed that when we pulled into town. Looks like

nothing ever took its place, either. Her last pie special signs look years faded in the windows."

"She left town over ten years ago. Said she couldn't make a go of it anymore. And we didn't go there, much, after that last time you were with us."

"Guess maybe we'll just eat at the inn, then, and maybe catch a few early-bird slots before check-in," T.J. said, nodding, and we pulled away into the rushing traffic down the four-lane highway back into town. The small man who was most likely my father disappeared, standing still, in the rearview mirror. I wondered how long he stood there before he took his first inevitable steps in that new role.

ACT THREE:

Action

CHAPTER SEVEN:

Call Back

o   o   o

Dear Son,

I am sorry I had to leave like this. I wish I had some answers for you, but I don't. I know you'll get lonely sometimes, but remember, your new dad is a good man. He saved me over there, in the war, and I never would have made it back without him. I have some things for you that I've asked your new dad to hang on to until you get to be a little older. I know twenty-one seems to be a long ways away, but even though you can smoke and drink and even get drafted to go fight in some other country, you aren't a man when you're eighteen. I know you're too young to read this letter now, but your new dad will read it to you, but Tommy Jack, and yes, I mean you, McMorsey, don't you let him read the rest of it until he's eighteen, or until he decides he's maybe going to try his skills at Fireball.

The things I'm leaving you, you'll probably run through them and say, what is this shit, but they're my things, the things I felt were important to pass on to you. The first is my only speaking part in the movies, though it isn't much and it never did even make it into the picture. It's a short reel, but I hope you like it, it's all I got. The second thing is the first picture I ever saw of you. Your grams didn't want to send it to me, she didn't want you anywhere near Vietnam, but I talked her into it anyway. I had to promise to send it right back, but when I saw you there in that little blanket, I

just had to keep you with me. It drove her crazy and she asked for it
back all the time, but I kept it with me. She believed a part of your
soul was trapped inside the picture. She always hung on to some of
those old beliefs, but I must have too. Hanging on to your picture,
guarding it, that was the one thing that kept me going over there.
There were lots of times I would just lay down at night, so tired I
almost didn't care if a sniper or some mortar got me in my sleep,
because it would mean I wouldn't have to get up and walk through
that damned jungle one more day, but then I would remember
your picture, in the pocket over my heart in the flak jacket, and
that would make me just that much more careful. I knew I had to
bring you back home, and I did just that. So, *nyah-wheh* for keeping me going. The other stuff, that's odds and ends, my draft card,
my dog tags, a beer can your new dad tried to play a joke on me
with, my call sheets from the movies I worked on, the little parts
of the costumes I walked off the set with. Wardrobe wouldn't miss
them. Just throw it out if you don't want it, probably won't mean
much to you anyway. I suppose that says something about a man,
if most of his life can be summed up in a box smaller than a rucksack. That last thing, though, that eagle feather with the beaded
and tanned hilt, you should either take that or give it to Hillman,
the medicine man. He was the one who gave it to me when I got
home, said sometimes I might need bad thoughts to take flight and
I could smudge them away with tobacco, let the feather push the
bad thoughts out into the sky on tobacco smoke. You can decide
if it did any good. If you want it, take it, but if you don't, return
it to him. Your cousin Brian Waterson will know how to find him.
They're related somehow, but I'm not exactly sure in what way. He
can tell you.

I imagine you'll be going home at some point, even if just to
visit, and if you decide to play in the Fireball game at the National
Picnic, here's a little piece of advice. If we all still went the old way,
you would have to wait until you had some kids of your own to be
considered on the Old Men's side of things, instead of the Young

Men's, and there's a reason for that. The Old Men are who they are because they are supposed to accept responsibility. I knew when I got back from the war, when I first saw you, sleeping in that laundry basket, just a little bundle, that I might have been an Old Man because I helped make you, but something changed in me, over there. I can't even say what it was, but I knew that I should have stayed a Young Man. I ain't saying you shouldn't have been born, I love you to pieces, but I knew that if I stayed there, at home, and you stayed with me, neither one of us was going to last long. So, I was looking out for both of us when I asked Tommy Jack to take you away, and go some place different. If you do go back and decide to play, you remember one thing. A lot of people play that game, knowing it's dark when they're on the field, and they try to settle some scores they don't have the nerve to when they're in the light. That's their business, but you remember, Fireball started off as a medicine game, one for healing. You play it with your heart, letting the good come out, and you live the rest of your life that way, too. I've played my last game of Fireball, past the point of any medicine, and I'm not going to ask you to forgive me, but just trust me when I say I know I made some mistakes, and I am sorry.

Love,
Dad

Tommy Jack McMorsey

Well, after that interview experience, Liza Jean is going to for sure get her dream come true this year. The road is a lonely place, and Liza Jean Bean never was much for traveling, even after she became Liza Jean McMorsey. She was the school nurse for all of Big Antler, such as it is, and that was a gig she loved a lot, because it gave her the summer off and we could head to our place in the mountains. Let me tell you, if you live in West Texas, you best find yourself a job that lets you get away in the summertimes, unless you want the soles of your shoes melting to the asphalt any time you just want to take yourself a walk on down the road. That's what it's like here, anyway, probably from the end of May right up to the beginning of the school year in August, at least. Really, more like Labor Day, and Liza Jean always said as soon as she retired, the one thing she most wanted to do was to stay at our place in the mountains through Labor Day to watch all the summer folks have to head on down to the flatlands while she kicked back on the porch, drinking herself a Big Red.

That seemed like it would have been a nice dream to me, too. But Labor Day is most like any other day, on the road. Maybe a little more traffic on the interstate, but not so's you'd remark on it. To the wife, though, that day always looked ugly on the calendar. It meant another full year of sticking thermometers under the tongues of kids who just wanted to get out of a test that day, and teaching the girls how to use one of those time-of-the-month devices properly. Mostly she liked her job but those older girls, the ones who were knowing their boyfriends in special ways before the wife could even explain the consequences, those girls seem to have worn her out, and Liza Jean's been looking forward to retirement the last few years.

The end of this summer her dream day would have arrived anyway, and I would have let her have it, but that was three months away, and just then, as always, I would have to get back to the flatlands and she knew it. She always took issue with the fact that my primary dispatch was out of Lubbock and that I could not get as flexibly hooked up in Cascabel. At first she was a little bent out of shape that we weren't going to be together on my birthday this coming week, but not bent enough to join me on the road. Birthdays never meant much to me anyway, but for sure we have already spent my last birthday together. At first, we'd decided to not head to Cascabel until after my birthday so we could have spent it together, but plans have a way of changing rapidly on you, sometimes. It was the end of Memorial Day weekend, but what I was doing here in Cascabel was gathering my things and by the time my birthday rolled around, we would be parted.

We didn't say much to one another after those reporters left. What more was there to say? We packed in silence and I drove us up here, so I could clean my stuff out of the cabin. The few brief conversations we had were about how to do this divorce clean. Yes, I know that sounds abrupt but there are some doors, once you walk through them, that is it, and I walked through a pretty big one on national TV Friday night and we both knew it was time for me to just keep walking.

She would keep the cabin in Cascabel and live there, as she'd always wanted to anyway, and I would keep the Big Antler house and the outbuildings. She could take whatever antiques she wanted from them to replace the things I was taking from the cabin that were mine. I didn't care, really, about whatever she might decide to take. I could replace most of it if I found the right things. She knew the curio was off-limits, but I didn't think I had to make that overly clear.

The temperature in the mountains was still a little chilly. Memorial Day was just as chilly as the folks we usually rent the mountain place out to always say it is. "Liza Jean, you want me to get the swamp cooler out for the season before I leave?" I asked.

"Well, yes, of course, I'll surely be getting a hot spell and then what would I do with no one to set it up for me?" This was one of those times she was asking a question but not really asking a question, like, wanting any kind of answer. "Make yourself useful as long as you're here." She sighed in that way that let me know I had wastefully used up some of the few words with her that I still had allotted to me, so I left her to the toast and tea I made for her each morning before she woke up. She was never going to forgive me for the end of the interview and I am sure that it would remain on the videotape she plays back in her head all the time even if I were to erase it from the VHS we made the night of the show. I can't imagine we will ever watch it. "And you be careful on the road tomorrow, Tommy Jack. The full moon's coming up and you know it makes all kinds of people get the most peculiar of notions." She was furious, but she was not letting me get away that easy. I still had a couple years of ass-chewing ahead of me, even if we were splitting up. I can't say as I blame her. Her place at the table warmed in the faint sun, even in the morning fog.

Since she was up, I put the phone back on the hook and as soon as it was back in the cradle that phone started to ringing, even in my hand. I left it there for a second too long, knowing that on the other end could only be bad news. Whoever was calling had been trying for a while. Some of our friends had called after the TV show a couple nights ago, though not really discussing the content, but none of them would be calling this time of day. Anyone who knows us is fully aware of Liza Jean's opinions on morning telephone calls.

"Tommy Jack McMorsey, answer that telephone! Someone's

trying to get through! I mean!" She turned her face and stared
out the kitchen window at the mist while I grabbed the receiver,
stepped into the living room, and mumbled a greeting, stretching
the cord, trying to disappear for her.

"Daddy? I'm home. I saw you on the TV and had to come back
and get things to right again. I can see Prime from here. Wasn't
hard to find at all." I knew the boy was closer immediately—not
just because the connection was clearer. The sounds of the city had
been gone from him for a few years, no more cabs, buses, ambu-
lances, that fear, but now even the sounds of New York period were
gone from him too. It was just him and a few voices—the customers who browse at the co-op flea market I sold junk from to support
my outbuilding projects. Nobody believed me when I told them I
financed all those restorations selling junk to other people looking
for their pasts, and that was fine. It meant nobody else would add
to my competition. All it takes is a few little gold mines someone is
tossing out with a seventy-five-cent tag on them, to really add up.
You just need some patience and a trained eye. And the search gave
me something to do with our mistake purchases or just other valuable stuff I found while I was out hunting for my own collection
when the haulers didn't need me so much and Liza Jean wanted
me out of her hair.

"Hello?" I repeated, louder, and as the boy matched my volume, thinking I hadn't heard him, I hung up the phone, cutting
him off in mid-repeat, and after a few seconds, I lifted the receiver
back off of the cradle, just a little bit. Then before the recorded
operator could tell me what to do in case I needed assistance, I
disconnected the cord linking the handset to the base. I for sure
needed assistance but I didn't think she could offer the kind necessary for this circumstance. The meteor Liza Jean McMorsey was
not one to be trifled with, and I don't know how the boy could have
forgotten that.

"Well, who needed us so urgently that they had to call us at 9:30
the day after Memorial Day?" Liza Jean asked, pressing her pointer

finger into her plate, lifting toast crumbs and licking them off her finger. "Someone wanting to talk about your new celebrity status?"

"Wrong number, I guess," I said, checking those little hang-up buttons to make sure they set right. "No one there. Listen, I got some stuff to take to Prime and get it all priced and such this morning. Don't worry. I won't ever ask you to check on it, and when I come to take inventory, I'll stay somewhere else." I was trying to avoid arguments any small place they might creep in.

"You've got that right, and just you remember that. These locks will be different by the time you come back up here, rest assured," she said, finding bitterness in the smallest openings I left.

"Anything you want from town or you wanna come?" She glared at me a minute, letting me know I could quit pretending right then and there that things between us were ever going to be all right again and when she knew she had done it long enough to sink in, she went back to staring out the window. In the past if I hadn't asked her to come, she'd be screeching her head off and running around to get dressed and go, and then complain to rush me at what I was doing the whole time, but if I asked her, I could just about be assured she'd be the first one to say no. Strangely, she reminded me to be back by one at the latest to take her out to lunch, so we could discuss who was getting what, but that was about it. It had been like this since the interview. I would get moments of the old life, then she would snatch them back and as soon as I got to accepting the new life alone, she would offer me up some shot of the old one again. I don't particularly want that shot, but maybe she needs to believe I do, and after all these years, I guess I can give her that for a little while.

"Okay, promise, be back by one," I said and leaned in, some part of me on autopilot while the rest of me wondered what I had in store for me down at Prime.

"Oh, Tommy Jack, you have got to be kidding," she said, before I realized what I had just done and could stop my movement. She pulled further away, pinching her lips tight, like a flower closing

against a night's cold. While this was understandable for our cur-
rent circumstance, I had been receiving that expression for a while
and was used to it, anyway.

All the way to Prime, I could not imagine what was on the boy's
mind that would bring him back here and think that we were just
going to pick up like a good old family again, like he had not chosen to reveal his knowledge at the worst time possible, like nothing had ever happened between the wife and him, like she hadn't
shattered some of her favorite things throwing them at him and
having them miss and explode, raining expensive porcelain shards
all over the wall-to-wall we'd laid just a couple years before, or like
any of that history would change just because I was on the damned
TV—particularly not because of that fact. Had he not watched the
whole thing?

Though really, the reason Liza Jean didn't love him like she
used to had more to do with me than with the boy. All those years
it had been my name on the mortgage with hers and the bank ac-
counts and all the other pieces of paper that keep two people together, even though all those things were about to change. What
I'm saying here is that all those pieces of paper sharing our names
and the hassle it would be to split them made it easier for her to
forgive me back then for doing the things I had done than to forgive the boy for keeping his mouth shut. There were promises I
had asked him to make. Maybe she was mad at his not keeping
his mouth shut, eventually, when she might have preferred that.
Maybe they had a chance now that there was nothing left to save
between her and me.

When I pulled into Prime's parking lot, there the boy stood,
big as life, with this redheaded woman who was dark enough to be
a Chihuahueño, but she looked too something. Too city, I guess.
Her clothes were maybe from Dillard's or Macy's, a store where
each item sits on its own damned little shelf, not being crowded by
anything else, the kind of store far away from this little mountain
town. And her lipstick, well, it wasn't the kind Liza Jean wore, that

I had to hand-scrub off all her cups whenever I did the damned dishes, that bright red making her lips look like she'd been kissing a freshly painted fire engine all night long. This woman's lips were soft, and not real shiny-like, natural colored, like if she kissed you, no one but you and her would know it and she wouldn't be telling and neither would you. The boy had good taste.

I know that kind of thinking is what got me in this situation in the first place but I have met all kinds of women and it had always seemed a crying shame to have to keep telling yourself no all your whole life because you said yes once. While I've gotten better as the years have gone on and I admit there are fewer women asking than used to, I never was that good at saying no. I guess I also said yes at the wrong time though there's no use in making that confession now.

This line of thinking of course changed as soon as he introduced her as Shirley's daughter. It seemed like all the bantams were coming home to roost today, and I could only thank the Lord that Liza Jean had decided to stay home. If she knew any of this was happening, she would be on that phone to a lawyer seeing what else she could get quicker than a cloud coming up in May and ripping your world apart, leaving your life a disheveled mess on the plains. I wouldn't even put it past her to get out a baseball bat. Her capacity for violence was not something I wanted to be the one to test.

I asked how Shirley was, finding myself wondering, picturing her as she was then, not unlike her daughter right now, in looks, mind you. I'd imagined her as she aged, like those computer simulations they have on the crime shows, but my memory was the way I liked her best. The Shirley I got to know then, okay, yes, the Shirley I had fallen in love with then, never saw this side of a thrift shop, and we spent lots of days driving around to any one we could find, me looking for junk and her looking for clothes. She would try them on for me at night after her kids had gone to bed and I would take them off of her and make love to her among those rumpled clothes and that Pendleton blanket on her living room floor. We always had to be quiet because it was a small apartment and those kids could have woken up at any time and when I would bring her right to the edge, I would always press my lips against those soft pink ones of hers, making sure she wouldn't let out a cry and wake those kids, and I never missed.

Later, I would head back out to the reservation to Fred's place, and we would spend the rest of the night around a bonfire, me and my old guitar that never played just right, Fred, his brother, and some others. I could still smell those thrift-shop clothes of hers on me into the morning hours when we would head to bed, that mixed perfume of mothballs, beer, and the blues, sending me off to sleep.

I wondered if this woman standing with the boy before me, all these years later, was one of the kids who was about to wake up as I was ordering corned beef hash and runny eggs a mile or so away from that apartment, or if she was a later kid, born after I went back to my other life. Well, even if she wasn't there the first time, no doubt she was the last time I returned.

When the boy ran into Prime, leaving us alone for a few minutes, she gave me an earful, and among that jam of information, she told me something that I wanted to hear but could never ask, myself, and something else I never expected to hear. The boy almost never talked about what he was doing when he called. I usually watched anything on the TV that had Indians in it, hoping I might catch him one of these days, but I ain't seen him anywhere, not even on the satellite dish. When he came back, the boy knew something was up, and looked down at the pavement. He knew that some kinds of words had passed between the girl and me, but I don't guess he knew ahead of time the direction the conversation had gone in his absence. A daughter. I still didn't fully believe it as they left me in the Prime parking lot, but it wasn't like I had a lot of choice in what I had to do next.

So when I got to the house I said the most neutral thing I could. "Well, things seem good at Prime, lots of customers for a weekday." Liza Jean could tell right away that something more than our dissolving marriage was up. I do not know how she tells these things but it's like she sniffs them out of me, like I have a cloud of lies or vague answers floating about me, giving off some noxious scent.

"Anyone besides Lurlene ask you about your big moment on TV?" she said, waiting for me to give some kind of deadly answer, so she could rehash my performance, conveniently forgetting her own. At that moment I saw Lurlene in my head picking up the phone earlier and calling the cabin, telling Liza Jean that Tommy Jack was standing outside with some man and woman she had never seen before and was just wondering if we had guests this holiday weekend and who they might be—nosy bitch. If she spent even a quarter of the time selling that she spent trying to keep tabs on every damned person in that town, I might actually turn a profit once in a while. I was trying to decide what I was going to say, when I glanced over at the phone and saw it was still disconnected, so Lurlene couldn't have called.

"Just a couple people." This was not technically a lie. "They didn't say anything. Maybe it didn't look the way you think it did on TV," I said, though I really didn't care anymore. We shouldn't have been together for, oh, the last ten years or so, easily, probably even more, probably from the time of Wanda's. "Well, did you decide where you want to have lunch to discuss who gets what?" I thought about reconnecting the phone, but sometimes, silence is the better option. This was one of those times.

"Foley's?" she said, making it a question, like pretending I was going to be the one who made the decision, but this time, I did.

"How about the inn, instead? We go to Foley's all the time."

"We won't be going there all the time anymore."

"And besides, I'm feeling lucky. We can play a few slots beforehand."

"Oh, all right, I guess we can go there. Whatever. Let's get this over with. Just know that I am not wasting my afternoon there while you play one more machine that turns into ten machines. My days of waiting for you are over, Tommy Jack."

"Yes, you have made that clear, but don't for one minute think you are the only one who is looking forward to not putting up with someone else's nonsense. Now come on, let's go and have lunch, play a few slots, like two people who've known each other almost fifty years. Just because we can't live together anymore, doesn't mean we have to be so damned snarly to each other."

"Maybe you should have thought of that before you went nuts on the damned TV!" she yelled.

"Maybe you should have, too," I said back, not shouting. In the past, our casino ritual had been a kind of foreplay, with her saying "I'm feeling a little lucky, myself" and pinching my ass. "Pinch to grow an inch," she'd say. She could be wildly forward that way, and I'd reach around and cup hers, back.

"Keep that up and your luck might deliver you more than one inch a little later," I'd say.

"Huh! You'd be the lucky one," she'd say back, and grab her purse. The pinch was always just a preview of what would come once we got back from the casino, but I guess my inch-growing days were over with Mrs. Liza Jean McMorsey.

The lot was jam-packed when we got there, even that early. All kinds of people wheeled their little oxygen tanks around in one hand and smoked a Pall Mall with the other and they came here from all over the damned country. When we walked by the boy's Blazer with New York plates on it, Liza Jean paid no notice to it. She was already rattling her little casino bucket of quarters, part of what she called her winner's ritual. But she did it with little enthusiasm, like she was sleepwalking almost. She always said her quarters called to the ones inside the slot machines, singing for them to join hers in this lucky bucket, but her quarters weren't singing very loud just then.

She roamed around the casino, trying a dollar's worth in the quarter machines and if they did not cough up anything, she moved on to another, as if the previous machine had slighted her somehow, but I always play the same machine. I even wait for this one, and as soon as some oxygen sucker moved, I would sit my ass down and would not move it until Liza Jean told me she was ready to hit it. My machine has three full moons as the big jackpot, and various phases of the moon as lesser jackpots. It was called High Tide, and the man in the moon smiled down his lucky face onto the ocean and my own face as I slid quarter after quarter in. I won five thousand on this machine early on—three half moons—and though I've probably put that much back into it over the years, I was certain it would pay off big time for me at some point. I guess, though, I had picked it in the first place because it reminded me of Fred, in both Vietnam and Hollywood.

"Tommy Jack, you are always hogging that machine," she said, after I had put in about thirty dollars' worth in a very short period. I kept looking around, but the boy didn't seem to be anywhere. Maybe they checked in. I wandered the floor, looking at the other machines, the other players winning and losing, and any distraction was mightily appreciated. I did not want a scene in public.

Liza Jean won a little, twenty-two dollars, enough to keep her interest for a short while. She never put the quarters on credit, cashing out every time she won a little, loving the sound of them falling into the stainless steel pit at the bottom of the machine. Scooping them into her bucket, she kept playing. She glanced up and saw what I saw, reflected in the glass man-in-the-moon's face. Surrounded by WIN! WIN! WIN!, my face, and the boy's face stood next to mine, for just a second, and then, when she turned to look at me, he was gone. He disappeared around a corner. The girl stood in front of me, at the edge of this bank of slots as Liza Jean frowned at me. The girl smiled, holding up a baseball cap of mine from home—Big Antler Tractor and Feed—then motioned her head for me to go outside and disappeared into the crowd, just like the boy must have.

"What?" I said, as Liza Jean continued to stare at me.

"Nothing, just been thinking about the boy, all day, since this morning. It's almost like I could hear his voice, and laws, I'm even seeing him now. I swear he was standing next to you a minute ago, I could see it in the glass, here, but when I turned, it was just you again. He looked different, though, older, not the way I usually think of him," she said, then added more quietly, "when I do." I said nothing. "Well," she continued, abruptly, "your machine, like you, has worn out its welcome. Let's get us that lunch and start sorting this out."

The casino restaurant was pretty good, but not cheap, like those ones in Vegas. The Mescalero reservation was the only game in town, so they felt no need to bribe you with dinner bargains. I wondered if the boy's tribe has done anything with casinos, like this tribe in Cascabel did. A lot of them worked there, but a fair number just lived off their casino profit dividend check at the start of each month. Maybe that was how he got through school. I still don't even know how he left our place that summer after high school, disappearing while we were away.

"Just a sec, I'll catch up with you, I want to go check the answering machine at home," I said, waving my cell phone. "Dispatch was gonna call, said maybe they were going to change my route a little." She was used to my eccentricities, and for the most part, didn't fight them too much these days. Maybe she just didn't care anymore as she was featuring her new life without my nonsense. She didn't even slow her stride.

In the parking lot, their Blazer was gone, but the girl leaned on a post at the entry.

"He's gone up to your place," she said.

"What's he doing up there?"

"Said he had to deliver something. We've come up with a compromise." I couldn't wait to hear it. It wasn't like I had a lot of choice in the matter. She said she'd tell me when I came back after dropping Liza Jean back at the cabin, and that I should plan to be gone for a bit. So after lunch, I asked Liza Jean if she wanted to take a ride up to Peter Creek, or maybe way down into Loborosa for some dessert, or even up to Crowd Loft for some fried pies. She just stared off. I tried to plan my exit already, telling her that dispatch had changed my plans and I had to leave a little later that very afternoon. Her lack of interest was clear, and I could only imagine how fast this was going to go from flatness to rage when we got to the cabin and saw the Blazer there in the drive, the New York plates shouting his return. I had about had my fill of her explosions by then and wanted to get my ass out of there. The boy could do what he wanted, I just did not want to be a participant.

But the Blazer wasn't at the cabin when we got there. No sign of it, or him, nothing, until we got in the house. Sitting on the kitchen table was a perfect-condition figurine, that limited edition model, "Over the Threshold," as if just out of the shipping box, bride and groom, frozen still, in that last moment before their lives get complicated in their own unique, intertwined way. No note, or anything else. It had been a long time since I had seen this particular item. When the boy would travel with me in the early years, one thing we did was to always bring back a new Lladró figurine for her collection. It seemed to make the hauls we did easier on her, becoming a game of sorts.

She had a collectibles book on them, and back then she would give us a list of three she was most looking for when we headed out, and we would try to find one of them. They were always so outrageously dear in price that it did not matter that we found them only rarely. If we had kept up with her desires, we would have been broke as a family, but the occasional porcelain figurines always delighted the wife when we returned. And if we didn't have one, she was still generally delighted to see us.

When we had come home with that "Over the Threshold," she had a present for him, too. Everyone from around his way, back in the east, had always said this one plastic Indian was his daddy, and the wife had gone to great lengths to get it for him and surprise him. I'm still not for sure how she did it. Back then, she had always taken a general disinterest in the junk business and seemed to pay less than half an attentive eye whenever I was doing some negotiating or on the trail of some elusive item. He had run into the house, holding the tiny just-married couple behind his back, and she had been standing in the kitchen, holding her arms behind her back too, the aroma of homemade macaroni-and-cheese casserole surrounding her. They both pulled out at the same time and the boy almost dropped that bride and groom, himself, when he saw that little plastic daddy of his in her hand. From that point on, it never left the top bookshelf above his bed, until around Memorial Day, the year he left.

"Tommy Jack! Where did you ever find it!" she said, memories flooding in, her old voice back for a minute, as she ran to the figurine immediately. "This must have cost you a small fortune." Then her tone changed, quieted. "It was always my favorite. But it's not going to change what happened between us. We just can't be together anymore. Really, you shouldn't have."

"I didn't," was all I said, and it was enough. She paused, thought for a minute, then set it down and looked at me again.

"That was him, this morning, wasn't it? On the phone?" This was also not really a question. She spoke a lot of these, over the years, but this time, I answered, anyway.

"Yes, it was."

"Back to your old ways? You must have acted pretty fast to try and pull this off. Well, like I just said, you really shouldn't have gone to the trouble, because it won't make any difference."

"No, I am not back to my old ways, damn it! He called and said he was down at Prime, so I went."

"Well, what did he say? Was he gloating that you had finally told me all the things you never had?" I expected something other than this from her, while not for sure what, or even what I was going to make up in an answer, but this was one question I could answer.

"He said he wanted to see you, so I arranged that, and let him make his own decision. I guess seeing you was enough. He said he wanted to leave something for you, too. This must have been it."

"That's it?"

"Yeah, pretty much. No, he also wants to read that letter his daddy wrote, you know, the letter."

"You gonna show it to him?"

"I don't know. It doesn't say much that he hasn't probably already guessed, but I suppose he deserves to see it. I told him it's at the house, and that I had to go pick it up. I imagine he's anxious. At first I was going to tell you that dispatch had called and I had to go. All bullshit. But it doesn't matter anymore. I'm going. We can sort through this another day. It's not like we're in any hurry, is it?"

"No, no hurry. Nothing is going to change the direction we're going," she said, shaking her head. "Truth be told, we've been going in this direction for a long, long time." I didn't know what her next sentence was going to be, and this lack of certainty was an odd sensation for me. Just then, the phone rang, and we both looked up. I hadn't put it back on the hook when we'd left for the casino.

We both knew who it was, but I was not taking the initiative this time. Though he hadn't called our numbers in over two years, the boy always said he'd like to come back. Whenever we'd get those calls and he'd sat there or stood there all still-like on the other end of the line and I could hear, beyond his breathing in the pay phone, the buses and cabs sliding by around him, we'd wait, him and me, until the wife spoke. Each time, she'd said something about the weather here, how the dust from the windstorms mats up the cat's fur, how the air-conditioning had been running for four days straight, how the cotton was going to give us a poor yield that year without the rain—whatever she could think of until he passed on some news about the weather up there, letting her know he had heard her shut the door and lock it one more time. She stared laser beams at me and her stare was like one of the forest fires that scorch through here in drought season. You could almost tell how mean they were going to be from the first few lines whispering out over the sky.

I remained where I was, and eventually, she picked up the phone.

"Hello," she said, in a quiet, timid voice, not at all her usual phone voice, the one she used to fend off telemarketers and errant adopted sons. Even from where I stood, I could hear him, and she nodded, as if he could see her.

"Momma? I'm home."

It wasn't always like this. When he was young, you could never speak a cross word to that boy without her getting her fur up and raking you sideways afterward. I should have just thrown out that letter when it came our way, those years ago, just noted it and touched a match to it. The boy was certainly all ours—mine initially, but eventually ours—fair and clear, and I had never hid his beginnings from him, either. But I had to do right by Fred, and who could have predicted I would wind up on national TV and start this mess a-rolling all over again almost twenty years later? The boy even talked to his real daddy on occasion back then when Fred made his own long-distance collect calls. So I never thought any-thing about bringing the boy back there for his daddy's funeral. I thought he should likely be there anyway to say good-bye proper but I never really thought of what might happen when we arrived, what would be reawakened in me, and then all the other things beyond—one stupid domino hitting the next and getting things rolling, slapping on down your future.

I did not think he should be going with me on the long haul that young and I for sure do not fly anymore. Nearly a part of every one of my days in the war was spent in the damned air, chopper up and chopper down, and once I landed back home after my dis-charge, I said I was never getting back into another. The sight of planes is not too bad and every once in a while when I am over to Lubbock on a local run, I go and park down to the airport, eat me a sandwich, and watch them come in, shifting in the winds like they do, reminding whoever's on them that they could still be dropped out of the air in a second's notice. That's what I always felt every time we went up.

So when me and the boy made that trip to New York we took

the train, a long, long ride, and then those rental cars that cost
so dear but my ass stayed planted right where it was supposed to,
nearly three feet off the ground and little more. Me and the boy, we
drove all through that reservation. Even in the couple years since
I had been up there visiting his daddy and Shirley, the place had
changed, lots. I showed the boy the place where he had been born.
The old house like so many others there burned down a year before
and all we could see were some charred boards sticking up from
the brush where the earth was taking back its own like blackened
bones reaching to the night.

A lot had happened in two years' time. His momma's new
address was tucked into my wallet where I keep my secret phone
numbers and we drove by it slowly but I never spoke to him about
that matter. A young lady hung some wash on a line as we glided
by, little jumpsuits in faded colors, like headless, faceless kids, but I
wasn't for sure if it was her or not. Could have been, from the girl I
remember, but those Indian girls, you know how lots of them look
so much the same and even if it was, it seemed pretty clear she had
moved beyond whatever the boy might have meant to her, breed-
ing different kids in a different time—kids she thought she had a
chance of raising right. So we came on home and didn't think too
much about what we saw.

It was just me and the boy before Liza Jean finally grew tired
of the Giant and called me up one Friday to see if I wanted to invite
her out for dinner like we used to. She pointed out that she was
still the woman I had first intended to marry. I had been with a few
women since returning from the reservation with that boy but after
my first time with Shirley Mounter I didn't really want any other
women except maybe Liza Jean Bean, or Liza Jean Montgomery,
as she was then. Sure, I went to bed with a few, you know, but there
was never a one I wanted to settle down with.

Liza Jean had offered to let the boy stay with her and the Giant
that time I went out and visited Fred in Hollywood, and maybe she
was testing life with the boy and had decided she could love him

after all. She left the Giant shortly after I got back from California
and then beyond that first Friday night, she would have us over for
dinner a lot, always making something special for the boy, some
kid food, and she would serve us up something fancy. More times
than not, I would have preferred the macaroni and cheese or fried
hamburgs she was serving him but I usually know when to keep
my mouth shut.

There were all kinds of pictures on her walls but they were
mostly of her with the other half of the picture cut out, and there
were some of her family where one person was carefully and neatly
cut out of the picture and the blank cardboard backing showed
through, a total absence where someone had once been. She was
mean with a scissors, I learned that early on.

That boy was playing with fire, here, on the other end of the
phone line, but at the cabin, we only had the one line. It was him
and her, but I guess he was ready to pick up the flaming ball, just
like his daddy used to. The last time he lighted this particular fuse
was in Wanda's, when all the shit started.

We had been at one of the other places I used to sell junk at,
that afternoon, before it closed and Prime opened up, and I had
been complaining that I was running out of stuff to sell. That's kind
of the way I get sometimes—itchy, even when I really don't have any
reason to be. One of the biggest garage sale weekends of the year
was coming up the weekend after, it was Memorial Day that year,
too, and this was the way I always jazzed myself for such things.
We had just blown into town from Texas, escaping the hot summer
that was frying itself up, over there, and the itch for change began
its creep on me like it did every year at the end of May.

I was saying how I was going to have to start filling the pump
house with junk again for my next big garage sale when we got
home. The shelves along the pump house's walls were gathering a
film they were so empty. You know me, laying it on thicker than a
dust storm covering a newly washed car just looking for an excuse
to hit every garage sale in town and even some out of town. My

holiday weekend was planned out sweet when the boy mentioned those two boxes of stuff sitting low on a back shelf behind some old tin advertising signs. He didn't know what was in them, mind you, but he knew they were there and once that was out, well, there were lots of questions flying around that table and Liza Jean, she did not even finish her strawberry glaze pie and that alone should suggest how grim the rest of my day was, but mine was not nearly as grim as the boy's.

All the way back to the house, and I mean the house in West Texas—yes, she made me pack us up and head on back, right then, needing to see what might be in those boxes before I had the chance to get one of them gone—she asked the same questions as many different ways as she could, trying to catch me in answers that didn't match up perfectly, and that was not too hard a thing for her to do usually. I don't know why I lie about all kinds of stupid little things, and she catches me nearly every damned time, but maybe it's because when I need to lie, when they really count, and she doesn't catch me, she gets thrown off.

So for the five-hour drive back to Big Antler, I recited the story of how the boxes were just pictures of the guys who were in the airborne with me, the can I had dented for Fred's head was in there, and the NVA flag I had saved, splitting the contents of one of those boxes, and making up other stuff, just to fill that second box in my head with anything other than what was really in there but none of that was filling the real box covered in dust we were driving toward. The boy listened, all excited, imagining that one I was making up in my head just then, wanting to go through it.

When we got there, she went right to the pump house and brought both boxes into the house and set them on the kitchen counter, not bothering to dust them off, coughing in the years' accumulation piled on top. Whenever I'd gone through them, I had always carefully removed the tops, so the dust always made them look like they had been sitting for the longest of times. I reached for the first one, the one I knew contained Fred's things, and when she saw that, naturally, she went to the other box instead. Lifting that lid, she opened up these brief bursts of my life, and she was never going to let me have them back. When she looked in that box and saw lots of nothing having to do with my life in Vietnam, and lots of nothing having to do with the men who were my family then, my squad, she was determined to make the things that were in there just as gone. She pulled the pair of panties out first, like I knew she would.

"Which one of the guys in your squad wore these, Tommy Jack, and why did he give them to you? Something you haven't told me about?" Shirley had given those to me that first time we had been together. Actually, I had asked for them. They were still lying on the floor next to that blanket when we had gotten dressed in the dark that morning, so pale they almost glowed there, in that hour before the sun rose. I saw her a lot more in the next months I stayed there on the reservation, collecting small pieces of her to take back with me, which Liza Jean was reconstructing here on our kitchen counter.

Books of matches I had lighted Shirley's cigarettes with, a scarf she had worn over her hair one rainy Saturday we chased garage sales all over the county, a napkin she had blotted her lipstick with, her deep-maroon kiss captured for me forever, the guitar pick I used when I tried to teach her "Ode to Joy." Though she had incredible rhythm beneath the sheets, she never had a drop of it on the guitar. Her phone number faded from the bottom of an Indian Head beer coaster, so old now it seemed not even like one, a ghost from those days before the distribution standard, when phone numbers were issued in exchanges. All these things were bad, particularly the panties, of course, but the worst was the strip of photos.

"Who is this, Tommy Jack? I don't remember you telling stories of any big-bosomed Vietnamese women in your squad. Would George remember her if I was to call him up right now?" You know the kind they were. You put a dollar in the booth, and you sit in front of this swirly satin curtain and get four opportunities to be

blinded by the flashbulb. Probably was a lot less, then. I can't remember for sure, but there we were, big as life, our heads together
in the first shot, my arm showing around her shoulder, then in the
second, me kissing her, but her with her eyes still staring at the
camera, and the last two, almost the same, us getting totally lost
in the kiss. And in each one of them, of course, since they are taken
only seconds apart, is the beard I grew while I was in Vietnam,
and the glasses that I only wore after I'd gotten married. Liza Jean
reached over to the wall-hanging Princess phone we kept in the
kitchen because she loved to talk on the phone when she put away
dishes, so I had gotten it installed for our anniversary at a time
when it was highly uncommon to have more than one phone in a
household.

I probably should have thrown all that out when Liza Jean
and I got hitched, and for sure shouldn't have added to the collection after, but you know how it is. I probably should not have gone
back and stayed at Shirley's apartment when we were there for the
funeral, either, knowing what was likely to happen. But not a lot
stops me when I have a drive and I have never been one of your
more introspective types.

"I don't know who that is, Liza Jean, it was a long time ago,
when you were married to the Giant. Remember that? You were
the one who left me, who wrote me the goddamned Dear Tommy
Jack letter while I was over there, being afraid of getting shot every
fucking night." I was in the clear on this. She put the phone back in
the cradle and though I would have to pay for sure and be sleeping
on the cold side of the bed for a while, it could have been much
worse than it was going. Then that fucking boy spoke up. The boy
never was all that smart, never knew when to go along with a lie in
just the right way.

"That woman's not Vietnamese. She's from the reservation.
Man, I haven't seen her since we stayed with her, when we went
back for my real daddy's funeral."

"We were married, then, Tommy Jack," was all the wife said to me, all quiet-like, and she didn't say anything to the boy. The woman in the photo was married then too, I thought, but obviously, that was something I did not say. Liza Jean dumped the box's contents into a trash bag, walked it out the car, and headed out down the road, I guess, in the general direction of the town dump. I made a quick phone call and then turned to the boy.

"Big mouth, I should have left your ass on that reservation, with your grandmother and all those others, hooting and hollering. Shit, your liver would be shot by now, and I would not be in this fucking mess. Now what am I going to do?"

"Well, I didn't know she was the reason we weren't supposed to talk about the funeral trip. You told me we weren't supposed to discuss that because it's like gossiping about the dead. And I was a little kid. How the hell was I supposed to know you were lying to me, and asking me to lie to Momma on your behalf?"

"Like you didn't know I was keeping time with Shirley, back then."

"Well, I never thought about it as a grown-up, Daddy, you know, I don't like to necessarily dwell on my real daddy eating the barrel of a pistol in some nasty L.A. project, and you and I having to go back there to watch them plant him. And back then, you know, what the hell did I know? I was sleeping with three strange kids in a bed in the other room. I guess I just thought you were sharing because there wasn't any other room."

"Well, you just keep your mouth shut from now on, mister, and maybe this will all just blow over. Maybe you should just stay here and get yourself ready for college, and I'll take your momma back to Cascabel, and maybe she'll be ready to see you off in the fall, and if not, well, you know, I'll move you by myself." That would have been good, had it worked out that way, but this world is never even close to being as neat as we would like.

Liza Jean came on home a little while later like we expected and she went to packing a few things she said she'd forgotten when we were first getting ready, putting them neatly in one of the empty boxes I kept in the pump house, acting like this was why we had come back to the house in the first place. Anytime I tried to put something in the box, though, thinking that might be a useful activity, she would smack my hand away and whatever I had held dropped to the floor. I almost wanted to go get one of those little Lladró porcelain statues she kept all about the place and see if she would be knocking that one out of my hand if I tried to put it in, but that day did not seem like a good one to be pressing my luck.

I went outside and tended to a few things out there that really didn't need tending to but it seemed like a good idea to keep busy out of the house while she did whatever she needed to do on the inside. No amount of straightening out the yard, though, was going to build me some armor to survive the trip. I could only hope for the best and pray the summer was going to work the magic on her it usually did.

I was not for sure where the boy disappeared to but hoped he had enough sense to make himself scarce. He had a good skill of turning himself invisible and it had served him well there on the reservation in that little while he was with his daddy, being one of the more obvious mixed bloods with that name. It had been a long time since then, though, and he had just gotten accepted to some college in the east. Said he was going to take up acting, which is like lying, so in some ways he is maybe more my son than Fred's, but, well, acting, that was supposedly Fred's profession when he used that revolver like a Whitman Sampler of bullets, so maybe in some ways we were equally his daddy after all. He was planning on going from invisible to totally visible. From the sound of things that day, while I moved benches from one spot in the flower garden to another, he decided it was no longer time to be unseen.

"How could you keep this from me, boy?" she asked. "After I took you in, raised you like my own, is this the way you repay me?" By then he should have been used to her questions that were not questions but started to answering the one question he for sure should have passed on.

"He took me in, not you. You just accepted the package so you could be married again, so you could have him again under your terms," the boy said, and I had to cringe at that one. He was getting to be big, though, and if those were the choices he was going to make, then he might as well get used to living that life, I thought, because it was going to be a hard one with that kind of attitude.

"That's not true. We were dating long before you came along, but I was willing, Lord I was willing, because I loved that man," she continued, getting a little louder, or maybe it was because I was creeping toward the screen door with the things I was moving in the gardens. "We probably weren't ready to get married so soon, I'll grant that, but we did it for you. You seem to have forgotten that."

"Maybe that was true for you, and I appreciate that, Momma," the boy said.

"Don't call me that anymore," she said. "I'm not your momma. Your momma left you at a house of drunks, away from your real daddy, just so she could get child support money to drink on. And that's the truth of the matter. Tommy Jack thought you shouldn't know that but it's the truth. I bet you don't even remember living with the drunks. He said you were in such a sad shape when he went to pick you up that he would do near anything to get you out of there. He said you were falling over drunk at the table, the day he picked you up, and when I heard that, of course I said yes to help him out, and you."

"Helping some kid isn't a reason to get married. And it wasn't your only reason, either. I saw those pictures from your first marriage that you have, those put away ones. You just needed another man to complete your perfect portraits from Sears. I know the real reason he married you," he said. There was a pause there, and yes, I know I should have stepped in, but I think I had used up any bravery I might have had, making it through all those nights over in the jungle, sharing a plastic poncho all night long, hoping to wake up and hoping not to wake up every damned day we were over there.

She continued to say nothing, afraid any word would cause him to continue but it didn't matter. He had already crossed that line.

"He asked you to marry him, because he finally figured out she was already married," he said, all quiet-like, but I heard it just the same, and of course, so did Liza Jean. "The woman who really loves him. He asked me to keep quiet, that they knew it couldn't work for them, that they'd met at the wrong time. I had to keep quiet. I saw her eyes when we left. It was a look I have never once seen you give him, in all these years. I couldn't tell you about her, because I couldn't do that to her, or him."

The first crashing sound might have been easy to ignore. It could have been any number of things and the way the wind is in West Texas, it even might have been somewhere down the road, but the neighbors are so far away, it was surely not from any domestic dispute and all you had to do was open your eyes and look to see no cars for miles around. By the time I could no longer ignore the realities and headed for the door, the fourth and fifth shattering had gone by in rapid succession. It was like those NVAs, trip wire–detonating our claymores, lighting up the night with their exploding bodies.

In the dining room, the boy stood near the far wall, haloed by lopsided family pictures on the wall, with the glass smashed out of them and surrounded on the floor by small broken figurines like some of the body fragments we would see over there after a mine went off. She was shouting by that point, crying words I couldn't understand around her sobbing as she heaved another one of the figures.

There was something in there about "goddamned Indians always sticking together, like a bunch of fucking cockroaches." She yelled as the figurine exploded around him and other things too. I had never in our marriage heard words like that come out of her. This was a very expensive fit on her part and there was no reason to make the day even worse in losses.

"I didn't know anything except they loved each other and I

wasn't supposed to say anything about it! I was a kid!" the boy kept shouting back to whatever it was she was saying. Maybe she was more coherent sounding when she pitched the first one at him. She was one powerful force when she wanted to be and by the time I had her buckled into the car with her box, my arms were killing me and I had sweated my clean shirt right on through. That last figurine she threw, "Over the Threshold," had cost me a couple hundred when I brought it back for her five years before.

"I'll be back to help you before summer's up," I said to the boy as I ran out the door before Liza Jean could reconsider. "You got my credit card and you can use the other car here, just be good, boy." This was the last thing I said before I climbed in the car and made my way out into that cold, silent summer. I did not want to walk out on him standing there in the mess of our obliterated dining room, small cuts on his arms and face from the tiny porcelain fragments, but choices here were of a limited nature. It might have seemed like a choice to him, since his memory would tell him he was in my life before she was, but that would not be fully accurate, so there he was, my boy, in the rearview mirror, as I left West Texas and our lives together that Memorial Day weekend. He and I had always talked about going to New York one Memorial Day after he graduated from high school to visit his real daddy's grave and maybe lay a wreath, but the odds of that happening grew abruptly long that day.

All that drive back to Cascabel, Liza Jean mentally sharpened her scissors, but it never happened, not for me, anyway. She stopped talking about the boy, period, as if he had never lived with us, like he was some International Care kid, a kid in some exotic and uncivilized place we paid a dollar a day for someone to feed a hot and nutritious meal, a kid whose picture we had, but with no sense of who he might be. Maybe he felt that way, too. I tried calling him from time to time on the ride out to Cascabel, drinking Coca-Colas all along the way so I would have an excuse in needing to piss at every rest area there was a pay phone. I tried off and on that summer, but from that first afternoon on, I only got the answering machine. The machines were new things then and by mid-June, I could not even leave messages, anymore, having already filled up the tape with my apologies and encouragements and vague promises to get back there as fast as I could. The credit card bill came and the only charges on it were those we had made in Cascabel.

I was always doing short-haul work from Cascabel and the wife knew that if I went back to West Texas, it was going to be to see the boy who did not exist anymore, and throughout that month, she kept those scissors at the ready, right next to the photo albums over on the bookshelf. I had asked the dispatch house if they had any haul assignment that would get me to Texas for a little bit, but their regular route was all tied up. One of the guys got sick and dispatch cut me a break if I was willing to leave right that moment and get the load there before sunup.

I took it and was relieved to see my other car there in the driveway when I pulled up the next morning. Inside the house, though, nearly everything about the boy was gone. He had cleaned up the mess Liza Jean had made of her figurines, and he had even spackled and painted the wall. It was a little whiter than the rest of the walls, but only because we had not painted in a very long time.

The pictures were back up but with no glass and they had curled and buckled some in the heavy sultry summer air around here, and though he had left all the pictures of me and Liza Jean and our various family members, every picture of him we had on the wall was gone but the one of him and me that Shirley Mounter had taken in New York. I had always told Liza Jean that Fred had taken the picture, but she probably knew better then. The boy's first-grade picture with the flattop that matched mine at the time, up to the thick braids he sported in his graduation picture, they were all gone, the holes also spackled and painted over, as if they had never been there in the first place. Everything in his room evaporated, as well, but the one thing he left was in the curio cabinet where she kept the figurines.

Little spots of lighter dust coatings surrounded the remaining figurines and in one circle, he had left her the little plastic Indian she had given him, and the Baby Snookum I had given him. I always have to wonder if that was the last thing he did before he left. I never had the nerve to ask him about that month, or even how he got out without my help, but he always was the resourceful sort. I played back all my messages, hoping one of them would be from him, telling me something, anything, but I just stood there in the cleaned-up dining room of my house in West Texas, smelling the fresh coat of white paint and listening to myself beg forgiveness of the son we shared until the tape ended and rewound itself, running left sprocket to right, back in time.

But anyway that was years ago and maybe now the boy has even found her, his real momma, and maybe she was ready to love him the way we did and the way I still do. That boy, well, even though it had all been different for many years, the wife used to think he just hung the moon for sure. Even later, when he left us only memories, a dusty toy, a picture, and occasional random phone calls, she would just talk and talk, as if he was supposed to walk in the house at any minute, throw his stuff on the kitchen breakfast counter, the way he always did, and leave his jacket dangling on the back of one of the counter stools, showing steel ribs through the material. But that boy she talked about was the one in her memory, not the one who continued to grow and who sometimes saw and said things she didn't take to at all.

In that first year, we got a few calls from him where we actually talked, a bit. Sometimes, Liza Jean would get a hang-up call and I imagine those times were him, too, but I never asked him. I figured those were his choices to make and I respected them. His calls were always short and informational. He would let me know he was eating, passing his classes, and so on, and then he would be gone again.

In the second year, occasionally Liza Jean would ask me, in a very bored voice, how the boy was doing, if she recognized by things I said on my end of the line that I had been talking to him. By the time he was in graduate school on a full scholarship, she would even pick up the other extension and say a few things to him and then get off abruptly, saying she had some such thing to do around the house that clearly needed no urgent tending to.

Eventually she would talk about all the good times, and her voice was filled with all the love it had whenever we would come back from long hauling, but her reflections always cut off the May he graduated. And for the last ten years or so, he's called to see if the door was open but so far it hadn't been and now I guess he finally got tired of knocking and was trying to use his own key again.

CHAPTER EIGHT:

Voice Over

o o o o

September 3, 1999

Dear Tommy Jack,

Just been wondering how you're doing, these days. After all these years, I finally moved back to the reservation. I suppose that is why I'm writing. So you'll at least have my new address, if you are ever inclined. Don't worry. I know you're not coming back, but I would have thought that twenty-five years later, I'd have moved beyond you. I felt fear, though, when I thought you might not have my address, I suppose that is why I put pen to paper, to put off pinching out that last hope like the ember of an unfiltered.

Also, you seem to be with me all the time, lately. Not sure why being here makes me think of you, of all people, must be that abundance of time you and I spent with Fred here before he left for Hollywood, driving around, building bonfires, listening to you on the guitar. Do you still have it or have you gone and sold it in a garage sale or antique shop somewhere? You know, I bet you don't read this letter, that you see my return address and my handwriting and throw it in the trash before you leave the post office, and I can't blame you. Back then, that night we met, I know I should have told you I was married, but it had been so long since anyone had invited me to dance, had wanted to hold me after the song was over, so long since anyone had even wanted to buy me a drink. I hope you can

understand how that was so very different from the life I had lived
for too long.

My old man loved the beer, that was so, but for some reason,
he never liked me to be in that space with him, never wanted to
buy me a drink. If I ever showed up with my friends in the same
bar that he had been in with his, oh how that frosted his ass, and
we wouldn't be looking at him, just visiting among ourselves. We'd
be over at our own table and he would come running over and cuss
me out for ruining his good time. Then he'd gather up his friends,
mostly his cousins from the bush, and they'd leave, go to some
other place. So to me it was like we really weren't married anymore,
almost like we never had been, like the days and nights we shared
before he put that ring on my finger had been with some other
man who just looked like him and who never came back, once we
had walked that aisle together.

I'm not crying in my beer here, just trying to explain why it
was so easy to be with you and not say anything, to let you rest your
hand on me that first night and not move, and why it was so easy
to fit into the crook of your arm anytime you came back around. I
know we didn't have much time together in those few years, probably less than three months, total, if you added up the days on a
calendar, certainly not even enough time to grow a baby, but those
three months, those are what I think about most these days and
I have for most of the last thirty years too, for that matter. Those
three months were my true lifetime.

I wish you would have let me pick you up at the train station
when you came back for Fred's funeral. We ended up together
anyway and though I had that sweet weekend with you, touching you, smelling you, just feeling that warmth of yours when we
lay there, skin to skin on my living room carpet, you know what I
thought of, watching you drive away? The things I could have done
in those remaining hours. And I don't mean only those kinds of
things, your ears and the rest of you got enough of a workout, ha-
ha. I mean holding your hand, feeling that little scar just over your

right thumb, where you said you had some shrapnel from the war, smoothing out some of those crooked parts of your mustache, to reveal those soft lips beneath, smelling that early morning scent of you, before you showered. Those things. I was jealous of your rental car, of all things, that it got to be with you from the moment you arrived here until the moment you left. Can you imagine that, a grown woman having such thoughts?

You know, I could tell you were always afraid Harris was going to come home, any one of those times we were together, but you want to know something? He left for good shortly after the last time I had seen you. He was gone on one of his usual Canada drunks around the time of Fred's funeral, didn't even make it home for that, as I'm sure you recall, and when he showed up, the next month, he was around for a couple weeks but he knew something in me had changed. Really, he hadn't lived with us for two years at that point, but now and again, he would come and stay for a week or three. That last one, though, was different.

Before that time, he could always read me, knew as he repacked the bag he'd brought with him each time that I wanted him back and would do nearly anything to keep him around and he loved that I could never figure out what the magic formula was. That night he came home, though, he wandered in sometime in the middle of the night and climbed on top of me, and I let him do what he wanted, until he was done, then I went back to sleep. He knew that I let him do it not because I wanted to keep him so bad but because I didn't care anymore, that being with him was like any of the rest of my chores, cleaning, cooking, sewing, and nothing more. He didn't know about you, that my heart had finally moved out on him without giving notice, but he knew something had changed in me, and it was not a change he could accept. He needed to be either loved or hated. Indifference—I learned that word in my crossword dictionary, impressive, huh?—that was what he couldn't stand. That time, when he packed, he knew it was for the last time. He had already taken his lucky work boots with him, the ones that had saved his feet when an I beam had landed on them. He never got them fixed, said he liked he way the steel peeked out from under the leather toes. When they were no longer in the closet, I knew that was it— knew that he wouldn't be back.

You would have no way of knowing but Harris died this year, which wasn't a surprise to anyone around here. What was a surprise was that he lasted as long as he did, what with the way he treated his body all these years. He was bad to everyone, himself included. So when it happened, most just nodded and went back to whatever they were doing. My kids all came home for the funeral, and it's a good thing they did, or the funeral parlor would have been pretty empty. Most of them are scattered around the country, and doing pretty well, I might add. The middle three have gone and settled down with families of their own, and I get school pictures every year, and some visits. Just about everyone comes home for the National Picnic, you remember that, where you played Fireball with Fred just before you left with the little boy. Did he play that night? I couldn't see him on the field, but then when you got hit, he was right there to help you. It's always so dark you can never really tell who's playing and who isn't. I assume the players must be able to keep each other straight, though.

My oldest boy, Royal, is still here, but he and his wife have split, for good this time. He'd spent an awful lot of time at my place after his dad died and his wife left but maybe that's to be expected. He and his dad had gotten close toward the end and that's where his dad came to die, to his place. I think that might have been it for Royal's wife. Suzy was always the spooky type and she was never such a big fan of Harris to begin with and I think she had a hard time getting into the same bathtub he had died in. Can you blame her? I sure can't. But then I've always been a little spooky, myself. So, when Royal asked me to come and live with him, I did. You wanna know what was hardest about that? Giving up my phone number in the city. Remember that coaster I gave you? The one with my number written on the back of it? You know, I was poor a lot through some of those years, but I never let my phone service lapse. I was always afraid I would lose that phone number, and then when you went to call me, you would get that operator, saying you had reached a number no longer in service, and then how could you call? Pretty stupid, I know.

My youngest is still here, too. You probably don't remember her, but maybe you've even heard little Tommy Jack mention her sometime when you're talking to him. They both work at the college. Can you imagine that, one of my kids, a college professor? You raised that boy right, Tommy Jack, the way he came back here to take care of his grams before she passed on, when she'd hardly looked at him all those years you had him, and then to get a good job like that on top?

Anyhow, this is going to be my last letter to you. I have written a ton of them over the years, but this one I'm going to really send. Don't worry, I don't expect anything from you, even a letter back. I know you have a different life, now, and when you were here before, back when you and Fred first came home from the war, I had a different life then, too. But there's no use crying over spilt milk, isn't that what they say? Though maybe in this case, it's like the whole dairy truck, but spilt milk is what it is, regardless of the amount. My new address is on the envelope, if you ever have the desire, but the phone is in Royal's name. It's listed.

Anyway, I better get going here. I was wondering if you still had the blanket. Just curious. Nice to visit with you.

Love, always,
Shirley

Annie Boans

There was so much to ask and almost no one to answer. The best place to start was with the man sitting next to me, driving me back to his home in West Texas. Two different sets of questions have taken turns prioritizing themselves as first in my mind during the last half hour, when Tommy Jack McMorsey had agreed to our compromise and showed up back in the casino parking lot more or less when he said he was going to. T.J. planned to wait somewhere in the upper canyon, where he could see their cabin, and was going in to speak to McMorsey's wife alone. He was probably knocking on her door now, walking in, perhaps sitting at the kitchen table. I wondered about the conversation they were about to have, what had transpired all those years ago that neither he nor McMorsey was willing to talk about, but that was also none of my business. I had enough of my own future awkward conversations to attend to. If T.J. ever got into a sharing mood, I imagine I'd be the first candidate for listening. Perhaps I'd even share my own story with him, though somehow I doubted it.

McMorsey unlocked the pickup's door when he pulled up and got out to help me with my bags, but I threw them in the backseat and tossed him the feed-store cap. "You want it? You can have it. I got plenty more," he said, as if we had known each other for years, instead of hours. I shook my head and he shrugged as I had seen him do on television and then he set the cap on the backseat.

"So why are you here?" he asked. "For me? For him? Your

momma? What is it you want? 'Cause I've been wracking my brain since y'all showed up this morning, and for the life of me, I still have no idea why you're here." He continued to maintain that air of defiant mystification that I'd seen on the television. I wondered if this were the general way he operated in the world. It seemed unlikely, though. My mother had, as far as I've known, suffered only one rigidly confrontational man in her life, and he slept forever in Calvary Cemetery over on the reservation's Torn Rock, along with Fred Howkowski and our other collected ghosts.

"Why did you do the things you did?" I asked, which seemed like a simple enough question to me and it made me feel suddenly powerful asking it, but his silence drained that feeling almost immediately. The smallish aging man sitting next to me, no matter how blustery he tried to be, didn't exactly align with the insensitive lout I had conjured. Even seeing him on television, I had still been able to cast him as some horny pig who was trying to unzip for any woman who might look his way with even the mildest of interest. Here, in person, he was somehow different.

He smelled of cologne and soap. The skin below his beard was a little pink. He had shaved before coming back to pick me up. He had neatened himself in that short while. It was a funny gesture, but somehow endearing. I didn't want him to be nice. I wanted him to be the cracker I had created, but that picture was getting harder to maintain. Perhaps he could help me keep him in that light, with his own words. Though there was a chance this would not be the case, I was here and so was he. It was time to ask.

"I've wanted to meet you for a long time, but not for the reasons you think," I started. I was trying to keep up my own front here, not wanting him to get even a little edge on me. He couldn't just start acting conversational on me and get away with it. There was much he had to explain. If he thought he was done being interviewed once that broadcast was over, he had better reevaluate what his next few hours were going to be. I engaged the one skill I've learned to use effectively during my post-college life. Any time someone thought he was going to get cocky on me, I offered the gesture I had learned from my mother. I reminded him that I was probably better armed than he was. "I'm an art . . ." I started, but chose to not fill in the rest of that sentence with the title I usually used. To acknowledge that, like this man, I was also a historian would give him some kind of relationship with me that I had no intention of revealing. In no way did I want him thinking his existence had any impact on my life, other than the obvious potential one caused by his trysts with my mother. "I study T.J.'s father's career as part of my career."

"Not much, is there?" he said, delivering this as a statement.

"No, there isn't. And his family, what family that's left, they're fairly closedmouthed."

"Can you blame them?"

"No, of course not. My family's on the quiet side too. I have four older siblings who probably could pick you out of a lineup, even today, but not one of them has ever spoken a word about you, at least to me. Nor have they spoken about Fred, and I imagine they know even more about him than they do about you, but I can't force them to do things they don't want to do. You know how stubborn members of my family can be when they want to be."

"Yes," he said immediately, but was no more forthcoming.

"That leaves T.J. Howkowski, who has probably by now shared every scrap of memory he has left, real and imagined, I suspect, and after him, there is only one other person who ever even sort of knew Fred Howkowski."

"Maybe you can tell me," he said, hatching an idea that second. "How did the boy get to New York, all those years ago? Do you know? When he left home for college?" I had no idea what to make of his question but thought I could answer it in a bland way.

"One of his cousins. You wouldn't know him."

"Brian Waterson?" he asked, immediately. I don't know how he could have possibly known that, and I considered lying, but then committed to the truths of this trip.

"Yes. Brian. How did you know?"

"I just remember a few folks from there. Thought that was the likeliest candidate. Thank you." He continued driving, saying nothing at first. We descended from Cascabel in silence and eventually out of the mountains altogether before he pulled over at a roadside park and got out to stretch his legs a little. "Pretty out here. I like it like this, no houses, no people, just land, wide open. The road can be an attractive place."

"Yes, it can. No one to question what you're doing, who you're talking to, who you are . . ." I said. There was more, of course, but I wanted to see where he went.

"I didn't do anything to that girl. The things I said on the television, that was the truth. You believe me?"

"Yes, I do." And that was true. I'd had my own experiences with the media, of course, curating visual art shows and film festivals. If you let them get the slightest foothold, they would use their reviews of your work as showcases for their own smug self-importance. One of the highest-profile reviewers at home insisted on using every review he wrote as a vehicle to brag about how he had met this famous actor or that high-profile director during the press junket he was afforded. I had allowed myself to be made a fool of once, while I was being interviewed about one of my earliest curatorial gigs. I had assumed the reviewer asked the questions he had asked out of real interest in the work, only to find myself looking like a moron with out-of-context quotations in the Sunday edition of the paper. That article was problematic in the tenure process. By that time, I'd had a stronger, more solid career, but a smudge is still a smudge.

"Okay, that's a start, then," he said. "And we have to start somewhere, I guess, but I can tell you, there are fewer paths than you might think there are."

"I think T.J.'s going to want to hear anything you have to say about his father, so we should wait on that until he joins us."

"Okay, but this is a long trip from—"

"Tell me about meeting my mother," I said. It seemed like the most logical starting point to me. If ever I was going to learn about the circumstances of my birth, this was the place. I closed my eyes to listen, to hear every nuance this man was willing to offer as he drove us back to him home.

"Your momma? Okay, I guess that's as good a place as any to begin, at least for me and you. I didn't know she was married, when we first got together, for one thing. That came out wrong. I am sorry. It's sounding like I am blaming your momma and that is for sure not at all even remotely the case. It was a different time, then, and I was a different person, and probably she was, too. Well, it goes back further than just meeting her."

He stopped, as if deciding on a point of origin for this answer before he began again. "When I got back, I had gone through the sketchiest debriefing process, Fred too. No exaggeration, one day, sleeping five to a hooch, rain tapping on that tin roof all damned night long, gut-punching anyone who dared to fart inside the walls, and having the job of lighting the big barrels of shit just a few yards away from where we slept. Man, I hated that detail. I was able to avoid it for the most part."

"This isn't really about my mother and you, now, is it?" I said. It seemed the indirect route wasn't going to work, but I was willing and able to prod as long as necessary.

"We'll get there, but for you to understand how things were when I got there, you need to know how I got there. And about the shit detail, maybe that's where I learned my way of life, trying to avoid the shit detail. We had to put on gloves and drag the half-barrel latrines out into the open and pour the diesel on them, light them up, stand back, and watch that nasty smoke fly out over the mountains. Usually the cherries had to do shit detail, break them in, but somehow I dodged that at first, and successfully stayed away until right at the very end before someone with a ridiculous memory couldn't recall me doing my part.

"Everyone tried to make that the shortest job possible, and

tried all kinds of things to avoid it, some even pouring the fuel into the barrels while they were still in use, until some idiot was smoking on the shitter and blew the whole fucking building apart. Had third-degree burns all over his ass and the other parts, so there was no way he slept comfortable for the longest time. We went back to the regular way, after that. So I had that detail one day, and the very next day, we were on the helipad watching artillery firing so we could get clean out, firing back, ourselves, from the choppers, and maybe a day and half later, hard to say—time was hazy then—those long flights between Vietnam and here.

"It was Da Nang to Japan to Hawaii, and then suddenly Fred and I were in Oakland. We had come in on the same day and we zeroed out on the same day. I was feeling pretty good, but then I saw it. They were taking some stuff out of the cargo bay while we were refueling and out of that cargo bay came one of those damned familiar boxes. I thought I had seen my last Gray's casket, but some poor fucker had flown all the way with us, silent and still, in the hold, making home but in such a fashion.

"They gave us a big steak dinner and told us there would be a movie later in the evening in the mess hall if we wanted. The next day they looked us over, gave us physicals, a dental exam—I had two cavities filled—then asked us a shitload of questions and afterward told us to pack up, that we were good to go, and that we'd be leaving for home shortly. Early the next day we had breakfast, shook hands, exchanged addresses, and headed to our separate planes, our homes just waiting for us.

"In El Paso, there wasn't enough time for me to wander around the airport between flight legs so I just sat there looking out the window, still hardly believing that I was back on U.S. soil, that there was no way this plane was going to be shot at as it took off and I could just sit and watch these people, walking, walking, not running, and it was such an amazing feeling. I must have woken up a million times each night, for all of a year, wondering where my rifle was, and I know Fred was the same way," he said in one long rush of a story and at that break, he sighed.

"Thank you for sharing that, Mr. McMorsey," I said. "I'm sorry. I know this is probably very difficult, but I would like you to go on if you could." He continued to drive, the muscles of his cheeks jumping beneath his coppery beard as he clenched his teeth and squinted into the afternoon sky.

"Tommy Jack, just call me Tommy Jack. Please don't call me Daddy, though. I am not sure I could handle that at this moment."

"No worries there, Mr. McMorsey." I could no more call him Tommy Jack than I could call him Dad or Daddy or whatever diminutive form was the norm in this part of the world. To call him any of those things would require much more from me than I had. I wasn't sure what substance was lacking within me that I couldn't make that leap, but the lack was there, as discernable as any other. "And I appreciate your taking the time. Thank you. And I don't mean to be rude, but while this story is very interesting and will likely be useful in my research, you aren't answering the question I asked."

"Miss, Annie, is that okay if I call you Annie?" I nodded. "Okay, look, I will go through this part as quick as I can, but like I said before, no story begins where you think it begins, and in order to know the story about me and your momma, you have to know this one first," he repeated, more forcefully, and then paused, as if searching in his mind for the place he had left off when I interrupted him.

"Okay. And then I came home and saw Liza Jean, that was my former fiancée, now my wife, soon to be my former wife, with that flat-footed giant she had married, the only woman I knew that I had pictured with me all that time in country." I wondered what that "former wife" comment was all about. They appeared to be fairly happily married in the interview we saw, and in the brief glimpses I caught of them at the casino, they seemed like a comfortable couple who have been together for many years and who know each other very well. Or more, they looked like I imagined couples like that are supposed to look.

"That ring I'd hung onto since I left for Fort Ord? I put that ring up, at my momma's, and I hightailed it out of there, heading straight across the state to Dallas, then Texarkana, and then like a bullet up through the country, passing by Memphis and Nashville, Louisville, Columbus, Cleveland, Erie, and Buffalo, until I reached Niagara Falls, and called old Fred Howkowski, pulling from my wallet that creased piece of Red Cross stationery he had put his momma's phone number on, just as we were leaving that airport in California. He had headed to Buffalo, and I'd gotten back to West Texas through Lubbock. He said to call him when I eventually got up there, so I could meet my namesake, but I bet he was not expecting to see me within a week of our last handshake, pretty sure that was going to be the last time we breathed the same air for a long time, both of us knowing the things space and time can do to your life.

"He of course was not at home when I called him, having no idea I was in town or anything, but his momma told me where I was likely to find him, once I told her who I was. She laughed and said the little boy carrying my name was fast asleep in her bed, and my picture was up on her wall, and I remembered the picture he had sent her. Jangle, this guy we had known over there, had taken it for us in one of his less paranoid moments, with the camera setup Fred had bought.

"We were both sitting on top of the sacks of sand we had lined the bunker tops with, practicing who could keep a semi-full can of beer on his head longer. Fred had the thickest hair and he could just about screw one of those beer cans on, but I was determined to win, just once, so I had dented the bottom of his can, first, and handed it to him, opening it. Jangle was in on this, and the goal was to catch a picture of Fred with the Schlitz toppling and spilling the can's contents all down his cocky face. He thought Fred called him Jangle just a little too often. It was not a name he was fond of."

"What did that nickname mean?" I asked. It seemed to be an invitation, since he had used it several times in just a few sentences, with no explanation.

"Not important," he said. "At least not important to this here story. The point is, it didn't work. Fred could even hold a dented can in that dense head of hair, so there we are sitting on the sandbags half a world away, him smirking and me frowning, and I guess we were now on his momma's wall, big as life. He said he always sent her pictures because she believed that old Indian gig that a picture captures your soul, so he said he was sending his soul back home airmail anytime he could, one piece at a time, and it made her feel he was safe, somehow. She laughed some more into the phone and said that since she had a part of my soul in her house, she supposed the rest of me was welcome there as well." I had seen this photo up at T.J.'s grandmother's house when I interviewed her years before.

Strange how I had not connected it to those photos of Fred and the red-bearded man we used to have in an old shoebox in our city apartment. Also strange, as I looked at him now, that I had known his face for almost my whole life. Though my mother talked about him sometimes when I was a child, and I had been free to examine those photos any time I wanted, I had never connected her stories of the funny man with the man in nearly every photo of Fred that we had from his war pictures. It would seem to anyone else now that I was an idiot all these years, but when the puzzle you've been given has a few substitute pieces in it, and no one acknowledges it, you try to find ways to make them fit.

"He was right where she said I would find him, at the end of the bar at the Circle Club, sitting next to an older white guy I would soon meet as his daddy, and a young woman who would change my life to this very day—yes, your momma was sitting at Fred's side, and I met her within minutes of arriving in Niagara Falls for the very first time. Of course, I didn't know Mounter was her married name, then, but I don't think we got much beyond the pleasantries of first names that night. We had other things in mind than genealogy."

"She knew you, then," I said.

"No, she didn't know me at all, but I knew her. I pretended that I didn't, that I'd never heard of her and such, but I knew many things about her that a stranger wouldn't know, not even a casual friend, really. Fred used to tell me stories about her every night once we got settled in the poncho tent for a few hours, during NDP."

"NDP?" I had to clarify constantly with him. He seemed to have little awareness that these memories of his were not universals. His use of the war's internal lingo was casual and automatic, as if we had both been there and he was merely asking me to remember.

"Sorry, night defense perimeter. Just what we did at night when we were out on patrols. The way we slept in the jungle. Anyway, in some ways, I had maybe fallen in love with her before I ever laid eyes on the real woman, just from Fred's stories."

"But you said earlier that your wife now was the only woman you could have imagined being with then," I said. He was a tough one, but he needed to know that I was just as tough, that no fabricated side trips were going to wash with my analytical skills.

"No, that's not what I said. I said Liza Jean was the only woman I *knew* that I could picture myself with. Your momma, I didn't really know at all then, and the women a soldier could dream up in his head while he was under enemy fire were most often for sure not at all like the women who existed in the real world. Fred must have known her pretty well, though, because when we finally met face-to-face, she was all I had imagined and more. As I said, I pretended I didn't know anything about her, didn't want to make her feel at a disadvantage."

"She knew about you," I repeated.

"No, we already went over this. She—"

"She knew. How much, I couldn't say, but she certainly knew what you looked like. Fred must have been working both directions, because we had pictures of you in our apartment the whole time I was growing up," I said, picturing some of our shared history I had inadvertently stored in my childhood memory.

"Well that's not too surprising. We did take some when I would visit, but before that night I met her—"

"We had pictures of you from the war, with Fred," I said.

"Hmm, well, that might change some parts of this story from her end, but I don't guess the events will unfold any differently, so I will just tell you what I know. As she sat at the bar that night, your momma was grumbling about her old man being out on a drunk for a week that day, and she had gone to the Circle to see if he was there, and, running into Fred, decided to have a couple with him to celebrate his safe return. She said nothing about being married to her old man, so I figured it was a casual thing when I asked her to dance.

"I found 'The Name Game' on the jukebox, and played it for her, so I could sing Shirley, Shirley, bo-birley to her." Funny, Doug and a number of others still call her Bo. I wondered if his doing that at the Circle Club was the origin of her reservation nickname. "I can't sing worth a flip, but she laughed, slapped me and called me a goof, but when I held her closer than a casual dance would warrant, a little later in the evening, she did not move away. In the john, Fred told me her man was only the first week into his drunk, and he generally spent them up in Quebec, on a reservation up there, and they also never finished in under a month, sometimes not even in two. I couldn't handle all that happened to me in those few short days home, and I had to find some warm arms to embrace, and there she was, your momma, dancing with me, my dream woman come alive in the middle of a bar in Niagara Falls, treating me like I was something special. I had never had that feeling before, from anyone in my life, except for maybe Fred, when I'd save his ass, but in country, that feeling fades, and saving someone's life becomes the everyday, the mundane. Fred gave me the address and directions to his momma's house, on a napkin, and told me there would be a sleeping bag on the floor in his room upstairs if I got in before the sun came up.

"That night I did not make it back before then. I had to get up and out just about as the sun came up. Your momma and I had slept on the living room floor of her apartment in the city, wrapped in an old wool Pendleton, but she shagged my ass out the door while the peepers were still calling, telling me her kids would be getting up in a little while. I hadn't even known any kids existed in that apartment, just thought she had something for sleeping on the floor, or maybe no bed, or who knows, I hadn't asked a lot of questions undressing her a few hours before. Sorry, you probably didn't need to hear that."

"I didn't think she had gotten pregnant by osmosis," I said. It would have been easier to imagine that route of pregnancy if Martha Boans had never written the note she did, or to assume she was mistaken, or taken with reservation gossip, which is about as abundant as commodity cheese at the beginning of the month. By now, I had to accept this man was at least possibly the man who had gotten my mother pregnant for the last time, and moving faster into the category of probably. I felt more and more stupid as the miles trailed out behind us, revisiting snide comment after snide comment at home, doing the math for the first time. I didn't know what I wanted at this moment. And I kept being brought back to Royal's question. Did I want to be ditched by two fathers?

I am guessing now that the stories my siblings told about our father, their father, never being around might have just been a lie, a story told for my benefit so our childhoods would match, as if I didn't notice how my mother never got pregnant again, and how that alone should have suggested there were discrepancies in their story.

"So anyway, that morning I got out and sat in my car for a little while, found a diner to get me some breakfast, and got ready to meet the kid who was not even born when it was decided he would be named after me. We weren't together for very long, her and I, and each morning, as I left her place before sunrise, I was afraid her old man would show up sometime and that would be it. Loving her was like being in the jungle again. Some parts were bad, for sure, I saw things I don't ever want to see again, but some days were peaceful, out there, away from the firebases and the rear, and all the bullshit orders and regs. Some days, we would find these beautiful little lakes, drop the gear, and I would just swim like I was in one of those holes back home, learning to not be aware of the moccasins swimming around below us or the snipers above us, maybe checking out that funny splashing sound. Her old man was like those moccasins. You could never count on even the fantasy of being safe. Unless you wanted to get yourself bit along the way."

He was silent for a while, and suddenly we were back in West Texas, oil well pumps and little else dotting the landscape, the hours vanishing in the way he told his story. I was kicking myself for not bringing a recorder along. These were questions I had been hunting answers for my whole life, and it seemed like experiences he had been waiting much of his adult life to tell. Though even if I had recorded the conversation, what would I do with it? Play it for my mother? "Thank you again," I said. I think I had enough information to sort through about him and my mother, at that point. I wanted a break to let it all sink in, hoping it would make more sense in retrospect, the way he told it. We still had a while to go, so I turned my thoughts back to my own special preoccupation, the place I went when the rest of the world stressed me out. I went back and forth in my mind for the rest of the trip, thinking out all possible scenarios, and in the end, I decided the direct approach was the way I had to go, even if directness was not a trait I inherited from either parent.

"I would like you to do one thing for me," I said, as we approached the patch of land where all his buildings slept. I had many of the answers I'd come for, regarding my mother, but there were a few more things I needed to do before T.J. got here. I imagined he would not be that far behind us, perhaps even more anxious than I was to see what would unspool before us, so that clock was ticking.

"Sure, if I can," he said, as we pulled into the driveway. Those worry lines were back in his forehead, but he didn't hesitate, despite not having any idea what I was about to ask him for.

"Okay," I said. We went into the house, and I walked directly into the den and his desk, which was kind of nervy, but I didn't have time to explain. I handed him his scissors and an envelope. "I would like you to cut some of your hair, here, just a little and put it in this envelope and seal it for me." He shrugged, and tugged at some of the hair hanging down across his forehead.

"Okay, you want me to wash it first?" he asked, taking the scissors and riding it up the lock an inch or so in front of him.

"No, that's fine the way it is, thanks." I took the envelope once he sealed it. "Also, sign the seal, here?" I said, setting it on the counter and pointing to the place he had just licked closed.

"Voodoo doll?" he asked, laughing.

"Sort of," I said, not laughing. "Blood tests might not have been conclusive, back then, but DNA is." He nodded.

"I hope you find what you're looking for," he said, walking his scissors back to the desk.

He brought two other envelopes back with him—they'd been sitting in the same drawer with the scissors, where he said he has always kept them. "These are the letters. Fred's letters. To the boy, and to me. I can copy them for you if you like. Be happy to. Well, not happy, but you know what I mean." He set them in my hand, and I didn't know which to read first. Since I knew him less than I knew T.J., that one felt somehow more private, and I couldn't read it. I read the letter written to T.J., several times, sitting on the kitchen stool where he'd said he always ate his breakfast when he was young, as Tommy Jack waited in the growing dark. "You want a light on?" he asked, as I started reading it again. I set it down and looked at him.

"Do you have the stuff he shipped you?" I asked eventually.

"He didn't ship me anything but the key to his apartment,

those letters, and the written right to take it all, with specific things for the boy. Didn't you read that?"

"I only read the letter to T.J, but that's what I meant, the things listed here. You have them? Here?" I had to calm down. I had never anticipated, first, that this box existed, and, second, the potential research treasure housed within.

"Yeah, they're out in the pump house. In a box. Why?"

"Can we bring it in here, look at it?"

"Well, I guess so. Figured you would want to spend more of this night talking about your momma, before he gets here. Also kind of thought you'd want to wait until he was here, since that seems to be a big part of his trip. Thought he could read the letter and then go look at the things mentioned there that he wanted, you know."

Headlights suddenly filled the room. It would be T.J., about on time. I suspected there was another story to be told, when he walked in the door. "Looks like your time alone is up, miss, sorry, Annie." I didn't say anything, but he took Fred's letter to him and slid it under the phone book, as T.J. walked up the back porch and came in.

"How did things go?" I asked.

"The porcelain's still in one piece, or it was when I left."

"That's a start," Tommy Jack said. "Here's that letter you wanted," he said, passing the single envelope to T.J. "The rest is out in the pump house. I'll go get it," he said and I followed him out. I went to the Blazer and retrieved my mother's letter from the glove compartment and then caught up to him.

"Here it is," he said, blowing dust off a box from among twenty or so on the shelf.

"How do you know it's the right one?"

"I know."

"This is for you. She wanted you to have it," I said. He nodded and slid it into the back pocket of his jeans. "She told me I could read it before I gave it to you, and I did."

"Did it give you any more answers than I did?"

"Not sure," I said. He set the box of Fred's belongings down outside the door and in the fading light pulled the envelope out of his pocket and gave it a quick once over, first the RETURN TO SENDER stamp. "In a town as small as Big Antler, it's useful to be friends with the postmaster. When I asked him to put that RETURN TO SENDER stamp on, he just gave me a wink and a nod then happily stamped it and threw it into his out bin." He blew into the end I had opened, slid out the letter, and read my mother's trained penmanship that was so perfectly neutral, it could only have been the professional sample they used in schools or her handwriting. "No one else on earth could make my name a work of art, but she could," he said, smiling and sliding the letter back in the envelope.

"I'm sorry," I said. "Just because she gave me permission doesn't really mean I should have read it." I had no idea what else to say. The world is never as easy as it seems, and this situation was no exception. I had wanted him to be evil, a bastard, someone who had used my mother and walked away, but he refused to conform to my version of him and transformed himself before my eyes, slowly, imperceptibly. It was like trying to watch the hour hand of a clock go by, or the opening of a flower. You could try and try and though you saw no movement whatsoever, the petals had transformed from bud to blossom, or a day had gone by and you still sat there staring.

"No big deal," he said, but I felt like it had been, just the same. The violated envelope said as much about me as the letter itself said about her, and the stamp said about him. I was in this, as much as I had believed I wasn't.

"Here, wait," he said. "Come back here with me." We went back to that wall of shelving and he reached down on the third shelf, pulling out another box. "I never look in this, but I can feel it, and if it wasn't here, I would know for sure, would sense it the minute it had disappeared. As it was, when the wife took off with it, I had to call in some favors, used up a lot of them, having a buddy of mine on the Big Antler P.D. trail her and snag the sack of stuff after she'd dumped it. She had dropped it in the car-wash Dumpster and I got it from my buddy a few days later. See that your momma gets this, please," he said, passing me the beer coaster with my mother's old phone number on it. He hadn't even needed to look. He could reach in and pull out exactly what he had wanted.

"I will. What blanket is she talking about in her letter? Is it the one in your den, that old fake Navajo?" I asked.

"No, that business is between me and your mother. Just because you might be connected to both of us, that don't make you, what's the word, that means you don't need to know everything about our lives. Some things are only supposed to be known between two people. Sometimes those two people are man and wife, sometimes not."

"Okay. Fair enough," I said. "Shall we take this inside?" I stood, tapping the box he had pulled the coaster from. He shook his head, knowing that I wanted to see the rest of that box of things from my mother, but I was sensible enough to know that he shared something big in even showing me where it was.

Some artists I've had to coax in order to get them to speak passionately and earnestly about their work, because so many people in their personal lives had laughed at them. When I did artist profiles, I was often the first person these artists had met in their lives who had taken their work seriously enough to attempt engagement in real dialogue, and once I got those doors open, it was frequently nearly impossible to end the interviews. They had that much to say about the work that they'd kept silent on for so long. At that moment, I didn't know if I wanted Tommy Jack to keep talking or never to speak to me again, but it seemed like I had hit the button that closes the door. I tried something new to get it back open.

"Fred kept saying you saved his life. So much so that he named T.J. after you. Would you mind telling me what that was all about?

It's okay if you don't want to go on. I understand," I said, lying. It was not okay, and if he didn't want to continue on his own, I was willing to prod a little, though it was growing more difficult with each small piece of himself he revealed. "Earlier, you guessed that Brian Waterson was the cousin who helped T.J. How?"

"That one's easy. When I moved him out here, I made some contact with his grandma, found a cousin who was around his age. Got them to be pen pals, so he would have a connection to home if he wanted."

"You know, you are truly a puzzle to me. When I got here, I wanted to hate you, tell you off, get my DNA sample and get the hell out of here. I guess I found it hard to believe that you had legitimate good qualities, earlier, and now . . ."

"I'm not the boogeyman you wanted me to be?" he said, smiling. At first I thought it was a smirk, but even my eyes would no longer lie to me. It was a smile, nothing less.

"Something like that, yes."

"Your momma's choices weren't all disasters, were they?"

"Enough of them were."

"Why don't we go into the house and take care of this box with the boy. I am sure you're both anxious, and then we can go from there," he said, not stopping, totally in control of the situation. He believed he was prepared to show me what frightened him most, and what frightened him deeply at that moment was the unexpected. He could accept what he was going to tell me about Vietnam, was willing to relive that experience for me and for T.J., to relive the countless dead bodies of anonymous humans. In some way, though, our sudden presence frightened him. The ways T.J. might view that box, or the ways I might complicate his life, those things caused Tommy Jack McMorsey great anxiety, and perhaps the unknown variable of my mother's continued life in New York did as well.

He promised or threatened to be as graphic and as blunt as he knew how on so many things. But as we sat at the counter with

Fred's box, I knew what frightened him was his own heart. Only when it came to the intimacies he shared with my mother did he demur, edit, riffle through a thesaurus in his head to conjure softer words than usually find their way running out of his mouth. The shapes of those words were unfamiliar to his tongue, but he had thought them, silently, for years, solidifying the memory of his encounters with my mother. He was a man still in love thirty years later and I don't think he even knew it.

We brought Fred's box in and by then T.J. had finished reading the letter Tommy Jack had given him and he was nodding though no one had said anything. We set the box on the counter and I blew the dust off and lifted the lid. On the very top was a stack of photographs. "Boy, I wondered where all these pictures went when I came home that June," Tommy Jack said. They were all of a younger T.J., often with Tommy Jack and his wife. T.J. shrugged his shoulders as Tommy Jack flipped through them, grinning. Immediately, though, his grin stopped and he pushed me away from the box.

"Whew, careful, there's likely a vinegarone in there," he said, getting a big wooden spoon and some paper towels. The sharp odor of vinegar emanated from the box and filled the room. I had been afraid of that. "Don't stick your hand in there."

"Vinegarone?" I asked.

"Whip scorpion," they said in unison. "We've both had enough experiences with those little buggers," Tommy Jack said, "and you don't want one in the house. They could move like a crazy bastard, and you'd never catch them, and just keep getting stung every now and then, and if it was a female with babies, I hate to think."

"It's not that," I said. "It's called vinegar syndrome. It happens to acetate film that hasn't been properly cared for." I pulled the canister from the box and dusted it off, tape curling around the label's edges. "If it's not in a cool, dry place, the film itself sweats out acetic acid inside the canister, in essence, eating itself. I was afraid of this when you told me where this box was." I opened the canister and touched the film in the reel. It looked almost corrugated and sounded brittle as I rubbed my fingers over its edges. "So, this is it. Do you have something to show this on?"

"A screen?"

"A projector. What is this?" I looked, flipping the canister lid over again. "Sixteen millimeter. I'm sure you don't but—"

"I do, actually. Got it when the school the next town over got swallowed up by ours. They had a going-out-of-business sale."

"Sound?"

"Yeah, pretty sure, yeah, got some movies, too, played 'em, some, mostly Laurel and Hardy type stuff. They're all in the basement with the projector. Boy, you wanna go get it?" They went down and hauled up an ancient A/V cart, wheeling it straight out into the yard. We could have set the projector up in the kitchen and watched the movie on the front of the fridge, but I thought if Fred's movie were finally getting a screening, it should play where we could experience it in the correct dimensions and scale. The only surface big enough was Tommy Jack's garage door.

While they linked an umbilicus of extension cords, I got the film up on the reel arm and waited to thread the leader. "You're hooking that up like a real pro," Tommy Jack yelled, snaking the cord through a cluster of potted cacti, trying to avoid the constellations of needles. "Liza Jean was always bitching about threading the leader when she showed the hygiene films up to the school, but that was a part of her job, so I taught her how on this old machine." It seemed not to occur to him that I would have done this professionally for years, but then, I never did clarify for him exactly what I do for a living. Once they established power, I had the leader on the uptake reel in a few seconds.

"Don't expect much," I said, and despite my efforts at appearing excited, fatigue was setting in, and the film's condition led me to grave doubts about what we would find. I suppose I almost didn't want to turn the machine on. "There's not a lot here, it isn't going to be long, and the stock—"

"Just turn it on and we shall see what we shall see," Tommy Jack said. "I'm kind of curious myself. Don't know why I never thought of this on my own." He killed the outside lights as I flipped the projector switch. The film fluttered a bit as the numbers counted down on this West Texas garage door. They beeped loudly, like Morse code pocking out concentrically into the night sky. I adjusted the lenses and the numbers blurred and sharpened before us. We saw a slate, from back when they still used actual slate, and hands holding it, Fred's name in faded chalk on the bottom half. Then they moved away and suddenly Fred stood in front of us, a giant, his face filling most of the garage door. I was surprised at how different he looked from any of the actual photos I had, or that T.J.'s family had shared with me. Certainly no publicity shots were produced in this era. I had always hoped to find a head shot, but one never surfaced in my research. Other braided men and women milled about near him, and he was practicing looking and not looking at the camera.

Fred looked like those last few music videos Queen made, when Freddie Mercury tried almost anything possible to disguise the path his life was charting—beards, wigs, masks, postproduction effects, kids playing the parts of all of the band members. They tried anything they could, even one video where the band did not appear at all, what they called a conceptual video. "I hope he doesn't have to smile wide, here," Tommy Jack said.

"Not likely, given the era of the stoic Indian," I said, "but why do you hope that?"

"His missing teeth would show, for sure. This is pretty much what he was beginning to look like the last time I saw him."

Fred Howkowski looked kind of white, almost blue, they all did, like ghosts wandering back and forth in the driveway. We heard some word that I imagine was *action* but it was so garbled, had you heard it under any other circumstance you would not have been able to isolate it. Fred suddenly came to life, filling the door, and I would have believed anything he said. He could tell me that he never really did kill himself and in reality, he had cashed in right and was now one of those secret film producers, the Sundance moguls who finance risky ventures because they believe in the work, and that he didn't want to blow his cover. He opened his mouth.

He sounded as if he had somehow learned to breathe underwater and was speaking from there, a voice like air bubbles popping on the water's surface, maybe the voice of a drowning man, nonsense words, that desperation just before the last held breath leaves his lungs. I tried adjusting the sound qualities, but this machine was fairly limited and it was no match for the decaying film. It never got any better in the three minutes he said whatever it was he was saying before the tailer came off and flapped around the uptake reel. We sat in the white light bouncing off the garage, listening to the clacking sound until I shut it off, and then we sat there some more.

"Maybe there's a script in the box," Tommy Jack said, after we'd sat in the dark for a while. "Or maybe we can try it again, on a different machine. Or maybe even have it restored."

"It doesn't really matter what words he spoke," T.J. said, all quiet, still sitting and staring at the darkened garage door. "It was cut, anyway. It was a glorified screen test. I always believed it was something more than that. You know, something they might put on a bonus feature, when they finally release a DVD, or director's cut, or whatever. I don't know what I expected to find here. Maybe I wanted the last few things that really belonged to him, something, some trail to follow. I wanted there to be some reason he found this more worthwhile than raising me."

"Some people just aren't meant to be parents, boy, and he tried to put you where people would take care of you, like your momma and me did. We did our best, but you know, even there, people mess up, they just do. It's in the nature." Sometimes it was good to be in the dark, and it was good at that moment.

"I still want to take it back with me," he said, hanging on.

"Sure, boy." Tommy Jack was visibly glad to have something

to do, and I rewound the film and handed it to him, and then he walked back to the house.

"Daddy?" T.J. said, as we followed him in through the door, dodging the cacti, "was there more to that letter?"

"No," Tommy Jack said.

"Was there another letter?" he asked after a few seconds.

"Yes, boy, there was another letter, but it's mine. It was written to me, not you."

"Does it say anything more about—"

"I know you came a long way for something that didn't turn out like you wanted, but that other letter, that's to me, boy," he said. T.J. nodded and turned to walk out, taking one of his bags. The film was fragile looking, even worse after we'd watched it. I packed the box up as best as I could, given the limited archiving materials he had here. Bubble Wrap is hardly ideal. I supposed carrying it with us into air-conditioned hotels was the best plan, and maybe when we got home, I could get in touch with some of the art preservationists at the university and persuade them to do a restoration. I'd probably have to apply for an NEH grant to accomplish that.

We loaded it into the back of the Blazer with the rest of our bags. Tommy Jack kept shining what seemed to be an industrial-strength spotlight all over the grounds, making sure no local nightlife wandered up to get better acquainted.

"Daddy, you're really not going to show me the other letter, after I came all this way?" T.J. said, leaning against the back hatch.

"Boy, it seems like you are intent on taking that stuff with you. It'll be funny not to have it here anymore. I guess there's a lot I'll have to get used to not being around here," Tommy Jack said. "If you want to come back inside, though, I think there is one more thing I can show you. And then, if you are really dedicated to getting Fred Howkowski's story straight, I'll tell you everything I know." While perhaps not wanting to admit it, Tommy Jack didn't want us to leave him there in that house, alone.

"Here," he said, reaching into the back of his truck's king cab, pulling out a backpack that had been with us the whole time. "I'm not for sure if this gets things straight for you, or if it just muddies things up further, but for what it's worth, I found it with the rest of his stuff. I tend to keep it with me. It reminds me of where we all go wrong sometimes."

CHAPTER NINE:

Head Shot

o o o o

This town is a harsh environment, everywhere I look. The first thing I have to do is get a permanent place. The residence motel address I give at any central casting office, they look at me and the address doubtfully and I'm certain that my application goes into the trash before I'm out the door. I hear from some of these other vets that there are places that aren't so great, but the rent is decent and they've agreed to introduce me to the person who can get me into one, or at least on the waiting list. I'll use this feeling if I ever get a role as someone who's been displaced. In the meantime, they've also taken me down to the soup kitchens with them, telling me I need to start saving up for rent. I feel a little guilty not revealing that I have some savings with me, but it won't last and I've got to think about my future here.

o o o o

I started to sleep in the bushes in some of the parks, deep enough where the police won't shag me out but I hear other things. Not sure what they are really, maybe the little people that everyone on the reservation believed protected lost children, or stole them if their parents were not responsible, or maybe there are bears here. The showers at Venice Beach are cold, but at six in the morning there's no one there to chase you away if you use soap and shampoo quickly, and a quick scrub inside the swim trunks generally keeps me decent enough looking for casting calls, but still the address issue is a problem.

o o o o

The rent-controlled place isn't bad. I spent some of my savings getting a couple of better locks put on, though. The super said it was okay, probably even smart, and though he wasn't in a position to provide locks for his tenants, he had no issues with us protecting ourselves. He seems like a nice enough guy, said he would invite me down to the VFW post but they don't let veterans of conflicts in, foreign wars only. He knew it was a shitty rule, because he knew if you were forced to wear a uniform and shoot at people who didn't share the opinions of those running your country, that sure sounded a lot like a war to him too, but he went along with it anyway. That was his advice. Indeed, a nice guy, which is more than I can say for some of my neighbors. I hear shouting from some of their places.

o o o o

I spent some more of my savings on a TV. It was really more than I should have, but I have got to get some sleep and all that shouting from the other apartments gets to me. Hard to believe this is what we were fighting for. Even over the TV, I'm beginning to hear some of what's going on in the apartment closest to me, and I wish I hadn't. Maybe they need bears to come and visit them, show them what's what. That might do it, but some people who need that lecture might need it more than once.

On the brighter side of things, even lacking sleep, I got my first job as an extra today. I report tomorrow. The casting agent said if I did well on that one, didn't mess up or get in anyone's way or stare into the cameras, she could probably send some work my way. She also said I might have a better chance if I cut my hair. That way I could pass for a white guy with a nice tan. She said in case I hadn't noticed, there weren't a lot of roles for Indian actors these days. I told her I couldn't and that Indians didn't need to be cast strictly in westerns. She said I could make those decisions when I was casting a picture, then told me to suit myself but that she would also send anything my way that looked like it had a need for Indians. There might be a few things. She said a couple of Westerns were in development and asked how I felt about doing scalping scenes and others along those lines. I told her I had bills to pay and she said okay. You only get one skin and you better respect its properties and values. Bears know that certainly and so do I.

o o o o

I am now as brown as I was in the jungles. Not like back home. If only my dad could see me now. All those years he made me wear long sleeves and jeans in the summer. He might have lived in the middle of the reservation but he didn't want any of his kids looking the part. He so liked introducing me to his friends pale that he would have made me wear gloves and a ski mask in the summer—considering how fast my Indian skin darkened—if he thought he could get away with it. My mom never knew any of this, naturally, always wondering why I never wore those skimpy muscle shirts and shorts she bought. She never knew I had to go through the no-tan test at least once a week with Dad and had to receive my appropriate punishment if I had gotten any darker. He made me wear a ring and on Saturday when she was gone shopping, I had to take it off to show that I had gotten no more tan. Sometimes I forgot and in the week following my forgetfulness, the long sleeves he made me wear covered up more than my relatively dark skin. They also covered those darker patches in different colors, shaped like his knuckles.

o o o o

The roles are coming pretty good these days, nothing big but I'm working fairly regularly. I spoke to the neighbor about all the noise and got a busted tooth for my troubles. The guy seemed calm when he answered the door, and I could see the little kid with the bloody nose in the background, pretending to watch cartoons, and when I yelled to him, he turned quickly back to the TV, right around the time his father sucker-punched me right across the left cheek. Calling the cops would probably just get me escorted out of here for causing trouble and I can't give up this address, so now I have two very good reasons to keep my mouth shut. The tooth was loose for a couple days and I hoped it would firm itself back up, but it never did and I think an infection must have crept its way in, so I took a tip from Jangle Kirby and yanked it myself with a pair of vise grips and then gargled with saltwater like crazy. It eventually healed up okay and I left the neighbors to themselves.

o   o   o   o

The side of the moon I used to see in the jungles has followed me here. This isn't the right moon for Los Angeles. It's closer. It's falling and one day, it will just land in the ocean and that'll be that. I keep watching the nightly national news to see if anyone else has noticed, but no one has. I'm sure the government knows and they're just not telling anyone. I mean, really, if they wouldn't tell the truth of all the things we had to do and the things that were done to us over in Vietnam, they sure weren't going to tell America that the moon was going to destroy us in a couple years. In the meantime, before it collides, it's trying to pull me out into the ocean again, trying to steal what little I have, like it did in China Beach. I lost that stupid ring my dad made me wear all those years at China Beach and I knew he'd look for it on my finger when I came home. That moon made me be who I am, embrace my skin like I never had before and that is one powerful thing that cannot be denied.

o   o   o   o

I think someone is dead next door. It's not just that the yelling stopped a few days ago. I can smell it coming up from the vents. At first I thought it was maybe a rat in the ductwork, but even rats don't have exactly the same smell as a dead human body. I knew I had heard a bear snuffling and what did I do? The same thing I have done all my life. When I don't like the words I hear, I just find some way of delivering different ones. This one was easy. All I had to do was turn up the volume.

o   o   o   o

That little boy's nose won't be bleeding anymore and I don't have to worry about losing any more teeth to my neighbor. They took them both away today, the boy in a bag, the father in cuffs. I could have stopped him, could have spoken to the super, the cops, any number of people. The bears sure came home and did it up right this time.

o   o   o   o

That little boy keeps talking to me through the ducts. I tried sealing the vent up with tape but it didn't help and now I just keep the TV on, blasting the snow when the TV is on a channel with no signal. That works most times, but I can still hear him a bit. He says the bears showed him how to do it and he said it was so much easier on that side. He gave me a couple options. He said I might go home or just head on over into the ducts with them. I thought about those things, even called people at home a couple times, my mom, Shirley, even tried to get Tom to come back out and see me, thought maybe he could help me, but it seems like those doors are gone, and all that's left is to slide through those slats in the vents and disappear down the ducts. I was holding out to hear on that speaking part but we all know how that turned out.

Time to write those letters.

Tommy Jack McMorsey

They read in the porch light, bugs swarming and mosquitoes like to carry you off if you don't watch out, but they both read, each holding the spiral-bound opened. "Daddy, he doesn't mention it here, but you said it often enough, about you saving him and that was how I got my name. Can you tell me about that?" the boy said, closing the notebook. I knew they were just going to ask more questions, and I guess it was finally time to answer what I could. He deserved answers because he is my son, and I suppose she deserved them because, like it or not, she is probably my daughter. And who is left to harm at this point except me, and maybe that's about the way things should be, considering all the hurt I have pushed out over the years. I decided I would answer any questions, but they had to figure out which questions to ask.

"Yeah, I'll tell you. But maybe in the house? I am getting eaten alive out here," I said and walked in. They could choose on their own which door they were ready to open, their car or my house. I figured I should probably start from the beginning, which kicked off, as so many things in my life did, with a letter.

o   o   o   o

We all knew what it was, as soon as the envelope came. It's not like the Selective Service was in the business of issuing invitations. At first, though, I thought for sure the draft notice I got didn't really mean anything. My daddy was confident, given his support of our local elected officials, that something could be done. In the meantime, we knew I had to tell the woman I was planning to marry.

"I need to see you," I said to Liza Jean over the phone, after my momma and daddy and me got our wind back.

"What is it, Tommy Jack?" she said, more annoyed than concerned. "Can't it wait? You know how I've got my standing appointment with the beauty operator."

"You're gonna want to cancel this one. I need to do this in person," I said.

"Supper?" she asked, her voice sliding up a few notes as if the words were greased. "Is there something you're going to ask me tonight, Tommy Jack?" Like most folks in Big Antler, hell, most of West Texas, she'd gotten it into her head that being coy was what a young woman did when she was talking with a man who was interested in her. It didn't matter that we'd known each other forever and were already settling down to our lives in the same workplace. The nurse's office was just down the hall from my classroom, and most had turned a blind eye when I'd slip down there during my prep period. We had both come home after college, and she took her expected place when Mrs. Moose retired from sticking thermometers up kids' butts to reduce the number who tried to fake being sick just to get out of school. I was a new history teacher with a fresh degree, returning to my old school. I would probably eventually coach JV football, and the like, or I would have, before getting that letter in the mail.

"Sure, supper," I said. "Sportsman's Club all right?"

"You can pick me up at six. I'll be ready," she said. This meant, more or less, that she would be decked out in pink with a fuzzy sweater on and no jewelry, so as not to conflict with whatever I might want to put on the ring finger of her left hand. I got there at six and, uncharacteristically, she was ready. She was not, however, wearing pink, had left on her old rings, and the look on her face told me that word had traveled fast in our little town. Only about half the houses had phones, but only the cattle didn't know I was leaving for basic training in a couple days.

"So I guess you've already heard," I said, letting her into my passenger's seat and closing the door as she nodded. "Good news is like a brushfire around here." We made our way to the Sportsman in silence, her hands making busy little adjustments to her skirt for the half-hour ride. The flatlands rolled out before us, interrupted only by the occasional house or mesquite.

"It's only two years," I said, when we were seated. "And usually, just one of them spent over there." Fortunately, no one in Cee City had heard yet, so the waitress just gave us the usual teasing she does, looking at Liza Jean's fingers for any updates. "I haven't talked to the principal yet, to see if they'll hold my job. Might be getting too much ahead of myself. Daddy's looking into what options we have. Maybe I won't have to go at all, what with having a necessary job here in town. Or they could station me somewhere close, if I absolutely have to go." Liza Jean's daddy held a lot more influence than mine; our whole cotton crop could fit inside just one of the nine patches he had all around Big Antler. She still said very little, nodding slightly. I guess they'd already had the conversation about how far Mr. Bean was willing to go to keep my ass out of Vietnam.

"When are you supposed to leave?" she said, finally, after moving the catfish strips around on her plate some.

"Have to be in Abilene to catch a plane the day after next. I think they don't give you much notice so you don't have time to plan some kind of escape. Basic training is, I think, something like two months, and then maybe more, depending . . ." I could hear in my own voice that I was already accepting this as my new life. Four years of college, and here I was, after a year of teaching, thinking they had surely passed me over, that I was beyond the point of snatching. They mostly wanted men who were eighteen, not so set in their ways. In my mid-twenties, I was already pretty set in concrete. People in town thought of me as a man instead of a boy. Hell, I even wore a tie to work every day.

"Depending on what, Tommy Jack?"

"I don't know. I do not know any of this stuff. I thought I was off the hook, that I could be done worrying about this. You know, I was planning our life," I said, reaching across the table to touch the hand that held the friendship ring she'd picked out for me to buy when we were still in high school. Even then, she began looking away.

My plane to Fort Ord left Abilene at 5:45 AM, so I had to get a room in town. And though she came with me to Abilene, agreeing to take my pickup back to my daddy's and leave him the keys, she stood at my room door in the early evening light and said her good-bye then. I thought, seeing it was my last night, we would have shared some time after supper together. She hugged me and turned from the motel balcony, not looking back until she was safely behind my pickup's windshield. Watching her taillights disappear on the horizon, I guess I had known she wouldn't stay. She still had that sense of privilege that came from being the daughter of the county's biggest landowner, and though we were over a hundred miles from home, she couldn't have anyone noticing that she'd taken me to a motel and not returned until the next morning. Vietnam or no Vietnam, it was not the appropriate action for a daughter of Marcourt Bean.

I'd never seen much of the country, so watching the sun rise over unfamiliar territory was at least a little pleasant. Heading due west, we stayed in a perpetual state of early morning for a couple hours. Shadows faded, grew, faded again as we passed time zones and state lines. Most of the others on the plane were quiet, some drinking coffee, some reading the papers. Most, though, were like me, not riding voluntarily. It looked like several guys wore the same "I got my draft notice" face I saw in the mirror all the time, and others, men and women, hunched, as if hoping not to be noticed. The only people flying in planes that early in the morning are those who are stuck with no other options. They had to get where they were going with no eye to pleasure.

See, my daddy could not do a thing for me, except get me a couple of days home between basic and advanced. Liza Jean and I went out for a date then too, but like the last time, it was more a dinner than anything else. She was different already, probably because I had been assigned back to Fort Ord after basic for advanced infantry training, which pretty much guaranteed I was going over. Almost nobody made it out of Ord and got a stateside assignment. I'm guessing she was maybe dating the Giant then, or at least considering it. This tall dork was the gym teacher and varsity football coach from the school. When that man was running, you could hear those flat feet slapping the floor across town, like a clown on the basketball court. I wondered if he had somehow busted his own arches just to keep his ass out of the draft. People do the funniest things in desperation.

All the time I was in basic, my daddy wrote to senators, representatives, anyone whose campaign he'd donated to, trying to pull me some strings to get my ass out of there, a deferment, anything. All these people around Big Antler looked at me like I was already a dead man. Everyone kept saying there was no politics in who had to go over, but there were lots of oil boys and rancher boys my age wandering around town, still holding hands with their girlfriends, even having the balls to smirk at me, in that last day before I had to leave. Lord, I did not want to go to Vietnam. At one point in basic, they had asked me if I was a conscientious objector. I said I was, and they had such a fit, telling me I should have said so a lot sooner than five weeks into training. They slammed phones and file cabinet drawers so hard that I said never mind. They had me convinced that I didn't want to make trouble for anyone above me. I wonder how many men they pulled that line of shit on, and of those, how many came home.

When I got over, in country, there were four black men, two Indians, and five rednecks, small-town farm types like me, in my immediate squad. I had never seen an Indian in my life at that point, and there I was, with two of them, all day long. You can't tell me there wasn't politics in who got drafted, and who had to go over and who got to serve stateside. I had never felt more alone in my life, and maybe it is that feeling that sends you out to even a remotely familiar face. I had met Fred Howkowski in basic, but we'd never spoken then. He was one of the idiots I went in with, paying a limousine to take us into Oakland. We didn't know a thing, scared shitless, giving up our own cash to get into the base when a free shuttle just passed us right on by.

I wondered then if he had recognized me, too, if he'd witnessed my last hope on the plane or if he had seen what I had seen just before we boarded. At the Oakland shipping post, we passed the truck they used to cart the bodies back, Gray's, I think was the company name—should have been Graves by my reckoning. That truck was mighty full of those special soldier caskets I would later get real familiar with over there, as if we didn't feel shitty enough, waiting to head on over.

So among those of us who were stringless, if a familiar face is all you got, that is what you go with. I'm not for sure when Fred and I moved from being friendly to being friends, but it was probably as soon as our second day over. We were out on the patrols. I never quite got exactly what we were supposed to be doing. It seemed like we were just showing other people we could walk around in their jungles, daring them to pick us off. Why they wanted to live there, I couldn't imagine.

We were going out on the "old NDP," which was new to us. The old-timers would just mock you to death if you asked questions. They called it Monopoly—ask too many questions, you go directly home, do not pass go, do not collect two hundred dollars. I wanted to go home, all right, but not the way the uninformed usually did. You know, in a plastic bag. We'd been walking all day when the first lieutenant called for NDP. All the other guys in the squad seemed to know what that meant and got to unloading their rucksacks.

"NDP?" Fred asked one of the old-timers.

"Night defense perimeter, cherry," he got back, and the other guy just shook his head at us.

"Well," I said, as we stood, "if we're going to die tonight, at least we'll know what duty we're dying on." Fred was the only one who laughed. I knew who I would stick with.

"You cherries watch out. Red Legs fired out into the bush all night long last night, and got a lot of enemy return. Might be a wounded VC or two out there. Happy hunting, boys," one of the old-timers said, as we walked out into the dark.

"Y'all head on over there in that patch." We were ordered somewhere along the trail, into the thick brush beyond our sight. "You two, you'll be up in three hours, then you watch for two hours, and then you wake these two up," the lieutenant whispered, and gave the same kinds of instructions all the way around. The firebases were made on the sheared-off tops of peaks that bulldozers had cleaned straightaway, but the rest of the mountainsides were as dangerous as ever. The only thing we had going for us was the dense brush we were tangled in nearly every moment of patrol. They said we could always grapple onto something as we fell, if need be, but the practical application of that was just a little different.

As we got into the shadows where we were supposed to set up our air mattresses and camouflage blankets, some rounds of ammo went off and we jumped to the ground, trying desperately to disappear into the bush. Fred suddenly sunk a lot lower into the ground than I did, almost a foot, nearly losing his balance. This low gurgly moan and a rush of foul air surrounded us. Fred snagged onto me, his arms pinwheeling. My mess hall lunch was rising inside me in that noxious cloud, my tongue thick and metallic, and my hands slick with sweat, but I held us steady. The tiny penlight my daddy had sent along with me showed us what he'd landed in. At that moment, I was wishing the light had been stolen along with the other shit that had been lifted from me by then. We would have been better off not knowing. Fred's rib cage expanded for one big scream and I clapped my free hand down on his mouth.

I kept it there, forcing him silent, so no one would hear him and get a bead on us. With one hand locked across his face, I yanked him out, threw him to the ground, and punched him, knocking the wind out of him. We lay there, and though my eyes were closed, I could still see perfectly what he had stepped in. Fred had sunk shin deep into the rotting belly of the dead NVA soldier buried in a grave under maybe three inches of dirt. His boots were glazed in maggots and dissolving organs, but we didn't dare move for a bit, until our quiet would cover us again. I hoped the body wouldn't shift any more and that we'd discharged the last of its belly gases when we'd disturbed it.

So, we lay there, listening to every sound around us, waiting to hear if there was more fire, afraid to move. Fred seemed spookier than me for some reason. I don't know if he didn't realize this was what our lives were going to be like or what. It was a jungle, at night, so there was not a scarcity of noises. Small, big, very big, you didn't know. Could have been wild dogs, or trained dogs. Lord, I was hoping it wasn't dogs, because if they can smell fear like it is said they can, we would have been radiating fear scent like a skunk spraying just then. Or boars, or bears. Of course the biggest concern was that it was NVA. Sound in the dark is a disorienting thing, and mystery sounds when you are afraid are even more disorienting.

I held him there, that night, my hand inches away from his mouth for hours, until we got the sound from the previous watchers and we got up to do our watch duty. I knew I could keep my mouth shut, but I had no idea what his capacity for restraint was, and I wasn't taking any chances. Throughout our watch and after we woke up the next shift, my hand stayed within grasping distance of Fred's mouth. We came in together, and I intended to make sure we finished our tours together. I don't know why. There were some more rounds of fire, and occasional flares.

"Some beginning, huh?" I whispered in the dark.

"Could be worse," he whispered back.

"How do you figure it could be worse?" His stained fatigues were still visible, even in the dark hooch.

"We're still alive. We just have to stay that way for three hundred and sixty-four more days. You and me? I think we might be able to accomplish that. So where you from? South somewhere, by your accent."

"Big Antler, Texas, population seven hundred and thirty-nine, I guess seven hundred and thirty-eight at the moment—"

"It'll be thirty-nine again, this time next year," he said. Whatever urge to scream he'd had was gone, like I had somehow discharged it from him with that one punch to the stomach. I'd heard bullshit bravado before, every fall Friday night in Big Antler, where most boys talked it on the football field and most men talked it right back from the sidelines, remembering their own days on the field. There was not a trace of it in Fred's voice. We talked through the night, quieter when we could hear others snoring. How they were able to sleep in that danger-filled night was beyond my comprehension. I was happy for the company, because I was pretty sure I wouldn't be sleeping again until I was back home in my bed in Big Antler.

I told him about Liza Jean, minus the fact that she was probably already moving on, told him about my momma and daddy, and in return he told me about his momma and daddy and brother and the girl back home who was going to have his baby soon. At first, it seemed like he didn't know about the deferment he could have gotten with that baby on the way, and at first I thought it best to keep quiet. I eventually mentioned it anyway, and he clarified that they weren't married. He added that it wasn't such a big deal on the reservation to have a kid without being married. People just raise their kids, sometimes together, sometimes not. To him, the deferment loophole being blocked to him was just another way the United States did not recognize the separate cultures. He then noted that it wasn't like they were going to hand it over now, anyway. Hours passed. It wasn't the worst thing we'd see over there in our time, but it was bad enough for the beginning.

"You cherries see anything interesting your first night?" one of the old-timers asked as we broke camp in the morning and began the next day's hump. All the others who had sent us out in that direction smirked, waiting for us to bitch or whine.

"Nothing to write home about," Fred said. We had wiped as much of the nastiness off as we could with foliage, and tried to wipe it from our minds. To this day, I don't know if those chumps set us up to get us in tune with life around the firebases or if we just got lucky. If they did, we passed their test, but only by working together.

Even as we bedded down the next night, when we were back to the firebase, in a hooch, I wasn't all that eager to sleep. I saw that poor rotting fucker every time I closed my eyes, and Fred wasn't too eager, either, so we spent most of that night listening to the sounds of gunfire and occasional flare shots.

"You know, the first chance I get," he said, "I'm going to write home and tell Nadine that we have to name the baby Thomas John if it's a boy. She's probably already had it by now and I just haven't heard."

"You and your girl already picked out names. That's real nice," I said. "What did you pick for a girl's name?"

"No, we didn't. I want him to be named after you." I had no response. What are you supposed to say to something like that? When too much time had passed in silence, I said the only reasonable thing I could.

"That's not my name. You gotta remember, Big Antler is in the state of Texas. My birth certificate, hell, even these here dog tags will tell you, my legal name is Tommy Jack."

"Okay, Tommy Jack it is, then."

"You like redneck names, do you?" I said.

"I'm serious."

"Did you not hear all the shit I got about my name through basic? If I thought I was a smart college graduate, they let me know that I was pure West Texas redneck deluxe, in and out. We didn't know each other then, but surely you could hear them."

"Tommy Jack," he said, quietly, frowning. "Yeah, I suppose I remember hearing something along those lines. I don't think I can call you that. That's a little-kid name, and brother, after this night, we are definitely not kids anymore."

"I'll agree to that like lightning."

"Just the same, I'm glad to know, and that will be the name I write to Nadine."

"I don't think that's probably such a good name for an Indian baby from New York."

"You saved my life, Tom. I may get the chance to repay you while we're here, probably will. But in case not, I want to honor your act. That little baby might not have ever had a father if you weren't so quick thinking. We're done talking about this," he said, but still insisted on showing me the letter before he mailed it off. I discouraged him, but it disappeared into the mail drop.

o   o   o   o

"So that's how you got your name," I said to the boy. "But you know, as I said before, I didn't do such a good job after all. It's amazing, the horrors that could bring people together, and sometimes all it took was just plain old loneliness."

"Thanks, Daddy. I'm also wondering, though, since we've come to this place, if you would also tell me what it was like, finding him that second time, in L.A.?" the boy asked.

"Is that really what you came all the way down here for?" I asked. I had made that silent promise that I would tell them what they wanted to know, but I suppose I wasn't prepared for them really to ask.

"I can't speak for T.J. here, but I'd like to know, too. If you can't, I understand," the girl said, as she had a number of times, but this moment, her voice softened for the first time. I could finally hear what it might be like to talk to her when she was not getting ready to give an ass-chewing the size of the Metroplex. "It is partly why I came," she added. "The other part is diminishing. I understand what he saw in you, enough, anyway."

"I said to myself a while earlier that I would answer whatever you wanted to ask. Both of you," I said, looking at her, letting her understand that no matter what she thought of me previously, I would go all the way to the end for her now. I would discuss whatever I had to about Fred and where he and I had been together. "This too, as you know, started with a letter," I said, and then paused, and decided to open that door explicitly. "Two letters. You've just read the one for you," I said to the boy.

o   o   o   o

Fred and I used to joke about just whatever we could while we were over and even later when we got back, but I guess Fred could find nothing to laugh at in his final situation. Things had somehow gotten that grim for him. Even in shooting himself, he didn't make the tabloids—passing without a smudge of national ink, lying in some little set of rooms, in a small corner of Los Angeles. Fred wasn't one of your better-known Indian actors in Hollywood. I think there was maybe one, then, maybe two. What I am saying is I never would have known had I not received the letters. Naturally, I immediately hopped in our sedan and drove as fast as I could. I wanted to believe, even as I drove from Big Antler, through El Paso, Phoenix, and finally into L.A., that this was some joke of Fred's, that I was going to get there, and he would jump out, say *surprise*, claim this was the only way he was going to get me to visit a second time, because he always knew what a stubborn son of a bitch I was. Of course, none of that happened, and I had pretty much faced that by the end of the long drive, but hope can be a strong presence when you need it, and for those hours I made that long stretch, I needed it.

I called the authorities when I got to L.A. and waited out front. When they arrived, I showed them the letter and handed over the key Fred had included in the envelope. They let me come with them, since someone had to identify the body. They asked why I hadn't called them as soon as I had received the letter, and I didn't have a very good answer for that, either. I guess I wanted to be there when they opened the door. I didn't want Fred to be dead with strangers even though that was the way he lived.

As we rode the elevator, strong odors of cheap cooking and other things came through the doors at each floor, until we reached the seventh, where Fred's apartment was, and I knew he was dead for sure. The hallway smelled like something I had tried to forget since we'd gotten home from the jungles. Though there was some other odor, one that was vaguely familiar, the overwhelming smell was that of death, and the smell of death is one you don't soon forget. It seemed impossible that no one else on this floor noticed; it was as if they chose to ignore that damned odor. Nearly a week's worth of newspapers were stacked in front of his door. How long was that paperboy going to keep delivering until he said something?

The officers removed some of those little masks they wear in surgery from a package they brought with them, and handed me one. It didn't help all that much, but we wore them anyway as they opened the door. Fred's apartment had gotten bad, even in the time since I had been there before. The furniture was all busted up, and the weird things Fred had collected the last time I'd seen him were all piled in one corner. The couch I'd stayed on was now saturated with piss and sat lopsided, one of its legs missing. I found it later in the bathtub, stuffed into the drainpipe hole. Copies of *Daily Variety* lay all over the place, some stacked and some randomly, specific pages that must have been meaningful to him folded over. Fred's right foot lay in sight, on the edge of his bed, as I walked by the bedroom door. There was a blanket covering some of him, but the foot was poked out, and I didn't go any farther in to see the rest.

The television was on, broadcasting snow and hissing, though it was midday. He must have turned it to a nonworking channel.

"You mind if I turn this off?" I asked them.

"Sure, go ahead, but try not to touch anything else," they said, entering the bedroom. The on/off/volume button was missing, and Fred had clamped a small pair of vise grips onto the recessed prong where the button had existed. I pushed the grips in and they dropped to the floor, coming loose from the internal piece.

"Mr. McMorsey, apparently we didn't need you here, after all," one of the officers said, coming out of the bedroom, and though he still had that little mask on, I could swear he was smirking beneath it. He passed me a copy of Fred's picture, what he used to call his head shot, the thing he sent out to casting directors on those movies he wanted to be in. "It's definitely him," one of them said as they walked me out the door, locking it behind us. "Is there anyone you know of we should call? Next of kin? The coroner will be by later, and things'll get taken care of."

"I'll make the calls, if you don't mind. I have his momma's number," I said, trying to remember if I had thought ahead enough to put it in my bag.

"She'll have to call us, for final arrangements. We understand you have this letter for his belongings, but a dead body of this type has different rules. We can be reached at this number," one of them said, handing me a business card. "Is there any particular funeral home you want to use, Mr. McMorsey?" he asked.

"I don't know a damn thing about Los Angeles. One is as good as another, I imagine. Would you mind if I—could you let me inside?" I asked. "I'm sorry. I promise not to touch anything, I just want to see him, you know, make sure it's him."

"It's him, all right. Are you sure you want to see this? It's not pleasant."

"We were in Vietnam together," I said, and I guess that was good enough. They unlocked the door and one came in with me and escorted me to the bedroom. One full look told me Fred was not having an open casket—that was for sure.

So I called Fred's momma and she did what she had to do, and had me make some arrangements out there in L.A., asking me to have him cremated and shipped back to the reservation. I offered to drive his ashes myself, really wanted to in fact, but she wanted them as soon as she could have them. I wasn't flying and besides I had to pick up the boy back at home in Texas to take him to the funeral and I asked her if she could wait until the end of the week for the services. She said sure, and I guess she likely kept him somewhere in her house until we made it.

By the time I got back to the apartment, the coroner, medical examiner, whoever, had already come and removed him. They let me in and said it was okay to take care of what he had asked me to do, to grant his last requests and deal with the mess he left behind.

Several pairs of nearly useless shoes lay strewn all over his floor, like a bunch of small dead animals that had been left to rot alongside a road. I could not imagine why he wouldn't have just thrown them out. The dresser drawers were more of the same. They were filled with clothes but most of them were dirty, smelling of piss and long days staying on the same body, just jammed into every damned drawer, as if you're supposed to put your dirty clothes in the dresser and somehow they were just going to clean themselves while they were stuffed away. Every dresser drawer was filled. There seemed to be some logic to it, which was kind of weird, but these clothes were threadbare and stained beyond belief. He should have told me he needed some new clothes when he'd called those times. I've never been what you would call rich but I could have afforded to help him out some. All I was spending money on was the junk-store business. I could have spared it, and would have spared anything, for him.

Something had happened to Fred in the time since I had last seen him and who could say what, really. The bathroom I had showered in a while back looked like it might have been last clean around that time. Now, I am the first to admit my aim is not always perfect, and Liza Jean confirmed this almost any opportunity she had, but how do you miss the toilet when you're sitting on it? That one, I just could not get. And even then, he just threw a towel over it, I guess hoping that would make it disappear somehow but it seemed like more had been wrong with Fred than he had ever let on.

I did notice on the shelf in there that he had gotten a partial plate. It was sitting in a glass of hazy water, the fake teeth embroidered with metal and plastic, fake gums. He for sure didn't need it anymore.

His bed was maybe the most revealing thing about those last few months of his life. Whoever had taken him away had lifted the blanket off of him and laid it crumpled near the pillow. But other than the bare pillow and blanket, the bed had no sheets, no headboard, not another damned thing. It was one of those bare mattresses and I suspect those little metal buttons all over holding it together had probably pinched him something hard any time he turned over in his sleep. It looked like he had tried sleeping on plastic sheets like storm-window treatment for a period right toward the end but even there it hadn't helped him out too much. There was shit everywhere, ground into the mattress and spattered on the plastic sheet crumpled in the corner. At first I tried to tell myself it was blood from his gunshot as that had turned brown already against the wall but there is no mistaking the smell of shit. I am sorry.

I am not given to thinking about such over and over and have been able to ignore lots of nasty things in my life but the thing that kept this exact scene in my head was not the shame of it, the humiliation, and the wondering what I could have done to change these things, but something else instead. I knew I was having him cremated, at the request of his momma and daddy, and though it would be closed casket and all, I was hoping there was something in that apartment to put a decent set of clothes on him before they sparked the burners. I didn't have much hope of finding anything in the dresser but he must have worn something reasonable to casting calls and I was desperately hoping whatever that was would be hanging in the closet.

The clothes on the hanger bar were in about the same condition. Above them, though, on the shelf, stacked neatly, in order of size, was gift box after gift box. I lifted one of the higher boxes, assuming it would either be empty or full of the same sorts of things that filled every drawer in the place. There was weight to it, and I carefully pulled it and the boxes on top of it down from their shelf, and set them on the dresser top. Maybe there was something salvageable in them. I was hoping. I opened the top one, and then the next and the next. I took the rest of the boxes, cleared the table in the other room, and spread them out there.

Each box still contained the exact contents the boy and I had carefully shopped for and packed over the previous year: shirts, pants, jackets, towels, undershorts, T-shirts. The other boxes held things from other people, his momma and daddy, his brother Gary, some other names I didn't recognize. I took one of the shirts the boy had given him from its box and shook it out but it didn't want to move. The pins and tissue paper were still in place, the arms folded neatly behind the back and the tags, too, still hung from the inside of the collar. The scent of commercial starch still hung on this shirt in the way those different scents clung to his other clothing.

I selected a set of clothes and put them aside, figuring I was going to have to get him shoes somewhere in town. Maybe the undertaker would have a suggestion but likely I would see a shoe store somewhere around the city without too much of a problem. The rest I threw into my trunk, assuming I could drop them off at one of those thrift-store donation boxes.

I took one last look around the apartment before I left for good and the super came to clean up the rest. I had the couple boxes of stuff Fred wanted me to take and I made one last sweep.

I guess I was looking for answers, knowing there probably weren't any, but hoping just the same. Walking through the bedroom door, I caught that familiar odd scent again, mingled with all the others, and looked down. I should have recognized it immediately. An open can of apricots sat on the nightstand, half empty, a fork handle leaning against the can's lip, its tines resting on the bottom, among the fruit. The few apricots sunk in the syrup were going bad in that stifling apartment.

In one of the kitchen cupboards, there were several more cans of apricots. Each had been punctured and the fruit inside was spoiling, as Fred had committed, inedible should anyone be tempted. I did the super a favor, collecting those cans and tossing them in the trash myself. I also didn't want anyone to be tempted.

The morticians let me see Fred when I got there. They didn't want to but when I explained that I had already seen him, they eased off a little. I had seen some of him but not all. He was semi-covered in a sheet when I went there and they had done some surgery on him, checking out what was left, determining a cause of death, that kind of stuff but really I didn't see why they had to cut up his belly when it should have been obvious that half the top of his head being missing was a pretty clear cause of death if there ever was one. I wondered if they had found fermenting undigested apricots in his belly, if he had done it before his body had begun absorbing their inherent bad luck.

The morticians had cleaned him pretty well but there was really no disguising what the bullet had done. I had not seen anything like that since we'd gotten back but I knew the look. It was always kind of weird any time we saw one in that condition and aside from this being my best friend—and that is a pretty big aside, I know—Fred didn't hardly look different from all those guys we had seen go, over there. From one angle you could see everything, the way the bullet spreads out on impact before its fragments knock the cap off your skull, and from another angle, it just looked like a photograph, where some of it has been ripped off, the skin, bone, hair, everything, just stopping abruptly along a jagged line.

I touched Fred's arm, the place I had pushed him and punched him joking around for so long and it wasn't really cold like people say about touching the dead. You always hear that but it isn't true. They are only cold compared to what you are used to when you touch someone. They aren't cold like from the fridge—more they are like furniture, a piece of wood, a table, a desk, a windowpane, a door.

I handed the clothes over, and told them I would go shopping for some shoes and bring them back shortly. They said I could do that if I wanted, but they added, politely, that he really didn't need shoes.

"I suppose it's not like he's going to get cold feet," I said, and they smiled, again, politely. I don't guess morticians joke too much with their customers, even if they're invited to. I smiled back and I said I would be back to pick him up the next day. In the parking lot, I reached for my keys and felt that other thing I had brought with me in my pocket and I ran back in, but strangely, one of those men in the black suits was running to meet me at the same time like he had known I had forgotten this one thing.

"Mr. McMorsey, I'm so glad we caught you," he said at the same time I said, "I forgot this."

"He no longer needs that, sir," the man said, looking into the folded paper towel I had given him, walking me back to the room where they were keeping Fred. "The entry wound was through the mouth. I'm so sorry, but really, there was little left to which this could even be mounted." He tried to hand it back to me.

"Well, it belongs with him, anyway," I said, refusing to take the partial plate from the man and he nodded once, indicating he heard me. I suspicion he might have just thrown it out after I walked back through that door but maybe he placed it with Fred in the casket.

"We found something in the clothing you left that might be important. It could always wait until you return to retrieve the cremains, but I am happy we were able to catch you before you left."

"Cremains? Is that what y'all call them?"

"Yes, sir, we do."

"Well, okay, sounds kind of funny, but that's your business. Anyway, what was it you—" I began and then I saw what they had found. It was resting on the tabletop next to the shirt. I recognized it immediately but that was probably because it was my own handwriting on the envelope. I flipped it over. Fred had never even opened the birthday card. I knew that was what it was because he had written on the back of it. His cursive said this was a pale-blue shirt, which was true, and that me and the boy had given it to him for his birthday the year before, which was also true.

"Thank you," I said. "Have you—"

"Yes, sir, there were others, as well," he said, handing me the sealed envelopes with similar information on them, from the pants, undershorts, and socks boxes.

"Thanks again," I said.

"We'll see you tomorrow, sir?" one asked, leading me back out the door I came in.

"Yes, tomorrow," I said and headed to my motel. There was a pool there and kids screaming as they jumped in it. Never quite understood why they felt a need to scream. The boy would never scream if he jumped in a pool. He was just not the kind.

I brought the boxes in and laid them all out on the other bed and went through each and every one of them to discover the same damned thing in each. The first box contained a full set of towels still folded exactly the way they fold them at the store. The ones I had used at his place had been threadbare beyond belief—I had to walk around the place with the windows open and air-dry, really, they were so useless—and when I was taking these boxes out I didn't even see a single towel other than the one he had thrown on the floor.

In the next box I found two funny things. The first was a pair of pajamas, which seemed damned odd for Fred, but who knows, I guess he could have been a pajamas kind of guy. But I have gotten pajamas, a robe, all that kind of craziness as gifts in the past too. People who maybe don't know you, have never seen you get ready for bed, these people think pajamas are safe gifts; they think everyone uses these kinds of things. The second thing I found was more interesting. The handwriting on the front of the envelope I recognized immediately and I did not at all need the confirmation on the back that this gift was from Shirley Mounter. I couldn't take something she had bought to a thrift shop, couldn't allow it to be lost forever.

Every gift anyone from home had sent to him, he had given up every damned one of them, like they were for someone else, someone he no longer was. He had put names and dates on the back of the cards' envelopes, who it had been from, what it was, and when they had mailed it. I guess maybe he figured if he ever ran into the man he used to be, he could pass them along to their rightful owner.

The next day, I picked up the little gray box they'd put Fred into. It seemed funny that he was reduced to something so small, but there was the evidence, in my hands. I wondered how intact the partial plate was, but not enough to open it and go through the stuff. Someone told me once almost everything is turned to ashes because the heat needed to be so intense to burn the heart down to ash. They said it was the toughest muscle but that didn't seem to be accurate to me. Hearts aren't so tough.

I bet there are all kinds of shards and things in the ashes, or the cremains, as seems to be the right word. I also wondered if Liza Jean knows that one, if it was in her crossword dictionary. Fred rode with me in the passenger's seat, all the way back through the route I had taken, L.A. to Phoenix to El Paso, and then I overshot Big Antler and headed on into Lubbock.

I could have just as easily sent him back to his place from any of those other airports but I wanted it to be Lubbock, something like home for me. It was strange, putting him on a plane in his condition. I couldn't bear to ship him UPS or through the mails, though, and there was probably even something illegal about that anyway.

o o o o

"That's it, you know the rest. He went home, and we went to see him off." What I didn't say was that as I headed home to get the boy ready for his daddy's funeral, mostly I got myself ready to see Shirley Mounter again for what I knew was going to be the last time, and I wasn't even for sure how I was going to walk away.

They both sat, looking at the counter, which was still a little dusty from Fred's box. They thanked me again, though the boy asked not one word about the letter to me. Maybe he had changed his mind. Maybe he'd heard enough.

"Mr. McMorsey, Tommy Jack, may I borrow this?" the girl asked. "I promise I'll take very good care of it. The place where my resources are, that would be the optimal place to study this journal of Fred Howkowski's last days," she said, the pleading leaking out, even as she still tried to sound professional and personal at the same time. She was right. That was indeed what the spiral-bound was, the journal of Fred's last days. "The glimpses I caught in my quick read indicate there's a lot more to his story than I had ever imagined—and I had imagined much over the years. I know what he means to T.J. here, and I have a little better understanding of what he meant to you, but his story also could be an immeasur-able contribution to Indian artists of the present and, more im-portantly, for generations to come." She paused and the boy raised his right eyebrow and lowered the left, giving me that little look he used to give when Liza Jean was talking crazy talk with us, trying to rationalize buying one of those Lladrós. This story was not going to be a contribution to any artist's career, except maybe the girl's Professor of Obscure Indian Actors career.

The girl noticed my pause, took it as a doorway, and then, more quietly, said, "The thought of filling the rest of my summer with Fred Howkowski in my apartment offers some comfort when I picture the emptiness awaiting me when I return home." She ducked her head, kind of delicate-like. "My husband and I have recently separated."

"I'm sorry. No. It never leaves me, hasn't in the last thirty or so years since it came into my possession. I'm sorry. I will make a copy of it for you, though, if you would like. That I can do." It sat on the table, an old red cardboard-covered stack of notebook paper, dog-eared and veined with creases from all the travels we've done together. I suppose the boy could have laid claim if he wanted, and grabbed it away from me right then and there. I didn't really like the idea of someone else even looking at the notebook, that someone else was sharing the history that only I have known for so long. Maybe it would be a relief at some point but just then, it only felt like a violation. To share even with them, given my long-held silence, might be the right thing, particularly in light of our complicated history. I had read every one of those entries. I knew Fred Howkowski had grown a bunker crop of odd ideas before he finally decided to harvest them. Sometimes the sharing of knowledge merely increased the burden. That book suggested the possibility of missed responsibility, the possibility that one could have made a difference. Maybe it could make a difference for some other lost kid out there, trying to find himself, or as here, herself.

"Thank you," she said. "Did you know?"

"No," I said immediately, then regretted it. Lying came so easily that it took easily five times the effort to tell the truth. "Maybe. Well, I don't know. I really don't know. Most of the letters he sent me? They didn't sound like the notebook. They sounded like your average guy, maybe frustrated, clowning to ease some tensions in his life. I guess if I had read them more carefully, maybe I would have seen what was there." I said that, but I have known some other people who've encountered suicides in their lives, and the one thing I have noticed is that we always question the act, even when we are given concrete answers. The one thing that remained

constant with Fred was that he always took the path of least resis-
tance. He didn't go to Canada to dodge the draft because he thought
it would be controversial. He just accepted that being drafted was
part of his life. I suppose it was part of why we got along. We were
a lot alike in that way. I don't know much about Hollywood but
what you see in the supermarket papers, but I never thought he
had even one chance. He was not a cutthroat enough person to
make the headway he would need out there, but who was I to tell
him that he couldn't chase a dream, wish upon a star?

"What are these bears Fred keeps referring to?" she asked.

"You know, I have no idea," I said, but of course I knew. The
way they crept into Fred's letters and notes to himself, like sneaky
spirits he had been unaware of. They were that way for me too, but
I had found a way to get rid of them. Maybe if I had told him what I
did, I could have brought him back. "Well, he did talk about the one
bear we had a real encounter with in his last letter to me too."

"Context?" she asked, back to her professional voice.

"Huh?" If I could do one thing for this young lady, it would be
to get her to understand that sometimes all probing does is start
up the bleeding again. Scar tissue might keep you together but it
doesn't make you like Superman.

"Why was he discussing that encounter, even as he was considering his final act?"

"Well, shit, I don't know. You read his notes. Does that sound
like someone who is seriously thinking about the subjects of
his letters?"

"Yes, it does," was all she said, and then she just waited, knowing I would come forward.

"Okay, yes it does," I said, finally.

o o o o

One time, a group of us had gotten away and stripped bare-ass
naked in a stream to swim, like I was telling you we did of an occasion, forgetting for a little while that we were probably giving

ourselves the worst cases of jock itch and ringworm, and every other nastiness you might want to think up, but we did it anyway.

We were only in for a little while when we heard a sound we were all too familiar with. Right quick after we heard a trip wire claymore go off, we grabbed our clothes and caught our asses up with the company again. Those mines, ball bearings and plastic explosive, would fuck up whoever had tripped them, and that person could just forget about survival for however many more minutes he had to live. Sometimes, though, even bleeding and in pieces, those NVA fuckers would still be trying to fire, or hold a grenade pin long enough to mess up whoever got close enough to inspect.

As soon as I heard it, I was back into my boxers and flak jacket, as were most of the others, and we made our way quietly up the hill to see what we could see. This time there was nothing for Jangle. For sure this one had no gold teeth. Bears rarely did as far as I knew.

Whenever we got a resupply, we'd sort out the things we liked from the things we didn't, making trades, back and forth, things like cans of chili, barbecued meat, ham and eggs. We called that last one ham and claymores because when you slid them out of the cans, they looked just like the trip wire mines we laid all over the hillsides. The worst was ham and limas. Everyone hated that. I used to like canned apricots before I got there, but some guy from our base, shortly after we were in country, had been shot in the head just after eating canned apricots, so from then on, everyone thought they were bad luck and no one would eat them. We didn't want the enemy to get ahold of this stuff, either, though—you don't want to be feeding your enemy—so we would puncture the cans and leave them to rot from the inside out in that sultry air. I am sure that was what attracted the wildlife we sometimes ran into.

This bear must have been five hundred pounds, and one of those bright guys in my company decided to skin it to give the skin to some higher-up and try to get a better deal. We were close enough to the worst, as near as any of us wanted to get to the DMZ, the demilitarized zone, where supposedly nobody's military was, but both sides were crawling around those hills, firing at each other, all the damned time. Every one of us wanted to get to any other base, but transfers almost never happened, unless you were being shipped out. I tried to tell him this but he said this bear was going to die anyway, which was more or less true. It couldn't survive the mine blast, but it didn't need to die the way it ended up dying. That guy, and jeez, I can't remember his name now, decided the dying bear was going to be his ticket out. He started to work on slicing that hide off, and the bear went to growling and moaning.

Some joker who'd had the radio while I was swimming thought he was going to be funny, called in a Whiskey India Alpha, a wounded in action, when we saw that the bear was still alive. Well, the base is nothing to fool with and we had to explain that there really wasn't a Whiskey India Alpha at all. They then ordered us to kill the bear, hack its head off along with the rest of the skin, and carry it back, which had been pretty much decided anyway. Though he hadn't come up with the bright idea of benefiting himself, that day's radioman got the honors of the lug and he was soaked in bear blood by the time we got back. The guy who received the call? He was the smart one. In order to forgive the paperwork, we had to give the skin up to him, and he was the one who got the better deal, and the rest of us, well, we got to see this bear, veins throbbing as we ripped its skin off, and we got to hear its last breaths gurgling out, as we slit its throat and worked our way deeper into its neck to sever its spine.

I didn't want to be thinking about those things, had not spoken of them for years, to almost anyone. It was like I was back there, suddenly. I could still smell the fear and panic on that bear as we killed it to save the stupid ass of one of us from being punished by regulations made by a bunch of idiots pretending there were rules and orders to be followed in a jungle where a bear on a walk gets wiped out by a C-4 charge, and then is tortured to death by a group of scared kids not wanting to get into trouble.

I saw lots of things over there that I didn't want to stick in my memory, and I think I probably got off lucky in wiping out some of them, but that bear, it would never leave, I think, because we were so much like it. Every day, I felt half dead, waiting for something worse to happen, waiting to be stripped alive, and then have some other inhumanity heaved onto me. I guess Fred must have felt that way too.

When you see that, every night, for months after, even back in your old bed where you know the springs that poke at you, almost taking comfort in their regularity, you try to find something to pull you back to the place you thought you lived, anything you can find. Even after I got home, I could still see that stupid bear, its eyes looking at us, not believing what we were doing to it, moving its mouth up and down and trying to growl, choking on its own blood in those last breaths. I would see it all over Big Antler, in shop windows, on my momma's TV, and everywhere else I went that summer, drifting through the country, but mostly behind my own eyelids.

For a while, I stopped seeing it when I worked on changing that humidor into a curio. Stripping it down was tough. When I'd get a layer of varnish loose with spirits, it would rub off in these clumpy sheets, like the layer of fat just below that bear's hide. But when I had gotten it down to the wood, I rubbed and rubbed oil into it, making it glow, rejuvenating it. That kept the bear away for a while, but it came back, showing up everywhere again. Eventually, there was one thing that grabbed onto me, pulled me back here long enough to stay here for good, to leave the bear behind.

o o o o

"That one thing was your mother," I said to the girl, and though she did not look up, she knew I was talking to her. The boy didn't say anything either. Finally, I think he understood that your life is your own, and no other person can know all of it. There were parts of his father that were his, and I guess parts that belonged to this girl and her world. Maybe he was finally okay knowing there were parts that were mine, and mine alone.

"Y'all are welcome to stay the night," I said, knowing in my heart that they wouldn't. "Plenty of room. You know, I might make it up to New York, sometime," I added, and though I doubted that, the picture of Shirley Mounter sitting in a window, sewing herself a new blouse, that had a powerful draw to it. I guess that was why I couldn't go back.

"Don't look me up," the girl said, and the boy laughed.

"You can look *me* up, Daddy," he said. "You'll always have a place to stay if you decide to come north."

"Could you tell me one last thing?" the girl said.

"I've told you all I've got," I said. "If there's something more, I can get in touch with you, but there just isn't any more."

"I'd like to know about the blanket. Is it here in this house? Can I see it?" she said.

"What blanket?" the boy asked.

"No," I said. She waited for more.

"We better get going if we're going to make Fouke tonight," she said, finally, which I knew was a lie. Fouke, Arkansas, was a good eight hours from Big Antler, easy. I know. I've done that haul. That's the little town where Bigfoot supposedly lives, where they made that *Legend of Boggy Creek* movie about him, years ago, but I didn't see much in that rinky-dink spot on the map except a couple barbecue places, a mini-mart, and a gas station. Her momma must have told her that was the movie we took all those kids to see at the drive-in, like a regular old family, that last weekend I ever saw her. If I've got my math right, the girl would have been too young to remember, but I'd bet a dollar she was among that tangle of kids in the back of my rented pickup that night. I hear they're gonna open up a little Bigfoot museum there in Fouke, sometime soon. Maybe the girl had heard the same thing.

"Okay, then," I said. "You drive safely." They started pulling out, and I shined my light at my feet while they turned around in the driveway. As they reached the bar ditch, I ran up to the passenger's side, flashing the light their way to get their attention. The boy pressed on the brakes and the girl rolled down her window.

"Boy, you just sit tight, I want to talk to your friend here," I said, and being the good boy he is, he just put it in park, so she could get out. "Why don't you come with me and get that letter for the boy," I said as we stepped into the house. If she hadn't been on the inside of that door, she might have just walked. But there we were, and she understood, even without reading, what I was offering to put in her hands. That it held some answers for the boy he was probably not going to want to know.

"As much as I want to read it, I imagine there's a reason you think T.J. shouldn't. I think there's something in here that you believe should be buried. Are you really changing your mind about what you want and don't want to share?" she asked. She finally understood that gaining knowledge is a state you cannot reverse.

"Well, you both came down here for answers, didn't you? You got yours, such as they are. I guess I'm not what you expected."

"I had no expectations."

"I don't think that's true," I said. "Why don't you want the boy to see that letter? I know why I don't think he should, but you of all people, I should think, might understand these pointless questions he's asking. No matter what's in there. I'm not going to tell you. You have to decide on your own if he should read it."

"Why is it my decision?"

"Because you've learned what happens when you find some answers you weren't exactly expecting," I said.

"What do you think T.J. would gain?" she asked. "He thinks he knows the way things are, and he does pretty well. Some people need to believe in things. He believes there's something in that letter, something that will clear up some itch for him, and perhaps there is. But I suspect there aren't any real answers for him there, only more questions, more itches. Or you would have shown it to him. There's a reason you've hidden it away."

"I'm not going to tell you. That's just the way life is."

"Do you truly believe T.J. will find meaningful answers on these pages?"

"Who's to say what a meaningful answer is?" I said.

"I can't give this to him," the girl said, snapping the envelope back down on the telephone table. "It's yours, for one thing, like this notebook. Some people have too many questions in their lives. More questions, more itches. If you want him to have that, you give it to him. I have enough unanswered questions, still."

She was of course talking about the stuff from her mother that I kept in the pump house, along with another hundred other similar-looking boxes. No one else would be able to tell it from any of the other junk, but I could spot it, and did, every time I walked in that door and pulled that light cord. And since Liza Jean thought she got rid of it the year the boy left, she didn't come a-looking too close of my stuff anymore. I supposed there was no need to hide it, now. In a few minutes, I could walk out to the pump house and just bring it in here, opening it like I did Fred's box. But what might happen inside me, when I touch those things? Fred is gone for good, but Shirley, that's a different matter.

o o o o

The morning after Shirley and I had made love that first time, I lifted her panties from the blanket and asked if I could take them.

"Don't you want a clean pair, handsome?" she'd asked, sliding a man's T-shirt on and stretching, her nipples rising in that cloth unfamiliar to her shape. I didn't really think of it, but that shirt must have belonged to her currently missing old man. "I wore those all day, yesterday."

"That's why I want them," I said, holding them up to my face, rubbing them against my beard. "I want to be able to smell your scent when I'm back on the plains. Be with you until I can smell you for real again, and who knows when that might be."

"Suit yourself," she said, and walked me to the door as I slipped them in my back pocket. "How long are you in town for? Maybe we could get you hooked up with some other memories of me to keep you warm on those lonely plains nights. You know, I've never been there. What's it like?" she whispered, all the while guiding me down the stairway in her apartment building.

"Flat. Not the way I like things," I said, reaching up to cup her breasts loose under that T-shirt.

"Not out here," was all she said, and I behaved, no questions asked. I walked out without answering her other question, and she didn't ask it again. Each time we'd been together, we traded a little something with each other and the last time, it had been that blanket.

It was what she had decided to give me, in the final few minutes we'd ever spent together. We'd made love on it and slept under it, that whole weekend, and nearly every time before. Just as me and the boy were leaving to take the rental car back, she folded it up, told me to take it. I didn't have the room, though I wanted to take it bad. Something of us would be on it forever. *Essence* sounds corny, but something like that. She was crying by then, holding it out in the air, and her arm, I bet, would have stayed like that, suspended. I took it, kissed the fingers holding the wool, and opened my suitcase. I left some clothes behind so I could stuff that blanket into the case and when we got back to West Texas that blanket went straight into my sleeper cab and it had stayed there until November of last year.

After I called the police from Detroit Lakes, it took the medical examiners forever to get to the cabin. They finally took the Japanese girl away by about ten o'clock. They had to ask a million questions of me and wanted me to stick around, in case they needed any further details, which I knew translated to "in case we decide that you killed her." I told them I would be in the Twin Cities for a few hours but that I would be back that night, to the same place. They wanted to know my route, and destination, and they let me go, but mostly, I think, because, like I said before, it is pretty damned hard to hide one of these big rigs.

When they lifted her out of my snow angel, there was not one impression of her in it, just mine. Her prints led up to it, but that was it. The snow and the wind had picked up again sometime in the day, and by the time I got back that evening, even the angel was gone.

That night I watched the meteors from the plate glass window of the cabin. The newspapers and all that mess came later, after the coroner's office had decided on an official cause and had released the story to the press, after her folks had flown in from Nagasaki, had her cremated in the Twin Cities, and had flown back to Japan with her. The medical examiners eventually said there was an unusual level of antidepressants in her toxicology report, but that overall, she had died of exposure, and I believe that to be true. They can say they meant it with regard to the weather, but to me, it was an exposure to this country and all of its crazy, casual violations of the soul that really did her in.

o o o o

"The blanket your momma asked about in her letter was a Pendleton, and it did have Indian designs on it. She had given it to me and I had given her a set of my clothes. Not really an even trade by anyone else's standards, but it worked for us. Our collecting of things from one another had begun the first night we'd been together, and sort of ended on that last night."

"Thank you," she said. Maybe that satisfied her. Maybe not. Whichever, it was close enough to the truth for her, even if it still left some of her spaces empty. If I gave her anything, it was the knowledge that sometimes, spaces are okay things to have. They make the other things tolerable. It must have nearly killed her to set that envelope down and walk out the door, but maybe not. Maybe the seventeen-hundred-mile drive was worth the effort. Maybe it takes that long a distance to know if you really want something, and to know what it was going to take to get it. I hoped she and the boy didn't find the drive to Fouke, or to home, one where they knew their spaces more sharply. Maybe she would learn to stop picking at other people's scabs, and maybe she would learn to stop picking at her own. I wondered how long it would take for that new spot to heal for me. The place where Fred's box slept all these years was bleeding out into the sultry night. I thought it would be easy. I hadn't looked at it in years, but to know it was gone was like losing him all over again. Maybe I should thank them for waking me up.

EPILOGUE:

Credits Roll

Dear Tommy Jack,

Enclosed please find one key to let you into my apartment. I know you're gonna hate me for this, but I'm asking you to come back to Hollywood, one last time. You're thinking there isn't a thing in the world I could say that could get you back here, but I bet you're wrong.

Remember that game I taught all of you, when we were in country? Fireball? Of course you do, you even played when you came out to my reservation, got your nose busted, as I remember it. Man, you should have gotten that fixed, but I always thought you were a little crooked anyway, and now your outsides match your personality. Isn't that a good one? I bet you don't remember that I didn't play, that night. You want to know why? Do you really remember what happened the last time we played in country? It was almost like the first time, but only almost.

You guys were always asking me to do a rain dance, and then later a stop-the-rain dance, asking me tips on tent-making with those damned ponchos, all that stupid shit you thought an Indian was supposed to know. Well, I wanted to show you a little bit of the real life—"like we didn't have enough reality," I bet you're saying. When I gave you guys a version of the medicine game, told you it was like soccer, only the ball and the goals were on fire, I figured that was good enough for you guys, give us something to do in the downtime, and give us a little medicine to go around.

That last time? Sure you remember how George said he was going to make the ball that time, use some special stabilizer for the bundle of rags. I imagine you remember what his secret ingredient was. He just laughed and laughed when the rags unraveled and that VC head rolled out from the middle, its jaw hanging sideways. I could never play again, after that. Not because that sight moved me, or anything. Just the opposite. For a second, I saw a human being who probably had a family somewhere not far from where he died, maybe looking up at familiar stars, even as his eyesight failed and he died, and then, someone laughed, probably George, first. Once someone started, everyone else joined it, me included.

I laughed right along, and so did you and Jangle and everyone else who played that day, both teams. And when we took a break? You remember that, too? Warming cans of C ration meat over the remains of that ball and eating from the can, not a yard away from that crooked head, with the broken jaw and the caved-in temple where someone had given it a good hard kick before everything had come unraveled. That day, I thought I had become an animal, eating because I was hungry, not caring what else was around.

You remember how I divided us up? Young Men and Old Men, those who had kids and those who didn't? Well, I know I went on the Old Men's team, but I was lying. I did the math, added up the months after the kiddo had been born, and I was seeing Nadine, his ma in those months, but we hadn't done anything then, not until later, so I don't think he could be mine, unless he was a preemie. I guess she turned out to be like some Donut Dolly but on the going-away end of the war effort, a last piece of reservation ass for anyone who got drafted.

Anyway, when I got that picture of the little guy, I hung on to it, made him mine, and he was what got me through, even in that period of not feeling anything, like that day in the chopper when Hughes turned to give me a little advice and that bullet rode up through the floor and straight up into the back of his helmet. Remember that? His face was there, and then it wasn't, and we just threw him in the back and held on while the pilots got us out of there as quick as they could.

You remember that bear? That one we skinned the month before, to save Hughes's ass after he had called it in WIA? You know, that bear blew bloody snot all over me, one of the last things it did, while I was lifting its head and you guys were cutting through. How long do you think its brain went on thinking while we carried it back to the rear? Do you think it saw its body, all blue veins and pink, bloody fat strings hanging off those thick muscles? I do. My ma's dad was a bear, did I ever tell you that? Not a real bear, of course, but his clan. I bet I did, one of those nights we spent under the poncho holding on to each other, silent in fear, hating the dark and the rain and those bugs, hating ourselves and holding on just the same for all we were worth until the sun came up. My clan was snipe, still is, for that matter, but not for long. I guess it's a good thing you take your clan from your ma and not your dad, because that little guy you're raising now, he would have no idea what clan he was supposed to be, if it was up to his dad's side of things.

No idea why Nadine picked me for the father, maybe she thought my ma would be a good babysitter. Who can say? When I got back, saw the possibilities from the other rez guys who made it home, I decided I wouldn't argue, and keep him, since he brought me home anyway. You take good care of him, Tommy Jack, just like you did me, because this time, I'm not coming back.

I just got word from one of the editing crew on that movie, you know, the one I had the speaking part in? Of course that one. Said he wanted to stop by for a minute. You've seen my place, I couldn't have that, so I met him in the lobby, invited him into the visitors' lounge. They shot me, all fine and nice, weeks before. I had rehearsed my lines, as few as they were, until I had them perfect, exactly right. You know what he brought me? A little can of film from the work print. The star, that nice guy, that up-and-comer who treated all the extras like they were real people, he decided it needed to be cut. Since when do the actors make those decisions? Since now, it looks like. He said I was messing up the tone of things, that I didn't look enough like the other extra Indians, like somehow they could see my dad was white, even though I'd already legally changed my last name to Eagle Cry.

Every one of the movies I've been in, they cover me in this orange dye, to make me darker for the screen, and it looks like blood every night when I try to wash it down the bathtub drain, like we had sometimes washing off us in those showers at Phu Bai. I feel like that bear, every night, scrubbing that stuff off until I am myself again, peeling my skin off me, layer by layer, and I don't have one inch left to call my own anymore. If I have to scrub it one more time, I think I'll look in the mirror to discover I'm not really there anymore.

I'll try not to make a mess, try to get it right on the first bullet, like Hughes did, but I have to warn you, my place here, it isn't in very good shape right now, so don't be shocked. I've left a few things here for the kiddo and you should take whatever you want except for those few things I noted. I know we used to fight over that NVA flag but it's yours now free and clear.

I bought some apricots a while ago and I think it's finally time for me to eat them. Don't worry, I've punctured the other cans so that by the time you get here, they'll be spoiled and no one else will be tempted to go near them.

I talked to my ma, the other day, using the last of my quarters, before calling her collect to finish things. She said she saw Shirley Mounter the other day, and that Shirley asked after you, wondering when you might make it back. I guess I'm giving you a reason to now. I want to be buried at home, on the rez. Okay? I would really appreciate that.

Have a good life, my friend.

Your very best friend,
Fred Howkowski

———————————————

Tommy Jack McMorsey

I ran outside, expecting to have to flag the boy's Blazer down again, but they were still there. The boy sat on the hood, watching the stars, and the girl leaned on it, following his gaze. She was waiting for me to give him the letter, but my hands were empty when I reached them.

"I had forgotten how clear the night skies are here," the boy said, climbing down. He didn't ask what we talked about, but he came around. I guess this really was it, for now. I stuck my hand out and he gently pushed it aside, hugging me, and I held him for a while. The girl just got in the passenger seat and waited for us to finish.

"You keep in touch, boy," I said, and he agreed to. "You are always welcome home," I added.

"My home is somewhere else, now. The place I came from."

"This is one of the places you came from, son," I said, shutting his door while he buckled in, and then I went to the other side and motioned for the girl to roll her window down.

"That blanket," I said, leaning in, "I don't have anymore. I used it to cover up the dead girl in Minnesota. Somehow reporters got there before the police did—I could tell they weren't official trucks as they pulled up, you know, some of them had those little satellite dishes on the top—and I didn't think she should be seen like that. At first, I put my old coat over her, but she looked ridiculous that way, the coat's arms stretching out in directions different from hers, and I knew the news stories were gonna have a field day with her anyway, so I gave her what little dignity I could. I ran back to my rig and got the only thing I had with me that I owned that seemed appropriate. I lay the blanket over her and guarded her until the police came, and when the ambulance people asked me if I wanted the blanket back, I said no, that it was hers now. I don't know what they did with it, maybe they gave it to her family, with the rucksack, and that little pink jacket, in one of those patient's belongings bags they give you when someone in your family dies in the hospital. For all I know, it's sitting in some little private shrine in Japan. Or maybe, they just threw it out."

"She would like to know that. Would you mind if I tell her?" the girl asked, almost shyly.

"That would be nice," I said.

She reached into her purse, handing me a little business card. "If you decide, here's how you can find me. I'll answer," she said.

"Thank you," I said and she patted my hand gently before rolling up the window. As they drove out, I shined my spotlight on their Blazer and followed it down my road and then onto the main road of the grid, until they disappeared near the entrance ramp to the interstate, miles away. I shut the spot off and walked back to the house in the dark, deciding I could probably make some selections of the things Liza Jean would want from this house.

That envelope the girl made me seal sat there, where we had left it, on the counter. I started to throw it out, but then I took her card from my wallet, addressed the envelope, put a stamp on it, and left it by the phone. Then I took that old letter Fred sent me and read it for myself one last time. I got a new envelope from my desk, put Fred's name and my address as the return and my own name, in care of the boy at his address and put a stamp on that one too.

I drove down toward the post office to drop those envelopes in the outgoing mailbox before I could find some reason to back out. Half a block before the post office, the parking lot lights outside the Allslip's mini-mart shone on the phone booth next to the ice machine, and I swung by there and called information. A few minutes later, Shirley answered the telephone, concern heavy in her voice. She sounded the same, but what would I say? Maybe I could ask her if she would put a bouquet of flowers on Fred's grave for me. It would be a little late for Memorial Day, but better late than never, am I right? But then what? It was late and I should have known better, so I hung up without saying a word.

The post office was dark. I let myself into the outer lobby, where the P.O. boxes were, and checked my mail. Liza Jean and I had left so abruptly that we'd forgotten to do our summer forwarding routine like we did every year. Just as well, since I was likely to be here. I dropped those letters in the post office's outgoing slot, sending my keys across the country. They could turn those locks if they wanted to. On the short drive home, I watched the night skies. There was no moon. Maybe it had already come crashing down in the ocean and the tidal wave had just not arrived here on the plains yet. I kept looking up anyway, hoping for one more shooting star, a fireball blazing across the dark, millions of miles away, arcing its way into my life. This time I would be fast enough to connect with it, deliver that wish, and wait for it to come true. I headed home and decided that if the phone was ringing, I would pick it up.

> May 9, 2001–January 8, 2003,
> Niagara Falls, New York

Author's Note

A true story: By the time you reached the end of chapter one of this novel, you may have dismissed a major premise as implausible, because this is a literary novel, and the outlandish is not generally considered the best fertilizer for literary novels, or so I am often told. Feel free to Google the most preposterous details and you will discover that sometimes, truth is stranger than fiction. In the late fall of 2001, a woman flew from Japan and according to initial media reports, did indeed head out for the wintry stretches of North Dakota and Minnesota, looking for the ransom from the film *Fargo*, to a tragic end. Google it; I'll be waiting here.

The day I read the newspaper article, I clipped it and stuck it on the bulletin board above my drawing table. This woman's experiences awoke in me a better understanding of where dreams become dangerous, and I more clearly grasped the dynamics of this trajectory, having chased some dubious dreams myself. Also, her story triggered an itch in my mind. I knew it meant something to me, but I couldn't say what, at the time. It seemed to have something to do with some unfinished business from my first novel.

Indian Summers was published in 1998, and I did a fair number of readings to promote it, tending to read one chapter in particular. It was the right length for an audience member's patience, and the right length for an audience member's gluteus maximus, teetering on the decrepit chairs used for many readings. It also had the right tone and enough shifts to keep a listener's attention. I should add that I had a strong feeling of allegiance to this chapter. It was the first short story I'd had accepted for publication, a few years before. It had served me well.

As a novel chapter, though, it was maybe a bit of a cheat. It was largely the story of a character who was dead from the opening sentence. People I've met after they've read this novel often ask about this character. They want to know what happened to him, and why he did the things he did. I wished back then that I had answers for them, but I didn't know, myself. The story had dropped like a bomb into my head one day, while I was struggling to write a different novel. I had sat at the computer, dreading that I was going back into a story I couldn't quite find. I opened up the file, and instead of typing "Chapter Seven" at the top of the page, which had been my plan, I typed "The Ballad of Plastic Fred," having only the vaguest notion of what that title meant. It clearly borrowed from the Beatles song "The Ballad of John and Yoko," music I tend to listen to when I am most stressed out.

At the end of that day, the story was done. With the exception of a few editorial suggestions, mostly about word repetition, it was published as written. This was one of those miracle stories I almost never speak about with students, because I don't want to encourage them into thinking this will happen often. It doesn't, at least not for me. The year I wrote that story was 1992. A story-bomb like that didn't happen again until 2004, but that's another tale.

As for "Chapter Seven," it never got written. The book died on the table. Somehow, the discovery of Fred Howkowski had shifted the way I looked at writing. The novel I had been writing was a horror novel, my second. The first one never saw publication, fortunately. I came to understand that, in the small story of children trying to understand a hero's suicide, there were scary enough things in the world I knew. I didn't need to invent unspeakable horrors. The speakable ones were bad enough, and worthy enough of exploration, if that were really the place I wanted to go.

After *Indian Summers,* I continued working, and I began to

understand that the story of Fred Howkowski was not over yet. He kept showing up, a ghost wandering at the fringes of my other work, asserting himself more frequently, more visibly, but I still could not find the right door to his life. It took the spark of that strange news story for me to find a way in. Somehow, the misguided passions of that Japanese woman, and the thoroughness with which she pursued them, allowed me to ask that secret part of my brain if it knew what really did happen to Fred in Hollywood.

The door opened, and I found my fictional narrative tied inextricably to the singularly odd and sorrowful events of the Japanese woman's journey. I think I was most attracted to this news story because I have done similar things, myself, just not to the point of flirting with disaster. In short, I could sympathize. When I understood this synthesis was happening, I chose not to research the details of this woman's death any further, figuring I knew enough for my purposes. The details here are mine, in service of Fred Howkowski's story. In addition to recasting this story loosely and fictionally, I've used actual locations, legal agreements, and historical events as part of this work's backdrop. Ultimately, though, this is a novel, a work of fiction, not reportage. Names, places, characters, and incidents either are products of my imagination or have been used fictitiously. Any resemblance to actual events or locales or persons, living or dead, is entirely coincidental. This is *not* based on a true story.

A project of this duration is never accomplished alone. As always, thank-you first and foremost to Larry Plant, co-dreamer from the start, hoping the long haul still stretches out on the horizon. Is there a limit to the number of conversations any two people can have about a project? I surely hope not, as we would have passed that number by now. A tremendous thank-you goes to Bill Haynes, who gave so freely over countless summer nights, revisiting details again and again, without asking for anything in return. We discussed his experiences in Vietnam at length, and spent great hours in the reconstructed and restored turn-of-the-century buildings at his patch of land in West Texas. How anyone was able to perform those miracles of re-creation on a teacher's salary and eBay profits was beyond me until we sat down and went over it, detail by detail. Thanks also to Robin Roberts of Snyder, Texas, who probably has no memory of the day he spontaneously agreed to teach me about the mechanics and logistics of life in the cab of a long-haul truck. It is not often I meet strangers as generous with their time. This novel could not have been written without these contributions.

Thank you to the following people, who read drafts of this book, in part or in whole, and offered valuable insights: Bob Baxter, Alan Adelson, Susan Bernardin, Gerald Vizenor, and Bob Morris. Thanks to Mark Hodin, for spotting *Loaded and Rollin'*, and picking it up for me, and for hours of discussion. A particular *nyah-wheh* to Mark Turcotte, for friendship of course, but also for the geography lesson, and for not letting me forget it, afterward. "Go Bears!" *Nyah-wheh* also goes to Heid E. Erdrich, for friendship and for the Detroit Lakes souvenir (Kwitchurbeliakin). Thanks to my friend, colleague, and fellow novelist Mick Cochrane, who shared memories of Detroit Lakes. A stunned thank-you to Jim Cihlar at Milkweed Editions, for offering the most thorough and amazing editorial exchange I have ever experienced.

Thank-you to Canisius College in Buffalo, New York, for its support of my work, specifically the Reverend Vincent M. Cooke, S.J., president; Herbert J. Nelson and, later, Scott A. Chadwick, vice president for academic affairs; Paula M. McNutt and, later, Leonid A. Khinkis, dean of arts and sciences; and the Joseph S. Lowery Estate for Funding Faculty Fellowship in Creative Writing. Thanks to the Seaside Institute's Escape to Create residency program, where this manuscript was partially composed.

Nyah-wheh forever to my family, always offering fireballs to reignite the story and particularly to my late brother, Tiff, for coming back to us from Vietnam. The rain is still washing away your prints.

Thanks again to the Jupiter 2, for the ever-rising moon, and to Japancakes, Explosions in the Sky, and Balmorhea, for providing exactly the right sound track music during the writing of this novel. Appreciation to the proprietors of Quaker Steak & Lube, in Erie, Pennsylvania, and the Monster Mart, in Fouke, Arkansas, and the owners of other places like these, who combat blandness in this country's landscape by following their own peculiar dreams. In addition to offering good food and cool drinks along the road, they have facilitated my passions with their sincere commitments to the odd. Finally, thanks to the Coen brothers, Joel and Ethan, for remaining faithful to their singular vision, a gift to all.

About the Author

Eric Gansworth (Onondaga) is Lowery Writer-in-Residence and professor of English at Canisius College in Buffalo, New York. He was born and raised at the Tuscarora Nation. The author of seven books, including the PEN Oakland Award–winning *Mending Skins*, and *A Half-Life of Cardio-Pulmonary Function* (National Book Critics Circle's "Good Reads List" for Spring 2008), Gansworth is also a visual artist, and generally incorporates paintings as integral elements into his narratives. In the fall of 2008, his first full-length dramatic work, *Re-Creation Story*, was part of the Public Theater's Native Theater Festival, in New York City. His work has been widely shown and anthologized and has appeared in *The Kenyon Review*, *Shenandoah*, *The Boston Review*, *Third Coast*, and *The Yellow Medicine Review*, among other publications. His most recent book, *From the Western Door to the Lower West Side*, is a collaboration with social documentary photographer Milton Rogovin.

MORE BOOKS FROM MILKWEED EDITIONS

To order books or for more information, contact Milkweed at
(800) 520-6455 or visit our Web site (www.milkweed.org).

The Farther Shore
Matthew Eck

The Hospital for Bad Poets
J. C. Hallman

Ordinary Wolves
Seth Kantner

Roofwalker
Susan Power

Driftless
David Rhodes

Cracking India
Bapsi Sidhwa

Gardenias
Faith Sullivan

MILKWEED EDITIONS

Milkweed Editions—an independent literary press—publishes with the intention of making a humane impact on society, in the belief that literature is a transformative art.

JOIN US

Milkweed depends on the generosity of foundations and individuals like you, in addition to the sales of its books. In an increasingly consolidated and bottom-line-driven publishing world, your support allows us to select and publish books on the basis of their literary quality and the depth of their message. Please visit our Web site (www.milkweed.org) or contact us at (800) 520-6455 to learn more about our donor program.

Milkweed Editions, a nonprofit publisher, gratefully acknowledges sustaining support from Emilie and Henry Buchwald; the Patrick and Aimee Butler Foundation; the Dougherty Family Foundation; the Ecolab Foundation; the General Mills Foundation; John and Joanne Gordon; William and Jeanne Grandy; the Jerome Foundation; Robert and Stephanie Karon; the Lerner Foundation; Sally Macut; Sanders and Tasha Marvin; the McKnight Foundation; Mid-Continent Engineering; the Minnesota State Arts Board, through an appropriation by the Minnesota State Legislature, a grant from the Wells Fargo Foundation Minnesota, and a grant from the National Endowment for the Arts; Kelly Morrison and John Willoughby; the National Endowment for the Arts, and the American Reinvestment and Recovery Act; the Navarre Corporation; Ann and Doug Ness; Jörg and Angie Pierach; the RBC Foundation USA; Ellen Sturgis; the Target Foundation; the James R. Thorpe Foundation; the Travelers Foundation; Moira and John Turner; and Edward and Jenny Wahl.

THE McKNIGHT FOUNDATION

Interior design by Connie Kuhnz
Typeset in Chaparral Pro
by BookMobile Design and Publishing Services
Printed on acid-free 100% post consumer waste paper
by Friesens Corporation

ENVIRONMENTAL BENEFITS STATEMENT

Milkweed Editions saved the following resources by printing the pages of this book on chlorine free paper made with 100% post-consumer waste.

TREES	WATER	SOLID WASTE	GREENHOUSE GASES
50	23,055	1,400	4,787
FULLY GROWN	GALLONS	POUNDS	POUNDS

Calculations based on research by Environmental Defense and the Paper Task Force.
Manufactured at Friesens Corporation